The
Red
Bird
Sings

AOIFE FITZPATRICK

virago

VIRAGO

First published in Great Britain in 2023 by Virago Press
This paperback edition published in Great Britain in 2024 by Virago Press

1 3 5 7 9 10 8 6 4 2

Copyright © 2023 by Aoife Fitzpatrick

The moral right of the author has been asserted.

A CIP catalogue record for this book
is available from the British Library.

Paperback ISBN 978-0-349-01667-2

Typeset in Perpetua by M Rules
Printed and bound in Great Britain by Clays Ltd, Elcograf, S.p.A.

Papers used by Virago are from well-managed forests
and other responsible sources.

Virago
An imprint of
Little, Brown Book Group
Carmelite House
50 Victoria Embankment
London EC4Y 0DZ

An Hachette UK Company
www.hachette.co.uk

www.virago.co.uk

For Peter

This story is inspired by real events that took place in Greenbrier County, West Virginia, in 1896 and 1897. In certain cases, incidents, characters and timelines have been altered for dramatic purposes. Certain characters may be composites, or entirely fictitious.

PART ONE

1896

Corn Harvest to Watchnight

from:

THE TRIAL OF TROUT SHUE

A TRUE STORY
CONTAINING HITHERTO
SUPPRESSED FACTS

---

by Lucia C. Frye

On June 22, 1897, Miss Minnie Grose, recently graduated from the Lewisburg Female Institute, took her seat in the Greenbrier County Circuit Court, and in the shadow of the bench where Justice Joseph McWhorter presided, she set her hands to the stenotype machine. The temperature was holding above ninety degrees, the paper wilting as Miss Grose struck the keys, feeding the narrow roll toward the floor. Upon this cream pulp was the court's official record – the only evidence that the jury would be allowed to consider in the trial of Trout Shue for the murder of his wife, Zona Heaster Shue.

This transcript was to make no mention of Mary Jane Heaster, mother of the victim, who rose from her seat in hatless dishevelment as the defendant took the stand. Dressed in full mourning, her percale unfashionably loose, she might have been painted, stark, upon the glowing summer air – the frock in blackened bone, the face and hands primed in grey, her expression uncommonly frank.

Mr Shue wore a fresh linen suit and a starched white shirt, both of which he had begged from his jailer, Constable Shawver. And with his mild gaze resting on the jury, he made his plea:

'Not guilty.'

This is Letter No. 1 of 5

My dear Elisabeth,

Where to start? I've never done this
before, and neither have you. It's one of
those things you can only risk once in a
lifetime. And maybe there's no right way.
So here goes.

I'm your mother, Zona. The one who
carried you for nine whole months
before you arrived screaming into the
Meadow Bluff dawn. Today is your first
birthday. But if you're reading this,
already the years have passed and you
are sixteen years old. My friend Lucy
Frye is taking down my words, being
better on her Remington than I will
ever be with pen and ink. She'll keep
my letters in store for you, Elisabeth,
because I might get too nervous to

send them when you're grown. That would
be like me.

You've no doubt become a fine young
woman of great accomplishment. A
Virginian wearing the fashions of the
twentieth century! Strange to say that
if you open this letter in 1911, I won't
be too much younger than your grandma
Mary Jane. Right now, I'm a score and
four. And when I last saw you, you were
smaller than I thought a human being
could be – moments into your life,
gumming the air like all creatures do
when they're fresh from the darkness.
Do you still have the name I gave you
when you were born, Elisabeth? Have you
been well and happy, in the way that
mothers dream of?

I owe you this letter now that you're
grown. Because there must be at least
one thing you want to ask me. Why did I
give you up? Well, if you're ready for the
answer, I will set it down.

The way that it happened, you and me
were separated all of a sudden. We were
over at the Harfords' farm – Bessie and
Armsted's place – staying in gentle
Ruth's old room, Lord rest her soul.
Four months I lay in bed, gazing out
over Miller Mountain, the boys looking

just as small and black as click beetles
where they worked the faraway fields.
I was hiding, Beth (if I may call you
by that sweet name). From everyone. Not
because I was ashamed of you – or even
of me – but because I didn't want to
hear the bad things people might say. Ma
and Bessie fussed, changing the linens
every day, scrubbing the walls and floors
with lye soap, until you arrived, early
one morning. A new person, so exactly
yourself. How you shrieked! And the
more you cried, the more I gave thanks
to the Lord.

Your first fit of bawling was only
just settled when that slip of a woman
from Richmond came to take you in your
swaddles. Whip-thin, she breezed through
the door just as Bessie was covering me
with a clean sheet. I remember how she
smelled: the August air, sweet and grassy,
rising from the folds of her skirt. This
woman was crisp as a paper swan, Beth,
while I sagged like an old ragdoll.

Ann Power, the Irish midwife, was there,
too, gathering her clattering wares into
her holdall. I watched how her lips parted
in her long face, the hard lines about her
eyes growing soft, making a more polite
arrangement of her features. 'Mrs Wylie,'

she said, nodding to our guest like she'd known her all her life.

I hauled myself up in the bed, and hissed to Ann, 'Is this she?'

For months, I'd been ready to hate whoever came for you, but I never expected them so soon. Ann stood back from the crib, and your new mother made for you with eager, but halting, steps. I don't mind telling you, I was shocked to see this Mrs Wylie's foot was dragging. And when she bent low to see you, I feared she'd fall into the crib. But then she swept you into the crook of her one strong arm. Beguiled by your little face, she didn't see me ogling everything from her scarlet cheeks, to her right arm dangling skinny and weak, to her boot, which was turned outward on the same side, the strap of her leg brace showing around the ankle. And the thing is, she fitted my ideal of motherhood exactly.

I've never seen a woman so able to love at first sight, drinking you in like a cool glass of water on the hottest day. Her sparse brows lifted, like some burden had been relieved. I know the size of it, because I felt it visiting upon me instead, my arms tingling and burning with the weight of your absence. Even now, the air is heavy as iron in the space where you are not.

'Missus,' I said, cold with the panic of losing you. 'Let me see my baby.'

That's when Ma came bustling in, efficient as always. Your grandma Mary Jane never tires of moving, right down to her black hair that was breaking free of its pins, stronger than corn shocks.

'You should be running along, Eugenia,' she said. Our visitor was Ma's junior by more than a decade, and she saw no boldness in grasping her withered arm and marching her to the door.

But that Richmond lady, she resisted! – setting her shoulder against the jamb like it was a magnet and she had metal bones. Lowering her narrow chin, she let those honest hazel eyes rest on mine. Eugenia Wylie knew your worth exactly, Beth – what she was taking and what I was losing. She was giving me one last chance to keep you.

With the thumb of her feeble arm, she tugged the linen back from your face. There were curls crusted on your temples, dark as molasses. You had a high bridge on your nose, just like your father's, and your eyes were set wide apart. (I've room for a silver dollar between my brows, and

now you're grown, I wonder if you do too.)
I have never seen anyone so gloriously
surprised by the world, little Beth. You
were a hodgepodge, and beautiful with it.

'Will you give me the child,
Miss Heaster?'

Her plain face held very still, as if
one flicker might cost a life. Eugenia
Wylie was afraid of nothing. She had the
courage to do what was right, no matter
what the price. That's why I let her take
you, Beth. I wanted you raised by someone
whole in spirit. And in that moment, I
believed myself to be less than I should
have been.

'Go,' I said. I saw the manacles
on Eugenia's soul cleave open,
and she slackened. 'Keep her safe.
Always,' I prayed.

Did Eugenia ever tell you about that
day? About me?

There's a hole in my mind. A place
called Missing You. And like a lens
bending the light, it changes how I see
things. I saw inside a bluegill's eyeball
once. I was feeding bones and fish heads
to the barn cats when your grandpa Jacob
came along with his penknife, and he
sank the blade into the shining dome of
a loosed eye. With one squeeze, out came

this little ball, cold in my palm, the
jelly hard and clear as glass. We held
it up to the sunset and it drank in the
light, blazing orange and peach. Then
we nudged it across the writing in Pa's
notebook – he's never without paper and
a bright yellow pencil – and it made
each letter look bigger. It was a piece
of magic in among the fish guts, Beth.
And you are the magic inside me. Nothing
looks the same since you were born. Not
even the past.

Before you, I did not know myself. That
I take things too much to heart. Every
punishment, every unkind word. I was
barely as high as Ma's hip that time
she sent me down the well. The dairy
had fallen from the bucket where it was
cooling, a mess of clabbering cow's milk
and rotting butter souring the water.
Every day for a week, I shinned down the
rope to skim the bobbing, stinking fat.
I worked the walls and soaked the smears
from the black liquid until it was a
polished mirror that I might slip through
and never come back – until the water was
good, and I hoped that I was too. A part
of me stayed in that half-lit, halfway
place. Until you showed me what innocence
is, and how much can be forgiven.

So please do not be hasty in deciding
who you are. If you hold strong opinions
on your nature, look them over, back and
front, to see if they were made by you, or
wrought by another hand.

There will be more to say, but the
paper's melting in all this heat and
Lucy's fingers have gone black from
changing the ribbon. Let me sign off with
wonderful news, my darling. I have met a
fine man from Droop Mountain. He loves
me, just as I love him, and with God's
grace, he will soon ask me to marry him.
His name is Edward Shue, but everyone
calls him Trout, just like the fish,
on account of how long he can hold his
breath underwater. He makes an honest
living at the forge in Livesay where,
being proud of his person, he is the
cleanest and most fastidious blacksmith
that anyone has ever seen. (He taught me
that word. It means that he's neat and
careful in everything he does.) But most
of all, Trout is kind. Maybe one day you
will visit us here in Meadow Bluff. Or
perhaps you will invite me to the fine
Wylie residence in Richmond.

I will send you a portrait so that you
might find some feature whereby you'll
recognise me. Until then, you have the

cardinal I've pressed inside these
pages. It has no seeds left in its big
pods because I set those golden specks
floating down the New River – praying for
them to make it through the mountains,
and along the waters of the Jackson until
they find you on the banks of the James.
The few petals that are left make little
velvet lanterns, as you can see. Trout
says the Catholic cardinals in Rome
wear hats and sashes in the same colour.
Daring and strange as that sounds, I
believe him. You will like Trout. He knows
things that nobody else does.

Go outside, Beth. Find cardinals by the
water. Towering and blazing like my love
for you. Lucy will seal my words now,
while I still have the nerve to leave
them from my grasp.

I will remain,

Yours ever truly,
Zona Heaster

1 | LUCY FRYE

Livesay/Meadow Bluff

September 16, 1896

Her mother kept urging her to get rid of the Remington, but Lucy couldn't imagine life without it sitting smart and modern on the dressing table.

Each silver letter was tiny and exquisite on the end of its own metal stalk, and there were few things more satisfying than firing them at the ink ribbon, punching words onto the page. She enjoyed the violence of the *click*; the permanence of the brand.

When she was buying the used typewriter from the *Greenbrier Independent*, the editor had doubted her stamina to wallop the stiff keys – questioned her ability to change the ribbon and align the arms so that the basket didn't end up in a snare. But after only a few months of practice, here she was typing more than seventy words per minute with as many as four cooperative fingers. The tower of writing beside her elbow was a triumph of sorts. Yet the higher this column grew, the worse she felt, riddled as it was with her failed attempts at newspaper articles.

She winced at the titles poking out of the dereliction. 'Have a Dirty Cut? Dial Franklin 448'. That was the one about the new antitoxin, written after little Prudie Thorne died of lockjaw. The *Independent* had turned its nose up, advising her to *stick to women's affairs*, before publishing an identical article under the editor's name. Dog-eared, near the top of the pile, she spied 'Neglect Felt by Society and Community', a report on the recent scandal at the State Fair when not one woman in the county had competed in the hosing or glove departments. If you were to believe the judges, it was a moral disaster. But the newspaper turned this down, too, telling her to come back with something *more cheerful, about fashion, or the household — maybe society*.

Dejected at the memory, she dropped onto the chair and grasped her tin of rouge, its equator seeping scarlet. She prised off the lid and leaned toward the mirror, daubing each cheek. It didn't look right, as usual, though her mother insisted that she try. The crimson might enhance the attractive cushion of a cheek like Zona's. On her own face, it highlighted her home-liness, and once she'd cycled as far as the Heasters' farm, it would double up on her redness, too.

Fingers greasy and lurid, she tugged at the paper in the typewriter carriage until it came free. When it was smoothed on the table, she had the strong urge to stay home and finesse her morning's writing. This hesitation to visit the Heasters was new. She had never felt it, nor any need to shore up her appearance, before meeting Trout Shue. The man had this subtle demeanour when he looked at her – eyes narrowed, always seeming to wish her different in some unspecified way. Whether she was reserved or outgoing, silly or serious, his little frowns and sighs told her that he was never happy. Meanwhile, he worshipped everything about Zona. Her best friend had been praying for Trout to propose marriage, while her own special wish was for the blacksmith to pack up and move on.

She wriggled into the neat jacket of her bicycle suit, regret hard and polished in her chest, because it was her own fault that they'd met. It shouldn't have mattered that her new bicycle lamp was swinging loose; not in July, when she was in bed every night before sunset. Yet it was she who had insisted on dragging Zona down to the blacksmith to have a wedge fitted to the clamp. That was where they'd found a new man tending the bellows, in the place where old amiable Jim used to be. And she'd acquired a wedge all right. One named Trout Shue, who was still driving himself in tight between her and Zona.

She started down the stairs, cringing at the stupidity of it all, trying not to wake her spoiled parents and beautiful black-haired sisters. In the hallway, her leather tool belt hung by its strap from the coat rack, and she checked inside the stiff pocket for her small tin of oil, her adjustable wrench, her screwdriver and the little .32 calibre revolver that she'd taken to carrying since that rabid fox emerged furious from the grass over at Fort Spring. Alongside these provisions, she squeezed in a small gift for Zona, wrapped in taffeta.

Her bicycle, greased wheels gleaming, was stored under the lean-to behind her mother's coop of ornamental fowl. The gold frame was shining after its recent wash, and the cork grips on the nickelled handlebars were smart and fresh. With her sleeve pulled over the heel of her hand, she wiped the saddle before hunkering beside the front wheel, a swipe of her thumb cleaning the glass face of her cyclometer. Its cream dial showed a series of small black digits, numbering the miles that she had travelled since midsummer – *0 3 1 7*. She was going to drive that number up to *2 0 0 0*, no matter how many bottles of Pond's Extract she needed to soothe her peeling face. Just a few more months on her silent steed and she would finish her best article yet: 'The Bicycle Woman in the Modern World'.

It was about the exhilaration of wheeling long-distance, and how she no longer felt obscure or uncertain when she was out on the road, in full occupation of her body. When she had told Zona about it, her friend's eyes had glinted with more kindness than faith. Still, she was encouraging, not believing in being shy or contrite about anything since the birth of her astonishing child. But confessing her ambition to her ma and step-pa had been different. While the pair sat rigid on the tapestry sofa, she had imagined that the painted walls were throbbing along with her pounding cheeks, her face perhaps turning the same shade of brutal magenta.

I can live with it, Lucia, her mother had said, *if you try descriptive writing. A bit of harmless showing off. These women journalists exist, but think how hard – and hardening – their lives must be. With all this bicycling, people will think you're depraved. Or deformed. For your own sake*, she had added, exasperation ripening to anger, *do something to preserve your . . . allurement. A woman never looks better than when she's on horseback.*

On the downhill toward Zona's house, she raised her feet

up onto the coasters. The air whistled by, sweet with summer's end; the scent of warm clay and wheat stubble and the last green cuttings of hay. The smell of windfall apples came in a sudden drift, and her soul took its first gentle shift into fall. Patches of crimson flashed amongst the oaks and hemlocks and birches and maples, heralding the march of scarlet and yellow and bronze that would soon flame across the hills.

God hadn't drawn many straight lines in Greenbrier County. The boundary between earth and sky was almost always curved and high. When she trundled off the Midland Trail, onto the slip for Meadow Bluff, her lungs and legs were blazing with the pain of riding over scores of bending horizons.

With her arms aching from the rutted road jerking the handlebars, she stalled in front of the old Burns house and reached into the pannier for an apple. Clean, sharp juice rinsed her mouth as she collapsed onto the verge, gazing up at the little building. The sashes were open onto the bedroom where she, Lucy Clementine Burns Frye, had been born one New Year's Day. The log walls were still exposed, the bark scrubbed and whitewashed. The glazing in the front door still had a red pane in the centre, and the same big black iron handle was screwed to the door, rust stains bleeding down the blue paint. Everything was much the same as it had been on that morning when she and her ma had moved out. The new inhabitants probably felt nothing of her father's spirit inside the house. To her, it had seemed that the walls and the wainscot and the shingles had been saturated with him; enough that when she left on her twelfth birthday, she had grieved the floorboards, the ceilings, the limestone hearth.

Her stepfather's white-colonnaded house had always been too grand, with its huge teeming pond and seven gleaming horses frisking about the paddock. It suited the character of her siblings very well. They were robust, vivacious children, while she, their half-sister, felt like a half-person in almost every respect.

Zona seemed to understand this without any explanation, meaning that she had never been jealous of Lucy. Not for living close to the painted shopfronts and restaurants of Lewisburg while she herself was left stranded way out in this hinterland. Not for suddenly having housemaids, or a leather-upholstered surrey. She didn't even mind that Lucy had no labour to do, not in house or field, remaining fashionably plump from one month to the next.

If anything, it was Lucy who was envious; who was some-times begrudging of Zona's easy nature, her confidence, her natural inclination toward happiness. And now here she was, nursing resentment against her friend's beau, dreaming of ways to come between them. With a groan of reluctance, she heaved herself to her feet. She would have to try harder to accept the blacksmith. After all, Trout and Zona seemed to set each other off, like sweet rhubarb and bitter orange. And nothing could be done about such affinity, no matter how bewildering.

She walked her bicycle up the big incline with lunging steps, jumping on when the road hit the level. After a mile of gouged and potholed road, the farm came into view. On the low ridge beyond the house, a spine of chestnut trees looked out over the acres beyond, their leaves already browning, a few of the Heasters' glossy hogs snuffling in their shade.

The side doors of the barn were open, channelling the cleansing westerly breeze, the building so vibrant in its fresh coat of red oxide that Lucy thought the milk paint might still be wet. The wooden star on the south wall had been revived, too, in a coat of green. Zona had collected a jar of emerald-coloured powder from the cinnamon ferns in the spring, explaining that the hue was a symbol of growth and fruitfulness and all the brothers and sisters she wanted for Elisabeth. And here it was, just as she had promised Lucy, mixed with linseed oil, radiating her hopes out over Greenbrier County.

Coasting through the open gate to the yard, Lucy saw Trout on the steps of the porch. He had a certain sense of occasion, dressed in a brown sack suit and a navy sateen tie with white stripes. He was ten years older than her and Zona, but something about him seemed immature; restless, as if there was always some other place he'd rather be.

'Lucy!' Shading her eyes, Zona came down the porch steps, clutching the plaid of her flannel skirts.

Stopping dead on the cracked earth, Lucy wiped her wet brow with her wrist. 'Happy birthday,' she said, as Zona ran and took her in a sudden embrace.

'All Trout's idea.' Zona kept her voice low. 'Let's call it a special occasion, but Ma's not really sure what day I was born.' She gripped Lucy's wrists, her broad grin almost taking her breath away. Strong and slender and tanned, with good colour in her cheeks. Lucy had not seen her this bright or happy since Elisabeth had been taken.

'What's with the ink?' she said, masking her relief by frowning at the big black marks on Zona's fingers.

'I'm helping Pa draw up one of his machines,' she said. 'The steam wagon, this time. He reckons a few good drawings will help him get a patent. You-Know-Who will be here in a few weeks to check over the paperwork.'

'Emory Snow?' Lucy grimaced. If ever a man knew how to abuse both hospitality and the people who offered it, it was Jacob Heaster's rich and thin-skinned inventor friend from Wilmington. A visit would be about as welcome as a blowfly in the larder.

'But speaking of machines.' Zona seized the handlebars, waiting for Lucy to dismount. 'I worry what this thing is doing to your insides.'

'I don't see why it should hurt my insides,' Lucy said, stretching her cramped legs, 'when it does nothing to a man's outsides. Lula Burr's given birth three times since Thomas got his bicycle, and his tyres aren't even pneumatic.'

Zona gave one of her big barking laughs, and wheeled the bicycle to the corner of the house. 'How you talk, Lucy Frye,' she said, parking it against the wall.

Together they walked around the corner, back into the sunlight, the scents of clay and bitumen and sawdust rising. The Heasters' rambling log house had always made Lucy feel safe. The way Zona's father, Jacob, had joined up the three old cabins, anyone might have thought he'd lifted the corners of the land and watched the buildings tumble into unexpected harmony. But today, she could not enjoy their sprawling charm because, as she followed her friend up the porch steps, here was Trout, blocking the way.

He gave Zona a fond smile, dimples showing, grazing the back of her hand with his own as she passed. But when Lucy lifted her face to greet him, he shuffled backward in exaggerated style, bowing in mock deference.

'Thank you,' she said, stiff. There was nothing else to do, what with Zona standing there, hands on her hips, beaming at them both. 'Good ride over from Livesay?' Lucy asked.

'Got here last night,' he said with a whiff of gloating. 'Mary Jane insisted I stay and bunk with the boys. You?' He rocked on his heels, his silence of that polite variety which verges on hostile.

'Good,' she said with a shrug.

Trout could be talkative. Friendly. But here he was again, watchful, getting ready to charm her flaws to the surface like worms out of dirt. She found Jacob's eye, where he stood puffing on his pipe. With the stem gripped between his teeth, he warned, 'Careful there,' as the door of the house banged open behind her.

Little Lenny burst out onto the porch, panting. 'Lucy,' he said, his small fingers clutching at her own. 'Emily Dove won't leap frog. Come show her how.' The tight curls of his black hair were damp, his grinning face flushed. Inside, there was the crash and roar of horseplay; the sound of the Heaster boys, big and small, winding up their humourless cousins.

'Not now,' Zona said, marching him by the shoulders. 'Lucy's staying out here with the grown-ups.' With the child delivered through the door, she slammed it. Lucy swallowed her disappointment, allowing her friend to grip her arm and pull her toward the swing seat. 'Forget them,' Zona said. 'You have to see this.'

They blundered past Mary Jane where she sat with her back to them, brass pins flashing in her thick hair as she pitched to and fro on the rocking chair. Her friend dragged her onto the swing, and Lucy's hand slid down its rough twists of rope. Fingers burning, she turned to scold Zona, but stopped when she saw the wry set of her friend's face, and the spectacular view that they had of Mrs Heaster.

Zona's mother was puffing on a cigarillo, looking more dishevelled than an infant just lifted from her nap. And, although such a thing hardly seemed possible, it was clear that she wasn't wearing a corset. Not even the healthy boneless kind, like Lucy's own stays, which were made of light summer netting.

'Lucy Frye,' Mary Jane said, squinting against a curl of smoke, her gaze very shameless. 'You took your time, girl. How's your ma?' As ever, her voice seemed to emanate from some basement of her being, gathering strange momentum around its walls before it emerged, fulsome and outsized.

'She's doing well,' Lucy said, unable to conceal her alarm. Beside her, Zona's shoulders twitched with mirth. 'But how are you, Mrs Heaster?'

Without her stays, Mary Jane's dress could not be fastened at the back, and the natural shape of her body was visible in all its glory. She slouched, a small mound of stomach protruding, the rounds of her breasts straining against that fabric where only a neatly tied waist should be showing. It gave the impression that she was a stranger to her right mind. And were it not for her familiar intelligence smouldering alongside her cigarette, Lucy would have thought her a lunatic.

'I am very well, thank you,' Mary Jane said. 'And I can see you, Zona Heaster, with your smirking. I haven't been on earth this long to have the like of you lecturing me. Lucy, darling, if you're wondering, I've decided to embrace my gift for spiritualism. It's a big relief, I can tell you, after a lifetime of denial.' Leaning to one side, she took an old postal card from her skirt pocket; a dog-eared image of a mild beatific girl with rag curls flowing over her shoulders. 'This is Cora Richmond,' she said. 'Me and her, we're close enough in age. I don't know how it happened, Lucy.' A note of bitterness entered her voice. 'Cora spent her girlhood channelling the finest doctors and judges and politicians – even has her own spiritualist church in Chicago now – while I gave up my talents to live this thankless life.'

'You think you can talk to the dead?' Lucy said. Mary Jane liked to raise hell, but this performance beat anything that had come before. 'Can't you do that in your stays?'

'Think about it,' Mary Jane said, as if the question were delinquent. 'Every woman has her craft for attracting the best souls. What if an important man like George Washington, or Benjamin Franklin, wants to possess my body to bring you consoling news from the After Life? You don't want him to find it too small or too stuffy.' She took another big draw on her cigarette before using it to gesture at Lucy's clothes. 'You understand. Same as you not wanting to be trussed up on that bicycle of yours. Ann Power helped me see it. She says the nuns don't wear corsets, and it has everything to do with communicating better with the Lord and the dearly departed.'

She leaned forward, pushing a vivid tray of raspberry lemonade a little closer to Lucy. The unfixed shoulder of her dress fell, revealing a glimpse of white cotton chemise and a stretch of sallow collarbone.

Lucy's eyes flicked to the ground, her brows rising without her bidding. 'And ... do you feel more ... holy?' she asked, doubtful.

Zona snorted. 'If you think she looks pious, you better get yourself over to Burdette's for some eyeglasses. Ann never said to go around dishabille, Ma. You're only doing it to annoy Pa.'

Sure enough, Jacob had positioned himself on the far side of the porch, as if to avoid friction with his wife; *a woman so loud and certain in her opinions*, Lucy's own mother said, *she's got to be shouting over some terrible noise inside.*

'And see up there?' Zona elbowed Lucy so that she might cast an eye to the porch ceiling.

'What about it?' she said, seeing nothing but white-washed boards.

'The colour. Remember? Used to be haint blue, to keep out wandering spirits. Now, Ma wants everyone on the Other Side tramping through the house.'

'What would you know about it?' Mary Jane shrugged her dress back onto her shoulder, and Lucy startled at the crinkle of onion-skin paper.

'Oh, that's right,' Zona said. 'I forgot to say, she's been carrying her caul around with her. You know, that nasty little thing she keeps in the Bible.'

'You still have your veil, Mrs Heaster?' Lucy pictured the dried morsel of birth sac, adhered to the same paper that had been used to lift it from Mary Jane's infant face. The membrane was as fragile as it was waxy, the brown of its curling edges a match for dried tobacco. 'I thought you might have sold it to a gullible sailor by now.'

'You'd better believe it could save any man from drowning,' Mary Jane said in a bragging tone. 'But it's the mark of a natural psychic, and I won't be parted from it.'

Zona shuddered. 'Might as well be carrying the skin off a rice pudding for all the good it'll do.'

Mary Jane stubbed her cigarette out in the ashtray. 'You'll never understand, because you're too closed to the spirit world.' She squeezed her eyes shut, a strong breath causing her nostrils to narrow. 'It won't be long now before a soul takes possession. I can feel it.'

Lucy watched Mary Jane flexing her hands in a strange expectant way. She'd always been fond of attention, and seemed to find it sweetest when it was stolen from Zona. As her eyes opened again, mother and daughter stared at each other, a hard glaze coming over both.

'Zona, darling?' Trout lowered himself onto the stool beside Lucy. 'Are you disrespecting your mother?'

His tone was playful, but Lucy could hear an earnest edge to his chiding. He'd been eavesdropping, listening to the whole of their conversation while appearing to be engaged in another.

'Pay no heed,' Lucy said. 'They like to fly mad at each other.' As if on cue, both women turned to her, chests rising and falling in a pair of matching vexed sighs. 'See?' she said. 'They can't stay sore for long.'

'Oh, you mind your own business,' Zona said, with mock anger, before linking Lucy's arm and setting the swing to gliding.

Lucy felt a petty wash of satisfaction; one that Trout seemed to notice. He watched her from the corner of his eye, waiting for the shine to go off her mood. Given his coolness, this took no time at all, and he seized the moment for himself.

'It's a great blessing to me,' he said, 'sharing the company of a happy family.'

He went quiet as a stone, studying his boots. It gave Zona and Mary Jane enough time to understand what he was really saying – *My own family is unhappy.*

Zona pulled her arm from Lucy's. 'We're blessed to have you,' she said. Rising from the cushions, she went to stand behind him, and there was something very frank and unsettling about their intimacy as she began to knead his shoulders.

He gave a little huff of laughter, and stayed her hands, as if he felt unworthy of the attention. 'I'm just saying how lucky I am.' He leaned against her belly, tilted his head back so that he might look into her eyes. 'I don't know, Mrs Heaster,' he said, 'how you managed to raise such a lovely daughter.'

Mary Jane went soft with delight, believing his compliment to be sincere. 'You just make yourself right at home, Trout Shue,' she said. 'Right. At. Home.'

Nettled, Lucy stood up and picked open the buckle of her tool belt, pushing her hand inside to claim the taffeta-wrapped parcel. 'I have a present for you, Zona,' she said. 'I got Pa to help me.' Her friend had always preferred any gift that was made by hand, no matter how ugly or amateur, and anything originating from William Frye, Watchmakers & Jewellers was especially welcome. 'It's a token. For good luck.'

Recognising the teal-blue wrapping, Zona said, 'Give it here,' and sought the parcel with wiggling fingers.

Trout grimaced as it passed under his nose. 'Smells bad,' he said.

'If I'm right,' Zona said, shimmying off the scarlet twine, 'that's the stink of burned cuttlefish. Meaning that Lucy carved a mould all by herself, and poured hot metal into the bone.'

His mouth twisted with derision, while she loosened the fabric and pinched open the layers of white tissue beneath. When her eyes met the object – a silver star, enamelled in green, strung on a green velvet ribbon – she glowed with sudden pleasure, its five neat points a twin for the star on the barn that she had painted in Elisabeth's memory. But then, to Lucy's horror, her expression decayed into a grand measure of pain.

Zona was biting hard on the inside of her cheek, trying to dismiss the lustre of tears. But there was no way that she could disguise the mixture of loss and hope and rage and love that sometimes possessed her when her baby came to mind. She nudged the pendant with her finger, in the same gentle way that she might have reached inside her daughter's blanket to explore her dark curls, and she hooked the ribbon, the enamel flashing as it rose into the air and spun into stillness.

'It's perfect,' she said, holding it out for Trout to see and by way of silent request for him to place it on her neck.

He rose to standing, wiping his palms on his pants, and gave Lucy a withering glance, one suggesting that he both understood the meaning of the gift and was opposed to the giving of it. And although she had begged Zona not to tell him anything about Elisabeth, she knew at once that her friend had revealed all.

He drew the ribbon neatly about Zona's throat, taking an age to primp the simple bow that he had formed. All the while, Lucy feared that her skin might blister under Mary Jane's ferocious gaze. Zona's mother worked her bottom lip against her teeth in this panicked way. And by the time her daughter had turned back to face them, there could be no denying it. The secret of Elisabeth was so open between them that the force of it might have conjured the child into their very midst.

Mary Jane scanned the porch, making sure that Jacob was gone from earshot. 'You told them?' she said to Zona in a coarse whisper. 'Both of them? Do you want the whole world to know?' She had a genuine look of dread, her complicity in Elisabeth's adoption a dangerous secret of its own.

'Listen,' Zona said, cheeks burning, 'today isn't about my birthday. I just wanted everyone to be here for our special news. Trout has proposed marriage. And I've accepted.'

Shock seized Lucy. How foolish she had been, believing that she had any chance of preventing this inevitable union. Without the stomach to offer any congratulation, she looked away before her friend could seek it. Meanwhile, Mary Jane's eyes filled with light, and there was a sudden ease to her bearing; quiet joy at her daughter's salvation.

'Not telling Trout about Elisabeth,' Zona continued, 'that would be the same as lying, and I couldn't do that to him. I might as well confess it to the trees. He won't breathe a word.'

'That's right,' Trout said, a supportive hand on the nape of her neck. 'Zona's been brave. And honest. And we're going to make a new start, just like she deserves.'

Mary Jane relaxed inside her brown linsey dress. But jerked her head in Lucy's direction to hiss, 'And what business did you have telling her?'

Sweat prickled in Lucy's armpits. She was the outsider now, with all three observing her, trying to weigh up her importance. Even Zona squinted, perhaps regretting their intimacy.

'Because,' her friend said, shaking her head, 'it's *Lucy*.' She threw her palms up then, as if no other explanation were needed.

'Exactly. I'd rather die than tell a soul,' Lucy said. 'Who'd have guessed anything from a necklace? Only you two. And that's because you already know.'

'It's between the four of us now,' Zona said, fingers pressed to the pendant. 'That's as far as it will ever go.'

'Maybe,' Trout said. 'But, darling' – with a firm hand, he lifted Zona's chin – 'it just goes to prove how hard it is for someone to keep a secret when they have less to lose.' He was using a special tone that seemed to imply, *Remember how we've talked about this before? And now look what's happened.*

Thoughtful, Zona gave a small nod, as much as his grip would allow. Then she stepped away, forcing a narrow stream of air through her lips that ended, finally, in a sigh.

'Let's take a stroll,' she said, extending her hand to Lucy. 'It's time we had a proper talk.'

They were both putting it off; waiting to find themselves beyond the stile at the end of the cornfield, or down the slope where the sheep were grazing, or past the sugar bush where the leaves were turning pink. Finally, the shallow creek at the farm's northern edge forced them to stop. Lucy watched the green water sliding to the east, amazed by the enormous discomfort between them.

It was Zona who broke the silence. 'You know,' she said. 'Trout's willing to make an effort if you are. The only reason he doesn't trust you is because he doesn't know you well enough yet.'

They looked at each other in hot astonishment; at real odds for the first time in their lives.

'Has he said something?'

'Only that he wants to be friends. Even if it's just for my sake. It doesn't matter to him, really, that you don't have much in common. He says,' she held up one of her long, pliant fingers, taking the trouble to recollect his words exactly, 'that he has no contempt for difference.'

Lucy could taste her own foolishness, sour on her tongue. She should have spoken up long ago, before Trout ever opened his big mouth. 'I've been friendly with him,' she said. 'But he judges me.'

'He said the very same about you.'

'But he's the wiseacre.' She mimicked Trout's scornful smile at her bloomers on that day when she first met him at the forge. *'At least you won't die of getting your skirts caught in your wheels.'*

Zona tried to affect good humour about it all. 'I know he rubbed you up the wrong way. But he's been working to make a good impression ever since. And you don't warm to him. Please. He's going to be my husband. Don't make me take sides.'

Lucy's thoughts were crowding. Any more grumbling about the blacksmith and she would be accused of bitterness. Worse still, if she pressured Zona to choose between them, her old friend would be loyal to Trout. 'Do you trust him?' she said.

Zona lifted her tanned face to the sky. Gone were the dark hollows that had lingered beneath her eyes for over a year. 'I know it sounds silly,' she said, 'but it's like we've known each other for ever. Since before we were even born.' Her shoulders crept up to her ears as she struggled to describe this phenomenon. 'I don't know. Everything about him is just so . . . familiar.' She relaxed, smile broadening.

Change comes, Lucy thought, whether you like it not. She was in no danger of acquiring her own husband and children, both wanting and not wanting these things in equal measure. But she had never considered that marriage for either of them might interfere with their long-standing affection. There was a quick unravelling in her gut; the unwelcome acceptance that comes with letting go.

'If he loves you, just as you are, I'll do my best to get along with him,' she said, the ache of loss already setting in. 'Can you ask him to meet me halfway?' She plastered on a smile, hiding her certainty that Trout would do no such thing.

'Yes,' Zona said. 'Oh, thank you.' She squeezed Lucy's hands, as if sealing a promise of sorts. 'Trout will be so happy, you've no idea.' Gladdened, she turned on her heel. 'There's a roll of blue velvet at Hansbarger's,' she said. 'Will you meet me there Friday? I've a pattern for my wedding dress and want it cut before Ma sticks her nose in.'

'You won't let her help?' Lucy said.

Zona gave a solemn glance in the direction of the house. 'She's so bitter, Lucy,' she said. 'I try to make light of it, but she keeps talking about Ruth.'

The sound of their departed friend's name brought a surge of grief between them. The morning that Ruth died, Zona and Mary Jane had been the ones to wash her ravaged remains, smoothing clean linen over her nose and fingertips that were black as the pulp of rotten fruit, destroyed by the slippery elm bark that, instead of ending her pregnancy, had ended her life.

'What's Mary Jane been saying?' Lucy said, her hackles rising.

'That I learned nothing from Ruth dying. That I disrespected her memory by getting myself pregnant. Imagine listening to that while you're stitching your wedding dress.'

'Don't let her get under your skin,' Lucy said, trying to quieten her own agitation. 'She couldn't be more wrong, Zona. Not if she tried. I think Mary Jane takes things too hard, is all.'

'What's she taking hard? Nothing happened to her.'

No stranger to resentment, Lucy believed that she could sense it in Mary Jane, too. 'Remember when you were lying in? How she bent over backward to keep the baby a secret. I bet that's eating her up now, thinking you got away with it scot-free.'

'There's no bigger price than the one I paid,' Zona said. 'I'd never treat Elisabeth the way Mary Jane does me.'

Lucy grasped her hand where anger had set it to hovering. And she felt a burst of sadness, realising that she could not comfort her friend with the same warmth and ease as before. The trust between them was not broken, but it was bruised and tender, the pain of it creeping into everything. 'Give it more time,' she said. 'When you've got your own house, things will settle.'

'Maybe.' Zona's sharp smile signalled the desire for a change of mood. 'It'll be a spring wedding,' she said, her gaze lengthening toward the future. 'End of April, the orchard in blossom.'

They started back toward the house. But as Zona described Trout's plans to build a cabin for them by a deep pool in the Meadow River, Lucy was too twisted up in her own concerns to join in the bride's excitement. When they reached the scalped stalks of the cornfield, there was a ruckus coming from the front porch, and she bubbled with relief, because here was the welcome promise of distraction.

All six of the Heaster boys had spilled out of the house, along with an assortment of Mary Jane's dreary nieces. The two eldest, Alfred and James – the former as swarthy as the latter was fair – were wrestling Trout, pulling at his jacket and mussing his long hair, so that he had to pull away and straighten his tie when he saw that Zona was coming.

He grabbed the cotton blanket from the swing seat and wrapped it about his fiancée's shoulders as if she were returning from the Arctic. Mary Jane was quick to join them all in a huddle, holding the front of her dress up by the frill of its yoke.

'Well?' she whispered, seeming eager for satisfaction from Lucy.

'Everything's fine, Ma,' Zona said, giving her mother's arm a dismissive pat. 'Everything's good.'

Alfred barged between them, linen vest rumpled, coarse curls springing as he pulled Lucy by the hand. 'Get Bertie,' he said, referring to her bicycle. 'I'll race you to the ridge.'

But before she could move, there was the sound of glass ringing. Jacob was tapping the rim of the cider jug with the yellow pencil he always kept tucked into his hatband. He didn't stop until silence had descended.

'Zona,' he said, solemn, 'Trout has told me your excellent news. Your ma and me, well, we're happy to welcome another son into the family. Boys, say congratulations to your new brother. Trout here's going to marry your sister.'

There was cheering, a melee of Heasters lifting the blacksmith onto their shoulders. Zona's brown eyes glittered with happiness as they carried him up and down the porch in triumph. From on high, Trout gave Lucy what might pass for a forgiving smile. But all she could see was a cowbird, sleek and devious, laying his own fat speckled egg as he got ready to throw her from the nest.

2 | Mary Jane Heaster

Lewisburg

October 3, 1896

Homer Woldridge tipped his cap as he passed them on Church Street, his wife, Amelia, clamped to his arm. 'Morning, Mary Jane,' he said. 'You too, Zona.'

Amelia gave a condescending nod, and Mary Jane managed a frosty hello. But Zona fell silent, her cheeks flushing scarlet.

'Quick now,' Mary Jane said, gripping her daughter's arm, walking out of earshot. 'Pull yourself together, before your father sees you. If I have to stomach the Woldridges, then you can too.'

Jacob was walking a little ahead, oblivious to the fact that he shared a grandchild with their smug neighbours. He knew nothing about the baby girl whose adoption Mary Jane had arranged after reading Eugenia Wylie's advertisement in *The Outlook* magazine. The plea for a child, printed in tiny writing amidst the news stories and pencil portraits, had seemed like a sign from God himself. And when that Wylie woman had arrived in Meadow Bluff, with her mealy face and the finest buggy Mary Jane had ever seen, she was that zealous you'd think the Star of Bethlehem had been hanging over Bessie Harford's house. *Elisabeth*, she had heard herself blurt as the child disappeared for ever. *For what it's worth, Mrs Wylie, Zona would've called her Elisabeth.*

She was at the mercy of these difficult memories every time a Woldridge shuffled into her church pew, or browsed alongside her at the general store, which was to say, very often. 'Why did you have to pick that George?' she said. 'I've seen maggots with more spine. No surprise, him leaving for California,' she said. 'Nobody buys a cow when they've had the milk for free.'

The sharp words tasted bitter on her lips as Zona lifted her nose in the air, marching faster so that they might catch up with Jacob.

It was all very far from the outcome that she had expected when she first agreed to help Zona with the baby; telling Jacob that his daughter was gone to Richmond for the summer to learn to bake fancy cakes. She'd imagined that the powerful secret would bond daughter to mother for ever. But no. Her girl was solo again, walking stainless in the light, basking every day in her father's affection. Jacob's endless doting was like an oyster knife sticking in Mary Jane, threatening to spring the truth about the child. She would have yielded long ago were it not for poor grieving Bessie. *It keeps me sane*, she'd said, *seeing Zona so well and happy and free. Is her good health not God's reward for laying out my darling Ruth on that terrible Easter morning?*

It was maddening, how Zona was able to pretend like none of it had ever happened; how she had landed a man even more devoted and adoring and forgiving than she deserved.

'Don't wait around for me after Pa's patent meeting,' Zona said. 'I'm going to meet Lucy for coffee in the Lewisburg Hotel.'

'So the whole of town will get to see those bags under your eyes?' Mary Jane said, taking in her daughter's sallow appearance. 'What time did Trout leave? Third night in a row you kept us all awake with your talking.' Instead of feeling secure, the blacksmith had taken to romancing Zona in an even more feverish way since their betrothal, wanting her all to himself in the small hours of the morning, keeping her drunk on love and lethargy.

'We've a life to plan,' her daughter said, through a contented yawn.

'The rest of us manage in daylight.'

Mary Jane turned the corner onto the bustle of Washington Street, the bright modern stores pristine. Gill Weber had filled his gleaming windows with tasselled gloves in impractical shades of pink and gold and palest green, and the cloying scent of honeysuckle was overwhelming where a vine had been trained about the little porch of The Sugar Plum. Beyond the cascade of flowers, Jacob used his sleeve to polish the brass plaque on the door of Frederic Wallace, Attorney at Law.

'Did you tarnish it just by reading it?' she said.

He looked them up and down, beady, assessing their value to his patent application. Zona's fresh, airy cape – the one Trout had bought for her – raised no objection. But the perished rubber of her own silver-grey gossamer provoked.

'It won't be raining inside, Mary Jane,' he said.

She pulled the fabric tight around her, ignoring its smell of rotten mushrooms and potato peel. 'I'm comfortable as I am.' If he'd had his way, she'd be home in Meadow Bluff, acting the drudge. It was better to be in town, tempering his vanity.

'Careful what you wish for, Pa.' Zona had the nerve to look exasperated. 'Nobody needs to see her without a corset. Go inside, now. And don't fret. Mr Snow will be here, just like he promised.'

Doubtful and mechanical as this reassurance was, Jacob brightened, and pushed through Wallace's door. Inside the shady room, he gave his name to the office girl, whose smile broadened with artificial cheer. To Mary Jane's surprise, she rose from her chair and ushered them straight through to the attorney's library, announcing them as *Your much-anticipated steam wagon party, sir.*

Behind the desk, Frederic Wallace's babyish face was shining with eagerness to meet them. 'You're the Snow Peeler man!' he said. As he stood to give Jacob's hand a brotherly shake, his expression filled with admiration and amazement. 'I hear they can't get enough of your machines in Kentucky. Shaving the bark off trees like they're paring pencils.' His tone turned confidential, then. 'I wonder,' he said, 'if we might speak about working together on future inventions.'

Jacob's fingers cramped as he withdrew his hand. The letter that he had recently received from Wallace had agreed to waive the fees for his patent application, but only if the esteemed inventor Emory Snow would vouch for his design. He tutted, shaking his head, as if he were the one guilty of a mistake.

'I wish I were the man of the moment,' he said. 'Mr Snow, he'll be along any minute. I'm Jacob Heaster, the applicant.'

At once, the attorney's good humour fizzled. Seeming blind to this alteration, Jacob continued. 'I'd like to introduce my wife, Mary Jane. And this is my daughter, Zona. She has all the drawings.'

Their daughter threw her cape over the back of a chair and picked several washed pebbles from her pocket: paper-weights for the corners of her big ink drawings. Jacob sat down beside her, doing a poor job of looking at home. Days of rehearsal turned into real performance as Zona eased the drawings from their cardboard tube. The attorney took no notice, instead becoming absorbed in the index of a large red book.

You couldn't throw a stone in Lewisburg these days without hitting a big-head jurist like him. He was the kind with clean hands and dirty money, most of it made off the back of others' misfortunes up at the county courthouse. His home, Mary Jane supposed, would be one of those mansions at the edge of town, with white terraces and red-brick wings, acres of fertile land wasted on nothing but lawn. His big green pond would be thick with fish caught only for sport. That was how rich town-folk spent their money from mining and logging and railroading and lawyering. And Jacob couldn't wait to be like them – lost for any real purpose, sneering at those honest people who worked God's good earth. Up at Little Sewell, both their fathers would be twirling in their graves.

'As I wrote you, Mr Wallace,' Jacob said, his manner very stiff and formal, 'the Heaster Steam Wagon will run on wheels, with no need of rails.'

Intent on impressing this stranger, he seemed oblivious to the attorney's despicable manners. And Mary Jane watched as his hunger for admiration grew even sharper. It caused her to remember, with a sudden stab of homesickness, their early days of marriage, when he had wanted to prove himself to nobody but her. He had been loyal, and ardent, and she had been his only girl, so happily capsized beneath him.

'This is Figure One,' Zona said, all business, elbowing the attorney's inkwell out of the way. Only as it squeaked across the embossed leather did Wallace pay attention. He darted forward to pin the brass with one hand, eyeing her as if she had meant to steal it.

'There is no meeting,' he said, as if they had missed the obvious, 'without Mr Snow.'

'Emory will be here,' Jacob said.

But the way he was hanging his head spoke of doubt. He rubbed the worn cloth of his good pants, the strokes small and apologetic. He was afraid, Mary Jane knew, of returning to their life exactly as he had left it. Their homespun seams and old-fashioned oil lamps, the old cradles and flails that they used at harvest, even Riley, their clever mare – all were out of date. Fire and rivets and cranks and the building up of steam were her husband's obsessions now, and he scorned the simple existence that he had once loved; perhaps along with the common-sense farm girl he had married.

'I have a proposition of my own, Mr Wallace,' Mary Jane said, her bold tone startling the attorney. Sweltering with embarrassment for her husband, she removed her gossamer, her daughter and husband staring in horror at her sweating face and her figure loose beneath her green frock. The pin that held her caul in place glinted in the strong light from the casement, and she laid her hand over it, as if for courage. 'My husband claims he has vision,' she said. 'But I have sight of a different kind. My gift is Interior Vision. Very useful to someone in your line of business.'

Jacob turned white, lips in a hard line, warning her to stop.

'Tell me, where do you keep Bill Moyers' will?' she asked.

'What should you know about Mr Moyers?' Wallace said, reproachful. But he was curious, too, she thought, because some subtle part of his mind had brought his hips to rest against a filing cabinet containing a drawer labelled *M through P*.

'Didn't Bill write you a letter before he passed?' she said. 'Asked his sister, Florrie, to send it to you.'

Wallace shrugged, giving nothing away.

'He left the farm and forest to his mother, Margret,' Mary Jane said. 'Everyone in Meadow Bluff knows that. But then there's Florrie. He asked that she be given – what were his words? – *special consideration for the rest of her days*. Poor Florrie's been waiting two whole years for the law to decide what her brother meant by that – to be granted some small piece of land or money to call her own.' She closed her eyes, and held her hands out, palms and fingers tingling. 'When I touch Bill's writing, his spirit will possess me. And you can ask him anything you like about his true intentions.'

'Ma?' Zona's voice held a small note of concern. Gentle, as if she were trying to wake her from a dream. 'Not here,' she said.

But, feeling brisk and fresh with relief, Mary Jane did not wish to relent. If Zona was not shy about her drawings, what reason was there to hide her own fledgling talent?

'I'm afraid, Mr Wallace,' Jacob said, 'my wife has taken to thinking she's a spirit medium.'

'Is that so? Or did Miss Moyers put you up to this?'

'Florrie doesn't have it in her. The truth is,' Mary Jane said, 'folks on the Other Side, they need mediums like me. Think of Bill, the comfort he'll have, finding a body to pass on his message.' Wallace's features hardened. 'You've heard of Cora Richmond? Emma Britten? I share the same gifts.'

Zona covered her mouth to snort with laughter, while Jacob tried to bottle his temper.

'Not only do you interrupt an important meeting,' he said, 'but you have to compare yourself with America's most famous spiritualists?'

He turned to Wallace with a sour smirk. Mary Jane was glad to see his rancour spilling over, scorching though it was. When they were alone, he would not admit his disapproval, though she suspected it from the way that he answered questions with a kind of long-suffering silence. Here was a rush of cold surety; a glimpse of the real man who was willing to hang her out to dry.

'Be careful not to deceive yourself, Ma,' Zona said, picking at her little fingernail. 'You don't want to end up being your own kind of fraud.'

'I'm the fraud?' Mary Jane said. 'But your pa's the next Thomas Edison? Don't listen to them, Mr Wallace. Let me hold the will. See for yourself.' She waggled her hand, demanding the paper.

For each step she took forward, the attorney took one back. She was not proud of looking peculiar; still she found that she could not stop. Since she was a girl, she had been ignoring this tension – this terrible whine – at the centre of her being. But lately it had grown too shrill. She felt as if she were a set of strings; a ragged harp catching every spirit breath and whisper that floated on the air.

'Open the drawer,' she said, pleading eyes fixed on Wallace. With a roll of her shoulders, she tried to get limber. It was easy to dispose of a corset, but flesh and bone were different; she would have to trust that they could not be stretched or torn. 'Clear some space, Zona,' she said. Bill Moyers had been a restless man with a clumsy gait. He was sure to thunder about this little room, stamping her feet and raising her fists in a way that no woman would ever dare, not unless she were a romp, or a lunatic.

Words rumbled in Wallace's throat, a flood ready to come downriver. 'Get out,' he said, contemptuous. 'And take all your scams with you.'

'Please,' Jacob said, face blanching. 'Wait for Mr Snow. He's a dear friend.'

'A dear friend who's not coming.' The way Zona snatched up her cape, and wrapped it about her drawings, anyone might have thought all disappointment belonged to her.

She marched for the door, and Jacob looked stricken. He stood up, his belittling glare ordering Mary Jane to follow their daughter. Queasy, she turned on her heel, nursing her stomach as she emerged into sunlight on the busy sidewalk.

The first face she saw was Trout's. He was standing on the kerb, a different light seeming to shine on him than upon everyone else; one that made him look healthy and happy and beyond the grasp of life's ordinary troubles.

'You're wearing the yellow?' he said in a playful voice, dark eyebrows raised at Zona.

'It's got full gigot sleeves,' she said, puffing up the fabric on one shoulder until it stood out like a balloon.

'But the drab is better on you. Flattering is better than flashy.' Zona seemed to sag, then. But Trout lowered the corners of his mouth, as if with comic sadness, until she laughed her assent.

'I've never met a man so interested in women's things,' Mary Jane said, glad of any distraction. 'What are you doing here? You're like the Holy Ghost.' He appeared out of nowhere, these days, when you least expected him, as if with some heightened sense of Zona's business.

'I heard all about your Mr Snow,' he said, drawing her daughter into the compass of his arm. 'You don't meet a man like that every day. I thought, why not stop by?'

Zona sighed. 'Hard to say if it's your lucky or unlucky day. Come meet Lucy at the hotel. I'll tell you all about it.' She took his hand, but he didn't budge.

'Darling,' he said, tender. 'You look exhausted. I'm going to leave a note for Lucy at reception.' The downturned mouth, again. 'I think it's best if I take you home.'

She looked uncertain. Still, she hugged him, as if he were welcome refuge.

Jacob travelled behind Trout's wagon, right along the Midland Trail, slowing around each bend, staying just out of sight. There could be little doubt that Wallace had chased him from his office like a rat from a springhouse. And as Trout drove up the incline to the farm, their changeless house and rolling fields coming into view, Mary Jane gave in to a quiet sense of triumph.

The air was sultry as they drew up alongside the barn. Zona and Trout jumped down to fuss over his thirsting mare, while Mary Jane ambled toward the porch, in festive mood. She took her time climbing the steps, happy to linger on any brink or margin where departed souls might cluster. Her honesty with Wallace – and with herself – had released something inside her; a kind of delicious momentum.

'Boys!' she called, surprised that none of the smaller ones had come out to greet her. But their absence made sense as she heard the familiar strains of tuneless singing. Each note was very high and thin, the lyrics piped in absent-minded fashion.

. . . *there on the carpet, dead and cold, lay the poor little fish in her frock of gold.*

Emory Snow held his strangled crescendo long enough that she was able to follow it to the only windowless room in their house; that cosy hub where three old cabins converged like the spokes of a big wheel. He was standing beside Jacob's charred whisky keg, holding a tall drink with the same lustre as garnets.

'I'm thirsty.' He raised the glass to her before draining it in one throatful. His accent was strangely old-fashioned for a young man from Wilmington. Everything was always *happ-ih* or *funn-ih* or *likel-ih.*

'Emory,' she said, the sight of him less welcome than a spill of blood. The morning had convinced her that their disastrous acquaintance was finally at an end, yet here he was, pouting, drawing his chin into his pudgy neck.

The languid tread of boots in the hall told her that Jacob was coming. He rounded the corner, trying to dodge past her, stalling only as Emory pitched into view.

'Jacob Hedges Heaster,' the inventor said. 'Where've you been?'

There was an agonised sound in her husband's throat, his eyes ticking over and back across the man's infuriatingly innocent expression.

'Go on, Jacob,' Mary Jane said, an urgent feeling lighting inside her. Before taking up with this witless city pigeon, her husband had been her wise grey fox; a man of good instinct. She wanted to see him redeemed, now, feathers between his teeth.

He mimed speech. But no words came. His eyes waxed glassy, noble rage fading. Perhaps he was not willing to snip the final thread; the one that Emory Snow had been using to dangle favours in front of him for years. They had all learned to tiptoe around the inventor, anticipating his every need, trying to avoid his malice and resentment, both of which were too easily stirred. And what had these sacrifices been worth, when the help he offered never came?

Jacob was silent, eyes downcast. Emory watched him, swirling whisky in his mouth, as if savouring both his betrayal and the lack of any consequence.

'Who's this?' Trout said, giving them all a jolt as he came from the direction of the kitchen. 'Why, it's Mr Snow,' he said, slapping Emory on the shoulder. Mary Jane supposed that Snow's oversized jacket had convinced him of his identity. Zona would have told him about his peculiar wardrobe. The labels of his jackets claimed that Everall Brothers made his suits to measure, yet they always drowned his stature. 'I'm Trout Shue,' he said, shaking the inventor's resistant paw. 'Zona's intended.'

'A wedding?' Emory said, cheerless. 'No one told me congratulations were in order. Tell me, sir, are you blushing with pride, or have you just scrubbed your face raw?' He squinted up at Trout's soap-tightened skin. 'You're burnished like a penny.'

'Hazard of the job,' Trout said with a thin smile. 'I'm a blacksmith, you see. Metalworking runs in my family. My brother, he's a riveter at the Brooklyn Navy Yard.'

'A riveter?' Jacob said. 'Your brother makes boilers?' The way her husband lifted his head, curiosity burning, unsettled Mary Jane. 'Your brother would have been useful,' he said, 'when I was planning on building a model.'

'A miniature steam wagon?' Emory said, seeming amused by Jacob's rallying.

'Small and simple,' Jacob said. 'Almost like a toy. One that could trundle around fancy boardrooms in the city. Imagine it – letting those rich investors feed it with spoonfuls of coal, how it would look like it was moving by magic, crossing the floor in any direction, tiny lamps blazing.'

Trout whistled. 'And I thought Mr Snow was the expert.' Mary Jane couldn't tell whether he was impressed or trying to aggravate their guest. 'They'd throw more capital at you than you could spend.'

Her husband chewed his lip, a sudden and terrible gleam of optimism in his eye. 'I'll give you a cut,' he said. 'If I can be sure the boiler won't explode. Your brother's help would be a great boon.'

At this, an empty laugh echoed along the hallway, making them all turn to see Zona where she stood, severe, the tube of drawings for the Heaster Wagon clutched in her hand. 'Why are you talking about money?' she said, her anger unmistakable as she glared at Snow. 'How could there be any money without a patent?' Her frankness astonished them all.

'Zona.' Trout spoke gently, just as he might to an anxious horse. 'Mr Snow will keep his word this time. Isn't that right, Emory? I know when Jacob first met you on the platform at Ronceverte station, with all your money left on the train for Chicago, he took you in. And here you are again, enjoying his hospitality. An honourable man like you won't be able to live with yourself until your debts are paid.'

Mary Jane smirked, impressed by his wiles.

'Well, of course,' Emory said, rocking on his heels. 'I believe in every man getting his just reward.'

Jacob grew a little taller, while Zona was colder and more rigid than ever.

'You don't get it,' she said, her face contorted with outrage. 'This man will *never* help us.'

She was right; there could be no doubt about it. Still, Mary Jane groaned to see her daughter's blundering honesty, the others suspending her in a kind of hostile silence, as if her outburst were an ugly sign of some deeper disturbance.

'Give me those,' Jacob said, grasping one end of the cardboard tube. 'We won't get anywhere without Mr Snow's opinion.'

Shocked, his daughter did not release it. But he happily overpowered her, twisting it from her grasp. Mary Jane watched as Zona's righteous anger receded to humiliation. Trout had been puffing her up these last couple of months, she supposed; making her believe her opinions should be held in higher regard. Well, she was learning some sense now. No woman could demand more room for herself in a man's world.

Not unless she was willing to pay some price that would leave her worse off than before.

Jacob smoothed one of the elegant ink drawings across the table in the whisky room; a fine, neat diagram in Zona's hand. The men huddled around it, their backs curved like pill bugs, little noticing as they shut her out completely.

Her daughter had the nerve to turn and meet her eye before hurrying toward her, as if any island in the storm, no matter how rocky, might be better than open water.

'What did you think would happen?' Mary Jane whispered, feeling the heat of her daughter's shame rising off her. 'It's embarrassing, at your age, not knowing when to hold your temper.'

'I don't feel well,' Zona said. And judging by her complexion, she really was sick to her stomach. 'Help me outside, Trout,' she said. 'I need some air.'

His fingers flickered by his sides. But after a moment, he abandoned his conversation, and sauntered over with more tolerance than affection.

Zona gripped his arm and rushed him out through the kitchen. Mary Jane found herself following them, spying through the window. In the blurry sunshine, the resemblance between daughter and mother was enough that she might have been gazing out on her own past; those early days when neither she nor Jacob had yet learned how to keep their powder dry.

She could imagine what Zona was saying. Perhaps the same words that were trapped in her own throat. *I know Emory of old. He'll never change. You're prolonging the agony.*

Trout was aloof, standing as tall as he could stretch, his arms crossed. Impatient, Mary Jane waited for him to cut loose, and for Zona to let him go, standing her ground. Instead, her daughter behaved like they were characters in a mushy dime novel. Seeing the blacksmith acting sore, she began ministering to him, as if he'd been wounded. Tentative, her fingers touched his arm, and a wave of alterations went through her body, chest sinking and shoulders narrowing. There was a twist in the meaning of things, as if she were seeking Trout's approval now. Or his forgiveness.

Mary Jane didn't think she'd ever seen anything more foolish or aggravating in her life. She seized the butter churn and yanked out the plunger, reaching in to scrub the staves. Maybe Zona didn't care how important it was for her to stay silvery cool, but she wasn't about to give in to rage, because there was no visiting soul – none of any quality – that would ever be willing to possess a body that blistered and burned.

from:

THE TRIAL OF TROUT SHUE

A TRUE STORY
CONTAINING HITHERTO
SUPPRESSED FACTS

by Lucia C. Frye

Trout Shue had no difficulty in marshalling character witnesses for his trial: local men, aiming to convince the jury of his inherent goodness. When the first such witness was called, his identity caused amazement in the gallery of the Greenbrier County Courthouse.

Thomas Gamble marched to the stand with a dress cane of polished ebony tucked under his arm. Given that Gamble is the wealthiest landowner in all of the county, those watching would have been right in assuming that few of his acquaintances were of the same slender means as Trout Shue. But, as the court was about to learn, the gentleman had genuine affection for the blacksmith, considering him to be an excellent farrier and horse medic who had made a great impression upon him in a short space of time.

The silver handle of Gamble's cane was in the shape of an Arabian horse's head, wrought in silver, and it glinted wealthily where he left it propped against the mahogany railing. The court transcript for the morning session of June 27, 1897, shows the following testimony, given to counsellor Rucker for the defence.

Last summer, my best horse – the one from Tennessee with the fast walking gait – went from gliding to moving with a kind of stuttering limp. That quack veterinarian over in Caldwell diagnosed Sweeney shoulder, and said I'd be putting her out of her misery before too long. But over in Livesay, Trout had me walk her around the yard before taking a look at her hoof. You could tell he had a skilled eye. There was no nonsense about blistering or bandaging. He made a well-fitting shoe, and applied an ointment of tar and lard, and a few weeks later, she was back to floating me along. The Bible says that 'a righteous man regardeth the life of his beast'. And I can tell you that Trout Shue has tenderness toward every vulnerable creature. I'd trust my animals to no one else, and any woman should praise the good Lord for finding herself in his care.

A note of emotion had entered Gamble's voice, as if Trout being on trial were a great injustice, and several jurors were seen to avert their gaze. It may have been that they struggled to remain objective, as receipts from Livesay forge have since shown that five of the twelve had also at some time given their custom to Mr Shue.

Walter Neely, a tall, lean and muscular man from Irish Corner, was next to take the stand. In a soft voice at odds with his size, he told the court:

Trout's just as good with a common horse as he is with those fancy breeds. First time I met him, I didn't know what was making my Jasper's belly sick. Trout reckoned bot fly, and gave me a syrup that settled him right down. And when he had that bad cough, he cleared it right up with aconite. And - hoping it won't get him in any trouble with the forge - he didn't charge me one cent.

Mr Neely supports a family of fourteen on a smallholding of little more than one acre. His testimony elicited the natural sympathy of all those who understand what is at stake when a farmer's only horse falls sick. And thus, every picture that the prosecution had painted of Trout's fickle-ness and cruelty was overlaid by another image of Trout as an equine apothecary - a wise man possessed with the knowledge and compassion of generations.

While Mr Neely is in many ways an ordi-nary citizen of Greenbrier County, he is unique in one aspect. In the course of the two-week trial, he was the only witness invited to give evidence of Trout's alleg-edly wholesome treatment of his deceased wife. The court transcript contains the following exchange between Mr Neely and co-counsel for the defence, Mr James Gardner.

Q: Mr Neely, please tell the court what you witnessed on January 19th of this year.

A: You mean when I saw the couple over at the forge?

Q: *That's right. How would you describe Mrs Shue's behaviour as you witnessed it on that afternoon?*
A: [Inaudible]

The Court: Mr Neely, if you could face the jury very directly, please, and speak up so that they might hear you.

A: I said that she was all lovey-dovey kissy-kissy with Trout.

Q: *Highly expressive of her affection.*
A: Yes.

Q: *And how did Mr Shue respond to his wife's devotion?*
A: I suppose he seemed pleased.

Q: *How do you know?*
A: He picked her up and sort of swung her around in this big hug.

Q: *A big hug. And did she seem like a woman who was afraid of her husband? Who felt herself to be in danger – or believed that he wanted to be rid of her?*

A: No. No, I would say that she was very happy. She came to the forge with bread and cheese and beef broth, very eager for his comfort. Mrs Shue was very warm and good-humoured with him.

Aside from her husband, Mr Walter Neely is the only person to have seen Zona Heaster Shue between the feast of St Stephen, 1896, and the time of her death on January 23, 1897. It seems that the couple had been living in total isolation in their new home. And Mr Neely could find no other explanation for what he had witnessed except to say that it was a moment of married bliss.

3 | LUCY FRYE

Livesay

November 9, 1896

Lucy awoke, head tender as a bruised plum. Her lamp was still burning on a low flame, and big shadows lurched up the wall, making her stomach sour.

A couple of weak punches knocked her pillow into shape, and she set her back against it. The taste of stale cinnamon was on her gums, her lips still glazed with sugar from Clara Burdette's spiced cider. It was barely midnight, or so said her wristwatch, its tiny dark hands twitching into union. And already the best things about the Burdettes' barbecue were curdling into the worst parts of the next day. Her hair smelled of bitter smoke and turkey fat. And the burn marks on her right arm were growing tighter.

It had been worth the spatter of boiling grease to stop Clara from falling into the firepit. Her old school friend had been zealous as Captain Ahab, spearing flanks of meat with her pitchfork and heaving them over. But she had been no match for a full side of blackened deer, and Lucy had rescued her, grabbing the tongue of her belt before she could tip, head first, into the white-hot wood.

This should have been the big story of the afternoon, but after coming from Gill Weber's store, her spirits had been too low to capitalise. *Did you hear about the new blacksmith and the Heaster girl?* he had said, conspiratorial, standing behind his forest of wooden hands.

She had pretended not to hear him, keeping desperate focus on the moon-white buttons of the glove that she had been easing over her wrist. It was too embarrassing to admit that she had heard nothing from Zona in over a month, and that the longer this silence went on, the more worried she had become that it might never end. But sensing that she was fresh prey for his gossip, Gill came waltzing out from behind his polished vitrines to tell her the whole horrible story.

It was on Halloween, he'd said. *That new blacksmith took his lovely girl down to the river and there was a pastor waiting. The groom brought her a white dress that he'd picked out in Hansbarger's. And they married at sunset. The mother was in yesterday.* He had raised a knowing eyebrow at this, perhaps hinting at Mary Jane's eccentric appearance. *Says she nearly fell in her corn when they rode up to tell her about it.*

Lucy remembered how stiff and peculiar her tone had been as she tried to conceal her shock. It was *very true and Christian*, she said, *for a couple to marry without fuss*. Then, to seem casual, she purchased the most expensive and impractical gloves in the store. French kid, in the palest blush, the seams whip-stitched in periwinkle so that they had the appearance of veins. A full two dollars fifty, her name a quavering scrawl as she put her signature to the account.

When she grasped the reins to climb up on Sugar, the fine, pink leather had bruised easily, and she had the sensation of having been turned inside out – everything tender on show. *They've rented Jim Cruikshanks' place, up behind the forge*, Gill had said. *The one with a scarlet oak, and stone chimneys.*

What a way to discover that Zona was living not ten minutes from her own home, in a house that Lucy had been riding by every day, little thinking that her friend might be watching her through its windows. She had slowed her mare outside it on the way to the Burdettes' house, half afraid and half wishing that Zona would appear at the door. The log house sat in a clement dip, facing south, its sashes reflecting a broad peach and salmon sky. A cloud of hens had billowed across the grassy yard – Zona's favourite Wyandottes – and when she saw someone bent double inside their enclosure, she'd walked Sugar in a tight pirouette. But it was only little Andy Jones in his oversized duster, filling a basket with warm eggs, just the same as he did up at Oakhurst every morning before running off to the Negro School, coat tails flying.

It was Zona who used to ground her, laughing away her anxieties when she felt awkward and surplus to requirements; as much an object of her family's unloving acceptance as the vast needlepoint ottoman in the drawing room. This bed had been the place where they shrank each other's problems down to size. Lucy pulled up the feather counterpane, inhaled its scent of washed down and silk. She could still feel Zona at the other end of the mattress, tugging the silver-sage expanse toward herself, trying to cover up her belly, that irresistible eminence that had been thrown up by her growing child, thrilling and shocking them both.

I could go to Wheeling. Rolling stogies is clean work, she'd said, twisting a corner of the duvet down as if it were sweet and smooth as a tobacco leaf. *I could make enough money for a flat. Put the baby out to nurse.* But the truth, with its coppery tang, had flavoured the air between them, impossible to ignore. The only things waiting for Zona on the banks of the fat green Ohio were slums propagating up the hills, homes that were new and rotten all at the same time, and women with vacant eyes who'd happily bleed her of every dollar without a drop of milk passing her baby's greying gums.

Perhaps this was the complicated thing between her and Zona. Folks don't want to be reminded of the hard times when the good ones roll back around. And those nights after Mary Jane Heaster had circled Eugenia Wylie's advertisement in *The Outlook* magazine, well, they had been the worst of all. The small print still lurked in the top drawer of Lucy's nightstand, quietly alive. *Baby Wanted – Good German family, Richmond, Va., seeks child born to clean healthy Christian mother of excellent background. Tuition in French, music and dance provided. Reply, Trinity Methodist Church.*

The bad memories scoured her veins, a raw feeling persisting as she heard a small strike at the window. The noise came again, making her heart go at a loose rattle. She untangled herself from the sheets and crossed the soft carpet, another missile striking as she edged in behind the golden drapes. Zona was on the lawn, her face brightly lit by the candle lantern held close by one cheek, and she was waving an urgent hello.

Lucy opened the drapes by way of reply. It would serve Zona right, she thought, to leave her outside in the freeze. But instead, she grabbed her oil lamp and made for the stairs, cursing her own weakness. Zona was on the porch now, peering through one of the small window panes. It rankled to see the apologetic smile on her face, begging forgiveness without first admitting her wrongs.

The big key turned neatly in the latch, and the door hinged silently open. Zona hurried inside, a veil of cold air rising from her coat. She was underdressed for the night: no scarf, no hat. Brown knitted gloves were the only concession she'd made to the weather, and her eyes were streaming. 'So . . . ' she said with happy expectation.

There was great pressure in Lucy's throat, the urge to soften the way with words. But for the first time in her life, she remained silent.

Zona gave her an accusing look. But Lucy did not give in, not even as her friend let her arms drop to her sides as if with hurt or disappointment.

'I see.' Zona's eyebrows lifted in aggravation and surprise as she plucked her gloves from her hands. With a sullen nod, she gestured toward the stair. 'Can we?'

Lucy swept past, a sickly tug in her chest as she guided her upward. She climbed back into bed, and turned up the flame of her lamp, watching her friend as she walked the brass screen away from the fireplace.

Zona rubbed her hands above the embers, as if their warmth might banish something of Lucy's coolness. 'Listen,' she said, sounding nervous and uncertain. Then, seeming to think better of things, she opened the buttons of her good overcoat, her numb fingers struggling with the loops of Hungarian braid. The wool crackled with static as she let it fall, and she stood there in her white silk tea dress. The frock was long and tasteful, with a pin-tucked bodice, all of it clean and bright as a snowdrop. She smoothed the crêpe over her hips, the simplicity of the design making her look tall and elegant and clever. And it occurred to Lucy that Trout must consider his wife to be all of these things, or else he could not have chosen this for her wedding dress.

'I wanted to surprise you with my news,' Zona said. 'Obviously someone else got there first.'

'A week is a long time around here,' Lucy said. 'You missed Clara's barbecue. And Mary Jane's so mad about missing your wedding that your folks didn't come either. Do you know where I actually got it from? Gill Weber told me.'

Zona grimaced. 'Oh, Lucy. Of all people.'

'Exactly. You know how much he loves sticking that snout in where it doesn't belong.'

Their shared disdain seemed to put Zona a little more at ease, and she stepped in front of the cheval mirror, the hinges squeaking as she tilted the glass. Lucy hoped that her friend was about to look herself in the eye; make a big show of confronting her mistake. Instead, she stood on her toes and lengthened her neck, engrossed by her reflection.

'First time I've seen it properly,' she said, silk dress whispering as she twisted into one pose after the next, studying it from every angle. 'It fits well. There's no way am I as skinny as Trout says.'

'Did he really buy it for you?' Lucy said. 'I mean, even my mother would be impressed.'

Zona spun around, lifted her skirts out to her sides until

they were a pair of immaculate wings. 'All his idea,' she said, seeming to float to the end of the bed. 'I had to change behind the pastor's muddy horse. Wore my old boots, too.' But she hastened to add, 'It was perfect, in its own way. Just me and him. Ma was getting on my nerves anyway.' She flopped backward onto the bed, the duvet dimpling beneath her. 'Kept going on about getting married on the farm, same as her and Pa. Anyway, Trout didn't want to wait. The longer we left it, the more people might have supposed he couldn't afford the wedding, or that I didn't trust him enough, what with him not being long in town. So here we are.'

'I can't believe he planned it all without telling you,' Lucy said, unable to decide if his actions had been a gift or a kind of robbery. 'Your wedding ring and everything?'

She tried to squint at the hoop on her friend's hand, but Zona was gripping the band, the silver very loose. 'It's not much to look at,' she said. 'I mean, not by William Frye's standards. But it's better in a way, because Trout made it himself.'

'Why didn't you tell me?' Lucy said, wintry. 'You weren't too busy, not if you had enough time to hire Andy Jones. I saw him down at your house, you know. He could've brought a note up any morning you liked.'

'I didn't know how to explain,' Zona said, lifting her hands in a gesture of helplessness.

'You just say it – the same way a person explains anything.'

'Don't be angry.' Zona shook her head, her faux-shell hair combs sliding out onto the bed. After a moment, she rolled over and propped herself on her elbows. 'I want to tell you something,' she said, a little downcast. 'But it has to stay between you and me.'

She was wearing the same tense and watchful expression that came before any discussion about Trout. Lucy turned steely. 'You know,' she blurted, 'you're only interested in me if you have a problem. Why should I listen? You'll only disappear as soon as you feel better.'

They both fell silent, surprised by this outpouring. And Zona seemed to swallow down those things that she might have said in her own defence.

'I promise you,' she said, holding Lucy's eye, 'that's not how I want things to be. I just wanted to tell you what happened. But you're right. I'm taking you for granted.'

Lucy softened, turbulent feeling giving way to curiosity. 'Go on, then,' she said, pulling the counterpane up tight to her chin.

Zona bit her lip. 'Well, since the wedding, Trout's been telling me more about his life. Things I didn't know before, about being a boy up on Droop Mountain. He never felt safe, Lucy. Can you understand? Bad things happened.' She paused in this significant way, as if urging Lucy to conjure terrible pictures of an unhappy home. 'It means everything to him that he has me, now. And the house. But that's the problem, too. Life is so much better that it's making the past rise up like a big wave, crashing down on him all at once.' She traced the arc of this colossal surge before landing a blow on the mattress. 'He needs me to spend more time with him – alone, in the quiet – until he's out of the woods.'

'What woods?' Lucy said, frowning.

'Melancholy, I suppose?' Zona shrugged. 'He's relaxed, mostly. Says it won't be long until he's settled and things will be better than ever.'

Lucy rubbed her face to hide her impatience. Trout's story

was a match for hundreds of others hereabouts, men who weren't asking their wives to stay home and nanny them. But what advice could she offer, knowing nothing about having a ring on her finger or wedding vows freshly spoken?

'I hope he's feeling . . . I don't know . . . happier soon,' she said. 'But, Zona, you could've had the manners to come to the barbecue. Everyone was waiting to congratulate you. Bessie Harford, Ann Power . . . Clara never stopped watching down the hill.' To a woman, they had given in to the hazard of missing the few who were absent instead of enjoying the company of those present.

Zona's eyes sparkled with disbelief. 'Have you seen what I'm wearing? You think I put this on to shovel dirt? I was ready before noon, planning on helping Clara. Trout was sorry to spoil things, but I don't think he can help it when he needs me.' She said this as if she were putting her husband's reasoning above her own. 'I came out tonight because I reckon he can't miss me when he's sleeping.'

For all their talk, they had arrived at a fresh standstill, neither quite understanding the other. Zona reached across the bed, trying to ease the tension. 'What time is it anyway?' She twisted Lucy's hand around, playfully, to get a look at her watch. 'Oh Lord,' she said, turning her nose up as she caught the hickory stench spilling from her hair. 'Did the Burdettes smoke you along with the deer?'

'Never mind that,' Lucy said, trying to pull free. A big dark smudge had caught her eye, on the counterpane where Zona's head had been resting. 'What's this?' She leaned forward and saw that the mark was wet – a slick glint in the pool of lamplight near her feet. 'But that's blood, Zona,' she said.

Her friend looked startled, even a little guilty. 'It's nothing.' She was touching her hand to her scalp, to a place just above her right ear, seeming surprised and embarrassed to have had some secret injury discovered. When her fingers emerged from the depths of her loose hair, a reddish-brown residue was shining on their tips.

'Let me see.'

'I'm telling you, it's fine,' Zona said. 'Look at the silk.' She was almost frantic where her hands hovered above the stain. 'I'll go get some salt water.'

'Forget that.' Lucy seized her arm, holding her back. Stern, she took a handkerchief from her nightstand and pressed it into Zona's fingers so that she might clean them. 'Show me.'

Gently she parted her friend's glistening black hair. There, on her white scalp, was a straight-edged furrow, the dark line seeping with fresh blood. 'That looks nasty,' she said. 'What happened? You should've had Dr Knapp put a stitch in it.'

Her friend shut her eyes and pinched the bridge of her nose; the air of someone about to confess their idiocy.

'It's so stupid,' she said. 'I fell on a lamp, and my big head broke the glass.'

Lucy sucked air through her teeth, wincing. 'When?'

'Night of the wedding,' Zona said, chewing her thumbnail. 'It was healing up well. I must've caught it when I was brushing my hair.'

'Oh, no. Zona. On your wedding night? Were you carrying the lamp? Did you trip?'

'What does it matter?' she said, bad-tempered.

'It doesn't matter. I'm interested, is all.'

'I fell over,' Zona said, sharp. 'Why do you want the gory details?'

'Why are you being so impatient?'

'Because – I already told you everything. Now stop making a fuss.'

'Well, now I feel like you're hiding something,' Lucy said, suspicious. 'What was Trout doing when all this was happening?'

Zona groaned, scrubbing the tips of her fingers with the handkerchief. 'Trout didn't do anything. It was all me. This is typical of you,' she said. 'What is wrong with you that you can't let things go?'

'Didn't seem to be much wrong with me until you met him,' Lucy said. 'You're the one who's acting different, doing everything his way. I'd bet my bicycle he did something stupid and he's too proud to admit it.'

Zona massaged her forehead. When she looked up again, it was with a kind of resignation. 'Don't mind me,' she said. 'I'm just having one of those days where I can't do right for doing wrong. And I'm plain sick of talking about myself. What about your writing? I've been thinking about it, you know, wondering how it's going.'

It was an attempt to reconcile, but as they both glanced at the Remington, sitting ever ready on the dressing table, Lucy had a hollow feeling in her chest.

'You know how these things are,' she said. 'It's all very up in the air.'

It was sinking in, as she looked at her friend, how Zona's life had begun in earnest. Marriage gave a woman authority overnight – the permission to command a home of her own and fill it with small people over whose lives she might solemnly rule. Meanwhile, Lucy's existence hummed the same laboured note from one day to the next, never breaking into melody.

'I sent a few pages to *Munsey's*,' she admitted. 'That letter on the dressing table? It's the editor's rejection.' It was face down, its white back to the ceiling, to stop the words from glaring into the room. 'Other people, they're writing about being friends with Bismarck and the Prince of Wales. About intrigue in the Balkans. My life's not exciting enough. And my instinct, it's not right, Zona. Remember that bird you found last winter, the indigo bunting that died because she didn't migrate before it got cold? That's me. Always heading in the wrong direction, until one day I'll find myself dead in a bush.'

'Listen to me,' Zona said, her tone unusually determined. 'If you want to write about something else, you'll do a good job. But don't let some editor from *Munsey's*, or anywhere else, start telling you what you should be doing or thinking about.'

'You mean it?' Lucy said. On most days, Zona put about as much effort into bolstering her own confidence as she put into making her liver or kidneys tick over, which was to say, none at all. It was a grand surprise that, for once, she might understand how fickle Lucy's courage could be.

'I've never meant anything more,' she said, her eyes shining clear for the first time since she'd come through the door. 'Actually, I was hoping you'd help me write another letter.'

'You want to write Elisabeth?'

'I do. Every day there's some new thing I want to tell her.'

Lucy climbed out of bed, stomach swilling and fizzing with the dregs of Clara's cider. As she eased her feet into her goatskin slippers, she imagined there was a film of spiritual armour glowing around her; an invincible shield. For all these weeks, she had pictured Trout as having a pair of special scissors that he could use to *snip snip* out those parts of Zona's life that were inconvenient to him, and in this picture, she was a paper doll that he dangled by its hand before dropping it in the trash. But she and her friend were knitted too fast, and he could not break one from the other.

The leather cushion was hard and cold as she settled onto the swivel seat. Fingers resting lightly on the keys, she said, 'Do it like last time.'

Zona looked uncertain, but Lucy encouraged her with a smart nod. Since they were children, the bed, with its cherry frame and barley-twist posts, had been a type of raft upon the sea of their lives. There was no better way for a person to think than to lie back and look up into its sky, to that calm place where the silk of the canopy gathered inward into a sort of blue infinity.

This is Letter No. 2 of 5

Dear Elisabeth,

How I wish I could start this letter in
the way that I begin all others - with a
response to some news or other that you
have sent me. I look forward to a day when
I might open a letter from you and have
the joy of seeing your name written in
your own hand.

If you wonder why I have let your
youngest years pass without any word
between us, it is because I fear
unsettling you, pulling you every which
way before you're fully grown. But I want
you to know, nothing would have made
me happier than sending encouragement
along the way. About your schooling, or
a troubled friendship, or some talent or
other that you have.

I wonder if you've ever played on
the violin? We don't have the fancy
kind here, polished like the ones in
Richmond. Still, I must tell you that
your family in Meadow Bluff is gifted
on the rough type of fiddle that we
sometimes make here in the mountains.
My Uncle Johnston isn't much for talking,
but once he tucks his fiddle under
his chin, the one he made from an old
cigar box, it makes up for every word
he's never said. A greater force works
through him and it's fair to say that he
holds us all in a type of rapture. If
you've not tried it already, it might be
worth your while lifting a bow some day,
just to see.

My little brother Lewis, your uncle, is
sixteen years old as I write this. When
I talk to him and his friends, it helps
me to imagine how you might be now that
you're a young woman. You are your own
self, of course, and quite unlike anyone
else. I knew that the first time I set
eyes on you. Yet there are some ways in
which we are, all of us, the same. Which
means there are certain things that we
all need to know. Such as –

> Love is
> The most important thing
> in the world
> It is also the hardest

Now, if I said this to Lewis, he'd roll
his eyes at me, and I don't mind if you do
too. He'd think I was talking about the
love stories in romance novels. Or the
way a girl might feel for an actor like
Maurice Barrymore if she has a cabinet
card of his handsome face hidden away in
her box of keepsakes. But that business of
finding someone fascinating and wishing
that they might find you fascinating, too,
is not the kind of thing I mean.

I'm talking about loving another person
with all of your soul. I am beloved to
Trout, and he is the one whom my soul
loves. And it is my dear hope that one
day you will find the soul who is right
for you, too.

It could be that you've met them
already. But how can you tell? I might be
able to explain.

Since my last letter, Trout and I have
married. We took our vows because when we
are together, each of us feels whole. He
does not pick and choose, accepting me for
one thing and shunning me for another.

Since the day we met, he has looked at every inch of my spirit, and no matter what imperfection he sees, he does not turn from me in contempt or judgement. Instead, he tells me that with the blessing of Our Lord, I will grow into the woman he knows I can be.

You will have no doubt, Beth, when you become one of two twinned souls. It is a full and satisfied feeling, a type of hunger sated. But remember - nothing has been perfect since Eden. And life will be hard sometimes, even when you are held within each other's grace.

When I fall, Trout forgives me. Likewise, when he fails me, I try to forgive him, too. There is give and take. Meaning sometimes you will give much more than you receive. But if God gave second chances to Jonah and David and Peter, should we not show the same mercy when we see a loved one's heart break in repentance? Should not the contrite be allowed to renew a steadfast spirit?

Though we are so far apart, my Elisabeth, I hold strong hopes of meeting one day. I think about getting to know you, and how nice it would be to see even a short way into your mind. And I think about ways of letting you see a little

further into mine. So how would it be if
I played a type of parlour game with you?
One that Trout taught me the first night
we met. We must have played it ten times
or more, but the point is that by the end,
we were no longer strangers. He calls it –

Two lies, one truth

Now. I'm going to tell you one thing about
me that is true, and two things that are
lies. And it's your job to guess which is
which. (The answer is at the end of this
letter, but no cheating, please.)

1 Last summer, I saw the ghost
  of a dead soldier over at
  Deitz Farm. He didn't see
  me, but I watched him walk
  along the south wall of the
  house, his chest open and
  thigh gashed.
2 When I was ten years old, me
  and my friend Ruth Harford
  found a golden eagle. A big
  female with an injured wing.
  I took her home until she
  got better.
3 I once galloped on a bay
  colt called Manuel. Not

                    long after, he won the
                    Kentucky Derby.

Which is the truth, Beth?
    I would like nothing more than to hear
some amazing truths about your life since
you left Meadow Bluff. There are days I
think I can feel you moving around in
the world, like the trace of a sharpened
pencil on my skin. How I miss you. But
I must be strong and courageous, not
frightened or dismayed, for the Lord our
God is with me wherever I go.
    As always, there is more to say, and I
could go on talking to you for ever. It's
getting late, though, and my friend Lucy
needs to sleep, and there is only time now
for the answer to our game.
    Well, No. 1 is a lie. I've never seen
a ghost, not the Civil War kind, or any
other kind for that matter. This is a
story that my pa – your grandpa Jacob –
told me. But when it happened, he was only
a boy, and close to starving. These days,
I don't think even he believes it.
    No. 2 is true! My friend Ruth, who is
now by the Lord's side, reckoned the bird
was trying to take one of our sheep when
she got hurt. So I hid that big eagle
in a copse, hoping nobody would find her

and wring her neck. I trapped an army of
squirrels to feed her but couldn't stop
her from screeching and squawking. She
ripped the skin on my arm, and I still
have red scars by my elbow.

No. 3 is a lie. I didn't ride a Derby
winner. But Trout did, when he worked
as a stable hand in Kentucky. It is the
first truth he ever told me. His lies were
that he'd been married twice and that
he'd been to prison for stealing a man's
horse. Turns out that these difficult
things really happened to his very
distant cousin Edward. I don't hold it
against him. They say there are skeletons
in every family closet if you look
deep enough.

Until the next time, darling girl.

I will remain,

Yours ever truly,
Zona Shue

4 | MARY JANE HEASTER

Meadow Bluff

Christmas Day, 1896

Jacob had sided with the boys this year, arriving at the door on Christmas Eve with a little white pine tree already uprooted, their three youngest marching behind as if he were the Pied Piper. Mary Jane had cursed the bushy sapling for taking up too much space where it stood in the alcove in its pail of sand, every branch terminating in a spray of long needles. Now, there were tapers glowing amidst its soft green falls, and it seemed to be the only other steady presence in the room, perhaps joining her in lamenting the scene at her Christmas table.

A big cardboard box sat empty in the middle, decorated with fountains of curling white ribbon and cherubs cut from silvered paper, while Zona and Lucy pulled the last of the ENGLISH-STYLE CRACKERS FROM WANAMAKERS. Each was holding one end of the bright parcel, and they engaged in a vulgar tug-of-war, grunting and straining until it came apart with a tiny explosion.

'I win,' Lucy hollered.

Trout and Jacob were the only ones not panting with excitement. Bad enough that Lucy had brought such expensive and wasteful trinkets, leaving the bones of the roast goose buried under a mountain of orange tissue paper. Worse still were the silly masks and hats that had burst from every package.

Lucy creaked open the folds of the final paper gewgaw and put her hand inside to punch out its corners. All at once, it was a tall hat, the letters *F. D.* shining in gold-foil print on its crown. The scarlet paper made it a counterfeit for a fireman's leather helmet, complete with a fat strap that fitted tight under her chin.

'Listen to this,' she said, and she tried to imitate a siren.

Zona snorted and cackled, making Mary Jane cringe. It was a type of mutiny, she supposed, everyone at the table emboldened by their disguise. Lenny, being the smallest, could be forgiven for pinning his arms by his sides and slithering his chest onto the crowded table, hissing behind his green snake mask with its shivering pink tongue. But even Jonny, the tallest and burliest of the boys, was trumpeting loudly, dipping his paper elephant trunk into the cider jug, a pair of big round ears eclipsing his own.

Mary Jane let her gaze settle on Zona, where she recoiled in mock fear from Lenny's writhing. Here was the brazen daughter who'd accepted an invitation to Christmas dinner even though she hadn't spoken one word to Mary Jane since moving out of the house; the one who had breezed into the parlour this morning, airy and cool as a skiff of snow. All smiles.

'Hey, Zona,' Mary Jane said. 'Who are you supposed to be?' Her daughter's party hat was in the Egyptian style. Made from blue paper, with a veil all the way to her shoulders, its gold-foil stripes shimmered in the candlelight. 'The Grand Poobah?'

Missing her dry tone, Zona knitted her brows and pointed to the rubber scarab that was glued above her forehead. 'I'm a pharaoh,' she said, condescending. 'Like Cleopatra.'

She took another swig of port, the chapped cushions of her lips darkly stained by the fortified wine. Trout was patient beside her, trying to be a good sport in his black bear mask with its short muzzle and rounded ears.

'You must have a lot of news from Livesay.' Mary Jane grasped her own glass of port, stamped its little foot on the table to catch the full of the couple's attention. 'After all this time.'

She might have been one of Lucy's crackers, waiting to spill her insides. The house hadn't stopped ringing and echoing since that day after her daughter's wedding when Zona came to ransack every cabinet and rifle every trunk, her face shrewd and intent as a mink in a henhouse. She'd left everything in a shambles, marching about while the obedient Trout packed every last button hook and flannel and brass pin that she'd ever owned into the beautiful leather-covered chest he had made as a wedding gift for his outrageous wife. Afterward, in Zona's cramped room beneath the eaves, Mary Jane had discovered the bed made, the corners sharply tucked, leaving no trace of her daughter's existence.

Zona scratched her neck in irritation, while Jacob plucked the cigar from his mouth.

'Can't be much to tell, Ma. There's nothing but work in

setting up house,' he said. The interruption, Mary Jane knew, was designed to put Zona's feelings above her own. And as he lifted his glass to toast their girl's efforts, he was uncharacteristically cheerful behind a clever mask that made him look part raven.

'Mind your business,' she said. 'And don't talk to me about housework when you insist on making it harder.'

That very morning, just as she was carrying the goose from the springhouse, Jacob had ambushed her with one of his new machines. A system of belts and pulleys, it was driven by two of her best nannies, both animals wild-eyed where they trotted on a wooden treadmill, the racket infernal. With a rubber belt around its middle, the barrel of a butter churn was lurching as if possessed, cream sloshing at low speed.

'Learn to use that treadmill and you'll have an easy life,' he said.

He tilted his big bird head, and she felt that emptiness in her stomach where faith in her husband used to reside. For months, she had been afraid to acknowledge this void. But today, as he had stung the goats' backsides with a birch, there had been little distress in acceptance. It wasn't painful in the way she had expected. Instead, it was fresh, like mint or wintergreen; an invigorating expanse that might prove to be exactly the sort of clean chamber favoured by visiting spirits.

She looked around to see Trout smiling at her, as if he understood her exasperation. 'Zona,' he said, 'why don't you tell your ma about the paintbox I got you. The paints come in these little tablets. Antwerp Blue, and Mars Yellow. And the brushes are real sable.'

It was polite of him to attempt grown-up conversation. But

instead of gushing about his thoughtful gift, Zona picked at a crease in the tablecloth. 'You know better than me,' she said, sounding childish and ungrateful. 'Why don't you tell her, in case I say all the wrong things.'

She lifted her glass to take another swig of port, and Trout pressed down on her wrist, as if to suggest, *You've had enough.* Instead of cooperating, Zona pulled away, but her discreet tug sent her drink leaping from the glass. A big slap of crimson landed on her blue puffed sleeve, another streak pattering onto Lucy's cheek. Everyone at the table went quiet, the boys wary of their sister's mood.

Before she could give it any thought, Mary Jane found herself standing up straighter than a Lewisburg telegraph pole, chair wobbling into stillness behind her.

'Come help me with the hard sauce,' she said. Her eyes pinned her daughter, warning that she would drag her if she had to.

As soon as they were across the threshold, the words escaped hotter and faster than steam from a boiler. 'You are a disgrace,' Mary Jane hissed, itching to twist Zona's hair and pull it hard. 'Making me ashamed to own you.'

Her daughter spun around and set her backside against the kitchen table. 'What about Trout?' she asked, incredulous. 'He's always ... just ... ' She groaned and balled her hands into fists, as if glad to have a chance to talk behind his back. 'You should go in there,' she said, throwing her arm out toward the parlour, 'and tell him that I'm not bad to drinking. I mentioned how fond Grandpa was of his corn whisky, and now he won't let up. Keeps saying it *runs in families.*'

Mary Jane felt her eyes grow round with amazement, not

just at Zona's impersonation of Trout's mild lisp, but at the fact that her daughter had suggested to her own husband that she had no breeding. 'You have to be simple, telling a man something like that,' she said. 'And don't let your pa hear you've been talking about your opa that way.'

Zona folded her arms in tight as plaited dough. 'He asks me questions then complains about the answers,' she said, voice lively with resentment. 'Only reason he's not drinking is because he's trying to make me look bad.'

'You don't need any help with that,' Mary Jane said. 'The terrible way you left here. And not a word since. Not even at Thanksgiving. You don't know how hard it was, inviting you for Christmas. It killed me, writing that letter. Down at the post office, let me tell you, Arthur Boggess got a kick out of stamping that envelope, addressed to you like you're a stranger I never lay eyes on.'

The way Zona rolled her eyes, anyone might have thought she was the hurt one. 'Do you even remember the mood you were in last time I saw you?' she said. 'Madder than a hornet, soon as we told you about the wedding.' She looked down at her nails, started pushing back the cuticles. 'Reason I stayed away is because Trout said it was unfair, the way you went off at me and not him. He's the one who arranged it all. I convinced him your letter was an apology, putting the past in the past and all that, or he wouldn't have come today.'

Mary Jane snorted so hard it hurt. 'He believes whatever nonsense you put in his head. There's no man, not in the history of husbands, who's ever been the real brains of a marriage. You encouraged him, or there wouldn't have been any wedding. People ask me how you're doing, how you're keeping the house, and I know about as much as one of those cows out in the field.'

Zona could do no more than croak by way of reply, showing how difficult it was to defend against the truth. And Mary Jane saw her chance to make her planned speech. 'Here's the good news.' She laid one hand to her chest, trying very hard to mean what she was about to say. 'It's almost new year. So, I've decided to forgive you.'

Watchnight, that most holy of nights, was coming all too soon. At the very moment when this stale year gave way to the hope of the next, she would clasp her hands in prayer to renew her promises of baptism. But there could be no baring of her spirit before God, no saying, *I am yours, and you are mine*, if her soul was still seething with ill will against her daughter.

'You forgive me?' Zona said, brassy. Instead of being grateful, she looked puzzled. 'For what?'

Mary Jane took a whisk down from its peg, drove her energy into mixing the bowl of powdered sugar and softened butter that was waiting on the table. 'Get the brandy,' she said, making a little dent in the sauce.

Zona's colour was high as she squeaked the cork out of the bottle, her fevered eyes glazed like two figs in syrup. She always looked this way when she thought she'd been misunderstood, when the real problem was her inability to listen.

'All right now,' Mary Jane said, taking a conciliatory tone. 'I'm just telling you not to carry any sins or debts into the new year. Every Christmastide, make sure your slate is clean. I don't want you fretting about owing me anything. All the good Lord wants is for you to get along with Trout. That'll make enough amends for all that's gone before.'

'Ma,' Zona said, 'tell me this isn't about the baby, again.' She kept her voice low, watching the door. 'It's not a virtue to help me if I'll never be done paying for it. Lucy was right. You look down on folks who choose different than you. Makes you feel big, judging me.'

'Lucy Frye?' Mary Jane said in a coarse whisper. She couldn't have imagined a more unworthy arbiter, not if she had until the end of time. 'If that girl had any sense, she'd tell you *I'm* the one who'll never be done paying. I'm the one lying to her husband every day – not you. You scold me, saying I'm unkind to your father. But you've no trouble with lies when they're for your own benefit. Trout Shue is your chance to start over. A better one than I ever thought you'd get. So I'm telling you to thank the Lord, have patience and stop poisoning your own well.'

This sound advice seemed to deliver more stings than a hill of ants, setting Zona to flinching and pacing the floor. 'What about the way he treats Lucy? He drove off this morning when he saw her coming over the hill. Not two minutes late, and he made her jog a half-mile alongside before he'd pick her up.'

Mary Jane laughed, and when she saw the thunder in her daughter's expression, she wondered what had happened to her sense of humour. 'It's not worth picking fights over her. Lucy should have taken one of the Fryes' phaetons and a couple of shiny ponies over to the Old White. She belongs at that fancy hotel, with her own family. Zona, she's got to let you get on with your life. She was a farm girl once, but that spoiled creature hasn't worked for anything in a long while. Normal folk like you and me, we have to make the most of what we've got. Wait and see. Things will be easier when you're settled and the Lord blesses you with children.'

The face of her absent grandchild floated into Mary Jane's mind, a sudden moon on a pond. In the raw silence, the struggle went out of Zona, too. And it caused a wave of spite to gather inside Mary Jane; the sort she had always been helpless to whenever harmony was descending. 'Remember,' she warned. 'Don't put all your hopes into having another daughter. If one comes along, you'll only be disappointed.'

Zona fixed her with a ferocious look, and she felt her insides going watery; the sensation of having gone too far.

'Good luck,' her daughter said, clear and cold, 'with getting that slate wiped clean.' She turned her back, her posture quite lovely, her gait very cool and graceful as she picked up her cerulean chambray skirts and pushed into the parlour.

The sound of chatter from the other room rose and fell with the swing of the door, and Mary Jane wiped her hands down her good apron as Lenny appeared, a tower of crockery loaded onto his little arms.

'Good boy,' she said, helping him to ease the plates onto the table. 'Take these out.' She handed him a clutch of silver spoons and stole a pinch of his soft freckled cheek before launching him gently by the shoulders.

The pudding was muslin-wrapped in a steamer on the stovetop. A stick of bamboo, prodded into the big white knot at the top, made it easy to lift. She set it onto a plate, pleased with its suety shine as she peeled away the cloth, the little jewels of candied lemon and orange bright against their dark bed of raisins, the soft-pepper and sweet-wood aromas of nutmeg and cinnamon rising. On top, she planted a sprig of holly with glossy berries, a ladle of brandy igniting very easily when warmed above a candle, electric-blue flames licking and purring as she spilled them over the pudding, the greenwood making a loud *snap*.

'Make way,' she shouted, lifting the plate high, carrying it fast before the fire could die. She kicked the door open and braced herself for the usual excitement and admiration. But the cheering that met her was lacklustre. Behind the short-lived sound, she heard Lucy's voice droning on, brittle in the strained atmosphere.

'Not at all,' she said, as if correcting someone. 'I mean exactly what I said – that you should stop interfering.'

She was fixed on Trout, who slid his mask upward from his face. His expression seemed to have gone beyond frustration and onward to a kind of quiet despair.

'What's this?' Mary Jane said.

'Don't you agree, Mrs Heaster,' Lucy said, 'that a woman should be able to make her own decisions? About drinking, and what have you?' She talked too loudly, her fireman's helmet gone. 'Zona managed well enough before they got married. Is she not entitled, still, to use her own judgement?'

Zona pushed her empty glass away, as if to disown it, her anxious gaze lifting to her father, who, instead of intervening, sat very calm at the head of the table, the tip of his cigar glowing orange beneath his raven's beak. He had always considered young women and small children to be prone to similar delinquencies, and had never been much good at counselling either.

Zona gripped the edge of the table. 'Lucy,' she said, as if warning her friend to get back in line, 'you promised me you'd try to get along. Remember? It's Christmas. Let's have some pudding, and toast Ma for a lovely dinner.'

'All right.' Lucy spat in her napkin and scrubbed her cheek

where it was still sticky with port. 'I'll let on I didn't see how much it annoyed you on the way over. All of that *Stick to the good news, don't tell anyone about your imagined troubles*, and *Don't let me catch you going gooey over your pa when you're ignoring me at home.*'

'Lucy Frye,' Mary Jane snapped. She set the pudding down so hard that the last of its ghostly fire sputtered out. 'Stop tattling about people's private business. Lenny, put Lucy's glass on the dresser. She's having coffee for the rest of the night.'

'Thanks, Ma,' Trout said, his expression brightening at last.

She turned toward him, a man barely a dozen years her junior. 'None of this *Ma*,' she said. 'It's Mary Jane to you.'

Their spark of amity and kinship set Lucy off again. 'Stop acting innocent, Trout Shue,' she said, 'when you know what I'm talking about.' Whatever minor charms were usually to be found in the girl's plain features, they had disappeared behind her ugly righteous expression. 'Wouldn't hurt for you to say you appreciate Zona. The sacrifices she makes for you.'

'Listen,' he said, holding his hands up in patient surrender. 'I've tried my best. Nothing is enough.'

Mary Jane's stomach tightened at the spectacle. But Lucy felt no discomfort at making a grown man explain himself.

'You never did a thing in your life that didn't suit you,' she said, vicious. 'You're only happy when Zona's dancing to whatever tune you're fiddling.'

Trout took a couple of pained breaths, and with that, Zona shot to standing, chair screeching across the floorboards.

'That's enough, Lucy,' she said. 'You have to go.' Her voice trembled with urgency as she turned to her nearest brother. 'Jonny, I'm sorry, will you drive her to her aunt Rose Ellen's?

Just over in Clintonville. Won't take more than half an hour. Get your things, Lucy. Go on.'

Lucy clamped her hands onto the table. The corners of her mouth went down, and Mary Jane could see that tears were coming, her pale eyebrows lifting into her square forehead.

'Why are you siding with him?' she said.

'Get out,' Zona said, flinty. 'Trout's been telling me all along.' She gave a little shake of her head, as if finally seeing the good sense of his reckoning. 'You're jealous. And lonely. You don't like to see me getting on with my life. It's not how a good friend should be.' She held Lucy's eye as she said these things, and Mary Jane thrilled to see her looming big and frank and powerful as any anvil cloud, finally choosing her battles wisely. 'I feel bad for you that there's nothing going on in your life. But I'm not standing for this.'

Trout leaned back in his chair, arms folded, his frown a study of concern as he waited for Lucy to get up from the table. The hurt on her face as she rose into the silence was horrible to see, grasping for some rope to pull herself back to shore.

'You wouldn't say that if he wasn't sitting right there,' she whined. 'You're saying everything he wants. Doing everything he tells you. You used to have backbone.'

Zona chewed on her cheek. 'Just go,' she said.

It was quiet, then, as if some flame had gone out, leaving them in the dark and cold. Her friendship with Lucy – once so wholesome and vital – had long since been picked clean of anything good. Bare as the white bones of the goose, all that was left was to slide it into the trash.

Jonny appeared with Lucy's coat, and he swept it through the air, draping her with its many yards of scarlet cashmere, trying to cover her humiliation. Trout reached for Zona's hand, twining his fingers with hers. But she didn't budge, waiting to see the job done, same as if a black widow spider were being shooed out of the room, little body skittering.

'You're lying to everyone, Zona,' Lucy said. 'He isn't what he pretends to be, and you know it.'

Trout met this with a good-humoured jut of his jaw. Next thing, Lucy and Jonny's boots were loud on the porch, scuffing quietly down the steps. And as if the evening were on a hinge, it swung back into place, everyone settling comfortable in their seats again.

Zona was flexing her hand in Trout's as Mary Jane turned back to the plum pudding with its crown of holly scorched. Taking her palette knife from her apron, she gave silent thanks to the Lord for the sacred ability of people to behave as if nothing has happened. 'You've worked up your appetites again,' she said, sinking the blade into the soft round.

Crumbling wedges of dessert were passed around the table, her heart lifting to see that Zona was not brooding, but smiling at Trout, blinking away tears until their shine did no more than add lustre to her fond gaze. She would feel sore in the morning. Perhaps they would all feel tender in that place where the roots of a friendship had been torn out. But here was new strength with Trout in place of a resentful girl egging Zona on to divorce and ruin.

'Time for scuppernong,' Jacob said, reaching for the bottle of sweet North Carolinian wine that Emory Snow had left behind on his last visit. He turned the corkscrew, the crisp *pop* a note of celebration, and Lenny was dispatched to pour the drinks for a toast. Zona declined by covering her glass, while her father raised his own, saying, 'It's good to have you, Trout. Here's to working on the Heaster Wagon.'

Everyone but Mary Jane and Zona joined in the chorus – 'To the Heaster Wagon.'

Jacob took his mask off, his thinning hair in damp ridges. 'And here's to a happy new year,' he said. 'Trout reckons his brother Patrick is willing to help me with the boiler.' He turned a gentle smile on Mary Jane. 'If I get my patent, we're going to make a scale model, and I'll be in New York soon, in one of those big steel buildings, raising money for the real thing.' He pulled an imaginary lever in the air, as if to open the valve on a steam whistle.

For the first time in many months, he gave her an intimate nod of approval. The steam wagon wasn't the only thing he had smug designs on. He'd made that very clear by leaving a little pine crate for her to discover on the footboard of the bed that morning, as if she might be an excited child waiting for St Nicholas. By the time she took her pocket knife to sever the string, she knew that nothing would do but to find it empty, because only this might signal a shared understanding; the need for a new beginning.

Instead, she spied something black tucked inside, her thumb tracing silky fabric and a row of fastened hooks and eyes. And when she emptied the box, she discovered not one, but three corsets. Each had padding for the hips, and for the bust, their tags informing her that the garments would REMEDY THE DEFECTS IN ORDINARY FIGURES.

With the stays fanned across the mattress, she had been able to see how tiny they were; smaller than any she had ever owned. All through the fall, Jacob had looked dismayed whenever her soft, loose body had strained against the wrong parts of every frock. Now, it seemed that winter, and her daughter leaving, had made her too slender. The slightness of the garments had made her laugh, and then laugh some more. With Watchnight coming, Jacob was playing his own game of forgiveness, giving her a chance to mend her ways. He was trying to wrap his compass tight around her, pursuing her shrinking form. But instead, he had helped her to see that she was like smoke, now. That she could not be held by any corset, nor handcuffs, nor even a prison cell if he had one, because the most important part of her was beyond his grasp – her spirit would slip through his fingers, bleed through the cracks of any cage or casement. Jacob, of all people, had shown her that she was ready.

Her last memory was of a sudden state of peace, her soul ebbing to the remotest corners of her flesh. She couldn't say what happened next. Only that she had come to again, her temples throbbing and her ears ringing, as the sky was making that near-imperceptible shift from indigo to grey. Rising into the winter freeze, she had cast about the room, lamenting the lack of any witness; someone to tell her if another soul had peered through the windows of her eyes, and stretched them-selves into the full length of her limbs, exclaiming through her lips with amazement before vanishing, once more, to the Other Side.

PART TWO

1897

New Year to Last Frost

from:

THE TRIAL OF TROUT SHUE

A TRUE STORY
CONTAINING HITHERTO
SUPPRESSED FACTS

---

by Lucia C. Frye

Trout Shue was held on remand for four months before his trial, occupying the 'Big Cell' at the Lewisburg jail, close by the Greenbrier County Courthouse. It is one of only two cells, and at 11ft x 12ft, it is four inches wider than its 'Little' neighbour.

The jail is in the basement of a stone building on a bright corner, a salutary place due to the renovations that Mrs Amelia Shawver insisted upon when her husband, Mr John Shawver, first took up the role of constable.

The Shawver family comprises the couple and their three small daughters. All are accommodated in six spacious rooms with four large fireplaces, laid out over three floors above the jail. According to Mrs Shawver, when they first arrived in the building, she was 'overcome by the stench of I don't know what ... ammonia, maybe sulphur, seeping up from the jail and through the whole house'. There was also the pressing matter of the 'dark peeling wallpaper and tobacco-stained distemper' in the residential rooms.

The upper floors were refinished in size paint and small-patterned chintzes, while the slabs and wainscot of the offending basement were scrubbed with lye water, each cell made like new with three coats of limewash. A notable entry in the accounts is the sum of $3 paid in settlement of a blacksmith's bill for fixing a new lock to the bars of the Big Cell. The work was carried out by a certain Trout Shue, his work skilled enough to later hold him captive.

Mrs Shawver 'cannot remember' how the habit formed, but admits to broiling the prisoner's 'favourite pork chops' for his dinner every Sunday during his incarceration. The constable denies the popular rumour that Mr Shue was at liberty to dine with the Shawver family in their neat parlour after church. However, the prisoner-jailer relationship appears to have been one of unusual intimacy, since the constable used his discretion to 'allow Trout a number of personal visitors', finding him to be 'patient, amiable and grateful for any little kindness that relieved his loneliness'.

In eccentric shorthand, the constable's ledger identifies four guests who were later called to the witness stand to speak in Trout's favour. Joseph Hansbarger from the dress store, Peter Rittenhouse from the hardware store, and the carriagemaker John Cunningham all praised the blacksmith under oath. But none of these is now willing to give an account of his visit to Trout's jail cell. There is only one man on Shawver's list who has agreed to speak freely of his audience with the prisoner.

On Tuesday, March 9, 1897, at 7.30 a.m., Mr Frederick Ballard arrived at the jailhouse in response to a note he had received from the accused. A clerk at the Bunger Store in Mill Creek, Ballard says that 'Shue's envelope stood out from the rest of the morning post, what with his handwriting being all pointed and sharp – even the "Os" looked like diamonds'. The prisoner, he says, asked him to visit as a matter of urgency, requesting that he bring the 'egg money and Duke of Durham cigarettes'.

The popular Bunger Store is housed in a long square-hewn cabin situated on Mill Creek, opposite the busy Bunger's Mill. Fred Ballard, a thin and precise man with a neat auburn moustache, works the dry goods counter at the store. Behind his station stands a high gallery of tins and bottles with paper labels announcing their contents – everything from peaches to tomatoes, and mustard powder to Japan tea, with the top shelf reserved for curative syrups. He is sombre as he leans on a bald patch of counter beside the weighing scale, describing how Zona Heaster Shue used to walk to the store 'twice a week, during that all-too-short time she lived nearby'.

The records at the Bunger Store show that the deceased sold an average of two dozen brown eggs to Ballard on each visit. She had 'rapport with the Wyandotte breed', according to the clerk, 'real skill with broody hens and nervous pullets'. But to the surprise of the scrupulous store-keeper, Zona never accepted the cash that he offered in payment for her produce. 'She didn't want me crediting her account either. Every time, she told me to put the money in an envelope and address it to her husband,' Ballard explains. 'I did what she asked, and set them all aside so he could collect them in what she called his "own good time".'

Ballard's wife, Mehitable, thought this peculiar. The only clerk on the haberdashery counter, Mrs Ballard is a short, amiable woman who is very spry on a stepladder, and who wears plain dresses for her work so that she might form a better backdrop against which to demonstrate the store's various laces, ribbons, braiding and buttons. 'I made some little joke,' she remembers, 'about her letting her husband think he was in charge. She went so pale, I regretted saying a word. I figured she was too proper to talk about money, and that seemed fair, and I was very sorry for causing her any discomfort.'

Shue arrived to collect the money at both Thanksgiving and Christmas. And when Frederick Ballard visited Mr Shue's jail cell in March, it fell to him to bring the money owed for January. He gave Trout the sum of $4, less the price of his cigarettes. When the prisoner pocketed the coins, Ballard says, it was 'without any of the grief or sorrow that I had felt in giving them. It didn't seem right or natural.'

Shue asked Ballard if he would testify in court; praise him as a good customer with clean accounts. 'It wouldn't have been a lie,' Frederick says, 'but after seeing him so uncaring about Zona, it didn't feel the proper thing to do.' We might wonder, then, why others agreed. Charisma is that spiritual power we associate with a certain kind of man. We all recognise the quality, though we might find it difficult to describe, and perhaps we allow the fellow who possesses it to have more influence than we might grant to a man of fewer charms.

'I couldn't believe that he had done it,' Mrs Shawver says. 'Only a monster could take a life that way. And Trout was such a thoughtful man. Even as a prisoner, he just couldn't do enough for you.'

5 | LUCY FRYE

Livesay

January 23, 1897

'Flesh of freshly fried flying fish . . . '

Lucy pushed open the stained-glass door to the back porch, struggling to master the tongue-twister. The painted rail was studded with opals of frozen dew, and she gripped it with her gloved hand, the leather soles of her boots skating about on each step as she descended. She had dressed hastily for the short outing. Legs flashing indigo beneath her pink silk nightdress, the train of her dressing gown was a froth of coral that dragged behind her no matter how she tried to gather it up, the fabric weighed down by the scarlet coat that she had belted above.

She peered into the lambent mist that obscured everything from the ice house to the stables, wondering what on earth had happened to little Anderson Jones. Every morning before breakfast, he called to the kitchen with a hickory basket dangling from the crook of his elbow, warm eggs nestled inside. He always had some new joke or game or tongue-twister to teach her, contagious laughter bubbling. But it was past nine already, and still no sign of Andy.

'A box of mixed biscuits, a mixed biscuit box.' She supposed the child was running late. If she was to keep him out of trouble, she'd have to take on the job herself: comb every roost, reach her hands in under those broody hens, who would peck at the knobs of her wrists before surrendering. It was the kind of work she liked best, but that she had avoided since scandalising her stepfather during her very first week at Oakhurst. His mouth had fallen open when he saw her tapping the heels of her boots on the inside of a steel bucket, collecting gobs of chicken dirt for the peach trees. He didn't have to say a word. She would never be one of those girls whose eccentricities were considered charming. And if she couldn't be handsome, it was her duty to be conventional.

The air stung as she picked her way out of the shade, toward the front of the house. The ice on the pond had thickened overnight, taking on the white lustre of porcelain, the glancing sunlight a spill of fire across its surface. The red bricks of the house had a warm ferrous glow, though every blade of grass between the house and the water's edge was standing at a frosted slant, each tuft a bouquet of glassy rods, as if God's glittering breath had purled across the earth.

Amidst all this brilliance was a fragile sense of growth. Wretchedness had been dining on her heart since she left the Heaster farm. But this morning she had confronted it by gathering those sour letters that she and Zona had been exchanging, feeding them to the fire before dawn could come and stay her hand. Flames had consumed the carbon copies of her own missives with their waxy black print. Zona's small notecards were slower to take. All of it a quiet and painful extinction.

January 5, 1897

Zona,

It's Twelfth Night and time for revelation. I've been so mad about the things you said at Christmas. But I'm not as angry as I am worried that our friendship might be over. Remember my last morning at the old house in Meadow Bluff? - how Ma took away my old clothes before making me pick a hideous dress from that big suitcase of silk and frills that William wanted me to wear? She started talking in that funny accent, saying I had to call her 'Mother' when we got to Oakhurst. If it hadn't been for you, I couldn't have laughed about all that. And you're the only one who says I look like my dear old pa while everyone else tries so hard to forget him. No one will ever know me the way you do. Just the same as I know you. Tell me how we can we fix things?

Your friend,
Lucy

January 7, 1897

Dear Lucy,

    Dont trespass on my porch any more, sliding letters under my door. I must put God first. Then my husband. All others come after. I told you before I will not let you get in the way. No matter how hard you try.

                                 Yours,
                                 Zona Shue

January 15, 1897

Dear Zona,

I was surprised when William came
to my room with a letter franked at
Livesay post office. Why not give the
envelope to Anderson, same as he'll
carry this to you? Maybe you want an
apology. Well, I am truly sorry for
saying that you have no mind or will
of your own. And I forgive you the
terrible things you said, too. If we
talk, I know we can put all of this
behind us.

                        Your friend,
                            Lucy

The last word. STOP writing me.

As Lucy remembered the scales of ash fluttering on the grate, she pulled her coat very tight, seized by a narrow kind of hope. This sharp feeling was interrupted by a flash of colour at the corner of her eye. On a bare branch of the locust tree was a brilliant-red bird. She looked closer, and saw that it was a cardinal, little crest raised. The astonishing creature was lost – perhaps carried across the mountains from Virginia by the last winter storm. And she felt a pang of desperation on its behalf, because what hope did it have of finding its way home? Stark on its thorny outpost, it broke into song. Not the lilting warbling kind that Lucy knew from her vacations on Chesapeake Bay. This was a slow and searching kind of melody, the red bird repeating the final note louder and louder, seeming to pierce through her optimism, and strike on some deeper melancholy.

'Miss Lucy.' Andy's voice came glancing across the pond, though he was not yet in sight. 'Miss Lucy,' he called again, his abandon causing her blood to cool.

He came racing up the hill, legs working harder than the cranks of a C&O steam engine, feet sliding on the pea gravel of the yard.

'What is it?' she said. She hunkered so that she might look very directly into his face, and when he skidded up close, she steadied him with a squeeze of his shoulders. 'Andy,' she said. 'What is it? You're shaking.'

It was certainly fright, and not cold, that had brought on these shivers. He swallowed hard, a knot rising and dipping in his throat.

'It's Miss Zona,' he said, his lips stretched in grief. 'Miss Zona, she's had an accident. She's out cold.'

Lucy had that same peculiar feeling as when her father was sick – as if she were in the steel jaws of a nutcracker, waiting to be broken. 'What do you mean, Andy? Where is she?'

'On the floor, in the Shues' parlour, pale like snow. I went home and told Ma. She's gone looking for Mr Trout. She said I wasn't to move, not till the soup beans came up to simmering. I left soon as I'd counted ten bubbles.' His tone was desperate.

Lucy tried to steady her breath, sifting Andy's few shards of information. Zona's not dead, she thought. There had been too much anger and hurt in the last words between them, and both would surely live until everything had been healed. 'Your ma and Trout,' she said, 'they'll have taken good care of Zona by now.' She pictured Aunt Martha kneeling by Zona's side, and Trout pressing two fingers to the hollow of his wife's throat before waking her with ammonia salts. 'Come on.' She grasped one of Andy's small, freezing hands, and they raced across the hard, glittering lawn, onward to the lean-to where her bicycle was waiting.

'Get in the basket,' she said. Fabric flew in scarlet and coral and pink as she threw one leg over the frame. She pushed off as Andy folded into the wicker, and they knifed through a curtain of frost-silvered webs. The road evened out beneath the glare of white sky, and she made every turn of the pedals a prayer, until one final bend brought them into that wide and shallow dip where Zona's house sat. She braked hard as they sailed in through the gate, and Andy scrambled free to race up the yard.

There was a small gathering of people on the scuffed grass, all of them standing just as quiet and still as if they were in chapel. Nobody budged as Lucy staggered forward, not even as Andy squeezed into their number and sidled up to his mother. They even kept their heads bowed as the heavy thud of boots came from above. It was Trout, shuttling to and fro in the slanting shadows of the porch. Lucy froze as he rushed the railing, glowering down the same as any zealous preacher in the pulpit.

'Don't touch her,' he said, a rope of spittle between his lips. All of him was pulled taut; eyes glaring, chin defiant. A streak of soot coated one jaw, his breath rasping as he used a blackened thumb to hike up the belt that was lashed above his leather apron. 'I said, don't touch her.' He pressed his hands forward, now, as if trying to hold back a crush of people. 'We have to be patient. Dr Knapp is on his way.'

The little group shuffled backward in unison. And to Lucy's dismay, she saw Charlie Tabscott – the youngest teacher in Lewisburg – holding his hat to his chest in a gesture of grief.

'Let me in,' she shouted, running full tilt across the yard. Her mouth tasted of metal as she started up the porch, but with nobody else trying, she had to push for remedy.

Trout blocked the way, cheeks flushed under a fine layer of soot, glaring at her with that kind of upset which is a close neighbour to rage. His silent congregation watched on, as darkly accepting as the mourners at any funeral. Before she knew it, she had grabbed one of his big wrists.

'Is she alive?' she said, squeezing the bones.

He looked through her, as if she were unworthy of any attention. She could smell him, even on the freezing air. The iron tang on his hands, his whisky breath, the sour sweat of his shirt. Beneath all of this, there was something else that she could not place. A base animal note. She released him with disgust, and ducked past him to rush the door. It was locked, its handle rattling to no avail, as she peered through one of the small window panes.

Trout's grip on her was so rough, then, that she might have cried out. First, he marched her. Next, he shoved her, right along the porch, his knuckles in the small of her back as if he were managing a disobedient child. But nothing he did could erase what she had seen. Just as looking into the sun might burn the eye, a picture of Zona was scorched into Lucy's mind: her friend, flat on her back at the bottom of the stairs. It grew stronger and clearer, like a photograph in a developing tray, coating Lucy's stomach with a silvery sickness.

Reality chased through her in one great shiver after another, making Trout's railing and chastising seem very far away. How wrong Zona looked. An effigy of herself, still and neat on the cherry floor. Her legs were lit, knee to boot, by the sun slanting in the window, her feet falling to either side. Her skirts were orderly, the hem rippling over her shins as if she had simply laid herself down for sleep. Her combed hair was flowing, black and shining, toward the door in girlish style, one arm soft and natural by her side, the other resting across her stomach. It was the ease of this pose that made the appearance of her throat even more unsettling – the way her skin had stretched to accommodate the lolling of her head. She was facing away, toward the kitchen, with a cord of muscle pulled just as taut – from ear to collarbone – as any steel cable on the Brooklyn suspension bridge. Standing long and proud, it gleamed white and hard in the dim of the room. And were there any feeling left in Zona's body, she could not have endured this contortion.

Hope spilled out of Lucy, the deluge leaving her weak. 'Trout?' she said. 'What happened? Did she fall on those steep steps?'

'None of your business,' he said in a warning tone. 'Leave her alone.'

Curiosity bloomed amongst their spectators, several of them shuffling forward, hoping to hear a snatch of whatever grief-stricken vaudeville was going on.

'Have you lost your reason?' she said in a low voice. 'Let me in. She shouldn't be alone.' With her heart small and wild in her chest, she had the strong feeling that she might be sick. Instead, with a burst of spleen, she spun back toward the house. Head pressed to the parlour window, she felt it vibrate. Trout had slammed the front door, and he was inside, now, drawing the short woollen drapes in front of her face. She rapped furiously on the glass. But Charlie Tabscott seized her hand, closing it tight in his fist.

'Miss Lucy,' he said, levering her arm down by her side. 'Leave him.' He gave her a patient look, as if waiting for some more sensible part of her to step to the fore. 'She's gone,' he said, with studied frankness. 'None of this will bring her back.'

'You're certain?' she said, working her hand free. 'Have you been inside?'

He nodded, and the full monstrous weight of grief made itself known inside her.

'I was down at the forge when Aunt Martha came looking for Trout,' he said. 'He can't accept it, Lucy. Not until Dr Knapp gets here.'

Although she hardly knew him, Charlie took on that rooted-but-yielding posture that is designed for ministering to the bereaved; against which she might throw the full of her despair. But she was not of a mind to use it.

'He's acting crazy,' she said. 'I can't stand here pretending there's hope.'

It was too grim. And cruel. Even now, Trout was enjoying his power to keep her from Zona, his grief tyrannical. And there was nobody else here with fury to match Lucy's own; who was gripped by the wantonness of loss.

She peered past the buckled seams of Zona's curtains. Her friend's second-rate sewing had left the panels off square, and she could see beyond the coarse green wool into that portion of room where the parlour table stood alongside the big stone fireplace, a small hand mirror suspended above the mantel by a slender black chain.

'What are you looking at?' Charlie said, watchful and disapproving.

'I don't know,' she said. 'Nothing.'

And yet, *everything*, because here was the room, exactly as it must have been when her friend had taken her last breath. The bitter realisation seemed to fasten her soul to Zona's, and she looked about as if with borrowed sight. A blue and white pottery cup was overturned on its matching saucer, its mouth silted with coffee grounds. The nickel-plated coffee pot was skewwise, too, as if it had sailed off its trivet to rest one sharp edge of its round foot on the table. Although it was long past breakfast, the fire was not yet lit in the hearth, and the previous night's char was lying cold in the grate. Beneath the rocking chair, there was a silver glint in the weak light. It was the sleeve for Zona's hair comb, the one that was etched with fine scrolls and fruits and flowers. While the disarray might have been mundane, it was heightened by the final touches of Zona's hands – by those ink-stained fingers with half-moons at their cuticles.

A black carriage came rattling along the road, its steel suspension no match for the rough limestone humps rising through the earth. The swift gig, with its single bay horse, was driven by Dr George Knapp, who bounced and leaned efficiently on the well-cushioned seat of Morocco leather. With great effort, he managed to steer his contraption into the yard, groaning as he clipped one brass wheel hub against the gatepost. His nose, which was always as red and pitted as a wild strawberry, was even more luminous in the cold where he climbed down from the two-wheeler.

'She needs water,' Knapp shouted to nobody in particular, patting his mare's wide barrel. 'Quickly now,' he said. 'There's been an accident over at the St Lawrence. No time to lose.'

Little Andy bolted toward the well to fetch a drink for the horse, the doctor huffing as the boy bowled past him. Knapp's exaggerated haste worried Lucy as he came striding across the yard. Yes, an accident at the sawmill could mean a bloody injury, but Zona deserved his solemn and unswerving attention, too.

'Who's the next of kin?' he said, struggling onto the porch with his heavy bag.

'You're looking for Trout Shue,' Lucy said. 'Zona's husband. He's locked himself inside.'

'Well.' The doctor bobbed his head, as if to say there was nothing strange that existed under the sun, and removed one shearling mitten to give a brisk rap on the door.

Lucy braced herself to see it flung open; for Trout to sweep Knapp inside with all the force of a spring flood, the relief and fresh agony of answers coming in a surge. Instead, Zona's husband opened the door in secret manner. The doctor squeezed in through the small gap allowed, leather bag scratching the wall. As soon as the latch clicked shut, she heard Knapp's muted tones, calm and kind, the slow rhythm and lilt of difficult questions.

'Come on, Miss Lucy,' Charlie said, walking down the steps. 'Time to let them be.'

But there was little chance of her relaxing her vigil – not with Trout raising his voice inside. At first he bellowed with a primitive groan. Then his voice took a shrill slide upward, landing on something approaching a child's howl. Zona's death, the fact of it, was as great and inflexible now as Weaver Mountain, its grey dome cresting to the east. Lucy kept her eyes on the receding sky as the widower grew more unreasonable still. There was the distressing sound of a scuffle, bodies moving fast and heavy toward the door. And she jumped backward as it was flung open on its hinges, striking the wall as Trout chased the doctor onto the porch.

Knapp scurried like a quail on his short legs. 'Take it easy, son,' he said, surprising Lucy with his composure. 'Do as you see fit.'

'I'll take care of her,' Trout said, striking his chest with the butt of his fist. 'She needs me. Leave her alone, all of you.'

He raised his arms to obscure his sobs, but while the

doctor's eyes glittered with concern for the widower, Lucy could not be moved to any tenderness. As Trout disappeared into the house, she had the shuddersome sense of an eel sliding back into dark water, the surface falling still and black.

'Well.' Knapp bobbed his head again, in solemn humour.

'Won't there be an inquiry?' Lucy pulled at the doctor's sleeve.

Knapp smacked his lips. 'It's sad for the family,' he said. 'But as far as this woman's passing goes, it couldn't have been helped, Miss . . . ?' He squinted, seeming to find her familiar in the same vague way as he might any other person he had treated around Lewisburg or Livesay or Ronceverte.

'Lucy Frye,' she offered. 'William's daughter.' He knew her stepfather, of course, having been to the store very lately to buy a Tahitian pearl for his wife, a peacock gem selected from the small vitrine where every piece cost thirty dollars.

'Ah, yes. Quinsy,' he said, remembering that night up at Oakhurst when he had treated her for the attendant fever. 'If you're not kin, Miss Frye, Mr Shue will have to tell you what happened.'

He swung his bag and descended the steps with awkward momentum. A shining penny winked in the sunlight as he flipped it to Anderson, and when he was settled on his buggy, he drove his mare in a wide circle, dispersing the little crowd on the lawn. The clatter of hoof and wheel faded into the distance, and Lucy stood destitute. She had no purchase on Trout. No way of making him answer any questions, and even less chance of gaining entry to the house.

Only the sight of Sam Withrow allowed hope to well. Newly arrived, Withrow was impossible to miss with one of his wife's colourful home-knit scarves pulled up over his face. This reticent man, in citrus stripes of lemon and orange, had been a neighbour to the Heasters all his life; had milled every kernel of wheat from their golden fields for more than twenty years. Standing near the gate, he tugged the yarn down from his hooked Withrow nose, choked with tears, as if at pains to bare his shock to her.

This shared heartbreak pulled Lucy back into her body, cold alarm giving way, at last, to the all-consuming heat of sadness. Here was permission, and release. And she returned his troubled smile, knowing what she must do.

She signalled for him to wait. Then she knocked very quietly on the door, as if trying not to startle Zona. 'Trout,' she said softly.

There would be no answer, she supposed. The silence was too deep. But the knob turned gently, and there he was, far more at ease than she had expected. He was a little sleepy, even, standing in stockinged feet, hair damp and face rinsed almost clean.

'What is it?' he said, as if it were an ordinary day, and this was just another of her intrusions.

'Do you want to send word to the Heasters? Sam Withrow will ride over, if I ask him,' she said. 'Mary Jane and Jacob . . . they know him. He'll be kind. And he'll make sure they don't hear it from someone else first.' She faltered, imagining how the ground might cleave open between the Heasters' farm and Livesay in that moment when Zona's parents heard the news. 'If you write them a note, I'll make sure they get it. Or I can put the words down for you. If you like. Just tell me what to say.'

He considered this with a low and sceptical hum, before closing the door without a word. Lucy hovered, unsure whether to try again or just send Sam on to Meadow Bluff. She wouldn't know what to tell him, except that her mind's eye was still pulsing with that pale, taut cord in Zona's neck. At last, Trout returned, holding a piece of paper that was torn roughly from some larger sheet.

'Here,' he said, blowing on the wet ink.

The note was written in fine, neat cursive, a mark of vanity that, along with the sharpness of each letter, should have been no surprise. Without any ceremony, he shut the door, scrubbing the nape of his neck with a huckaback towel. And here it was, Lucy thought, her ribs too tight to breathe. Here was the page that would tell her the truth.

She stretched the paper between her thumbs and mouthed the words. His report was as brief as any telegram, as if she had charged him dearly for the inclusion of every character.

'Will bring Zona after first light. Knapp says everlasting faint. Your son, Trout.'

6 | MARY JANE HEASTER

Meadow Bluff

January 24, 1897

They were thrown together now, into this cold and glassy place.

Jacob sat hollow by the fire, not a word going in and not one coming out. Mary Jane took his old pocket watch from where it was hanging on the mantel and saw that it was almost five o'clock. She closed the timepiece inside their old tinder box, fighting the urge to set it on the hearth and crush it with her heel; to stop its shifting hands from consigning their daughter to the past.

Through the parlour window, the sky was smeared with stars, the moon's third quarter sharp-edged. It had been wrong, perhaps, to make everyone leave, to send them out into the January freeze. She might have let them rest until the light came. Until Trout brought her daughter home.

It didn't seem possible – that she could give birth to Zona

yet be absent when she departed. She reeled from the swerve of this, the polished steel of the blow. She'd known something was wrong as soon as she saw Sam Withrow riding over the hard ground to the house, even before he stuttered through frozen jaws, telling them that she was gone.

No, she had said with certainty.

No.

And still. *No.*

The force should have been fatal, yet body and soul persisted when she wished that they would fly apart.

Time softened. Grew hard again. Grew more solid and resisting still. The hens stirred outside, and Mary Jane wondered if Jacob, too, was falling and falling, hitting the ground, and falling again.

Her husband couldn't look at her. Nor she at him. When she exhaled, there was a gap in the pain, making it sharper still when she breathed in. And the sun was a hum below the horizon.

Clouds stretched in luminous fingers of pink and peach, beautiful between the hills. The sky sailed from indigo to white, washing out the last of the stars. And merciless daylight pushed and packed the truth into every terminus of her body, spilling into her corners.

The boys were up and moving around, warming grits on the stove. There was butter melting on the pan, the scent sweet and light and at odds with everything. Lenny came in to lay a small hand on hers, a grown-up expression plastered over his shattered heart. Lewis stood at the kitchen door, gazing at his father, working on that difficult man's business of helping without touching. She could feel them – her sons – constellated through the house and across the yard, smouldering with grief. But none of these living souls could sing as loud to Mary Jane as the one that was gone.

Lenny was formal as he set an overflowing bowl of yellow onto each of their laps. Despite her waves of sickness, she said, 'Eat,' trying to make Jacob pick up his fork, because nothing could sustain them, now, except full stomachs.

She forced the stodge down in tight swallows to dampen the smallest part of the morning's shrillness. She should not be trembling when she washed her daughter with fresh linen and soft water; not shaking as she dressed her, carefully looping every button for the last time.

She imagined Zona lying quiet in the frost, perhaps somewhere behind the house in Livesay. The cold, and the thin slats of pinewood that Trout had surely used to cradle her, would keep her immaculate for her mother. It was a shame for Jacob that he would play no part in this women's ritual. He sat as if blinded to the world, crossing his legs with no mind for the bowl that was resting on his thighs. It rolled off and smashed against the hearth, the cornmeal turning out onto the floor. But nobody moved to fetch it, because there could be no order until Zona was back with them.

Through the small east window, Mary Jane watched daylight broaden. Trout would be making preparations for the journey now. Before he carried her daughter to the bed of the wagon, he would try to gather the clothes for her burial. But in his grief, he might not choose the right garment. Still, if he didn't bring the wedding dress, they would manage. Her niece, Eulalia, would surely offer the plum silk gown with scalloped ruffles that Zona had so often borrowed. You cannot know the destiny of things; that this dress, or those shoes, that flattered a person so well in life and in which you had seen them so happy, might join them in the ground.

'Everlasting faint,' she muttered. She eyed Trout's note where she had crumpled and thrown it onto the stacked firewood. Jacob had to be wondering about it, too. 'What on God's good earth is an everlasting faint?' It was bad enough for Zona to be snatched away, worse still for Dr Knapp to have given such an obscure reason. This was the fate of a hapless princess; of a woman in one of those fairy tales that Jacob used to tell. It hinted at hope and romance where there was none. 'There was nothing wrong with her at Christmas,' Mary Jane said. 'She looked better than ever.'

Jacob winced, closed his eyes. They could both picture it. Zona sitting right there at the parlour table. There had been that little argument with Lucy, of course. But she had been quiet and settled by the time she left with Trout on St Stephen's Day. As Mary Jane remembered it, her daughter had begun to accept that no life, not even hers, could be without compromise.

Questions persisted, nosing under her skin. Did it hurt when she died? Did she know what was happening? Was she afraid?

Withrow said that a negro child, the one who collected Zona's eggs each morning, had found her at the foot of the stair. But, never having met the boy, Mary Jane couldn't picture him. Nor could she imagine Zona's parlour, because she had never been inside it.

The hunger for every detail was sharp, now. She needed to be sure that all things had been perfect yesterday morning; that when Zona collapsed, her world had been in a state of grace.

Alfred tried. Lewis tried. Lenny tried. But no one other than Zona could have gotten her father into his good clothes. His clean union suit was still stretched across the bed where Mary Jane had left it, starched and blued, but he refused to change even his under-things.

The fabric whispered as she eased into her old-fashioned mourning dress — one of those that she had dyed for her father's funeral. It had been bad luck to keep it, she could see that now. Back then, she had worn her weeds for a full year, leaving three black dresses threadbare. And as she wriggled her shoulders into this one, she felt as if there might be no end to the stewing of frocks and the sharp stink of logwood dye.

Small as she was, this little dress would not button without a corset beneath, so she left the crêpe to flutter at her back. On this day, of all days, she could not think of strapping her ribs, or squeezing tight her lungs. The cord between her and Zona might be thinning and fraying, but she did not believe it to be severed. The spirit world felt too close by, and her daughter's soul would linger, surely, until there had been some kind of farewell. She would hear the sound of her voice. Or catch the scent of lily of the valley. Or see the rare flash of a cardinal in a wild grapevine, just like the one they had seen around the time of Zona's tenth birthday, brightly singing.

Her caul sat paper-wrapped on the dressing table. A few days' wear had left the envelope oily and dog-eared and curved in the shape of her breast. She gently tore it open to reveal the yellowed membrane. New cracks had appeared in its surface, their edges buttery. Taking a fresh sheet of onion-skin paper from the drawer, she transferred the caul, shrouding it with a series of practised folds. The ritual finished, she pinned the packet inside her dress.

Every corner of the bedroom seemed to shimmer, as if brimming with Zona. It was a small but sovereign comfort that if her daughter was watching from the boundary between worlds, her kindness and wisdom would be perfect. By now, she had shed the ignorance of life, just as the copperhead sheds its skin. All stubbornness, impatience and superior attitudes would be gone. And as water finds its level, so it must be that Zona finally understood her mother.

At last, and without undue favour toward her father, her daughter must have some grasp of her festering sadness with Jacob. As she sat on the bed to button her boots, she could see her husband where he stood in the ragged stubble of the cornfield, holding his head with both hands. Perhaps it was where he felt closest to Zona — out there on the land that they had planned to conquer, together. But what care had he for his living wife? He indulged his grief while she was left to summon her courage, to make her heart stout for that moment when Trout's wagon would climb to the house, and she would take possession of her daughter's body.

Hot with exhaustion, she stood to smooth her dress. But every joint stiffened as she saw Bessie Harford walking up to the porch. For six months, her friend had been easing herself out of full mourning. She had been persuaded, finally, to wear nothing more than a black band on her arm in memory of Ruth. Mary Jane grew weak at the sight of her black leghorn bonnet, and her overcoat, darker than bitumen. A stooped grey ghost of herself, Bessie was carrying a pewter bowl. And when Mary Jane recognised it, she went rigid and cold as the metal itself.

Bessie gave a muted knock on the door, and Mary Jane hovered on the landing, pulling on a black-fringed shawl to hide her bare shoulder blades. By the time she took the first step, her friend was already in the parlour, Lenny closing the latch behind her.

'What happened?' Bessie said, watching her descend. Her eyes, though shining, were too shocked for tears. She held the bowl – that same vessel they had used to wash Ruth – as if she were begging Mary Jane to place magical alms inside it, undoing what they both knew to be true.

And all at once, there was the heat of her. The clamminess under Bessie's arms, the give in her belly, her hot, sour breath. Grief oozed at the lightest touch. Until there was a roaring channel, a flood of meltwater, clear and daughterless.

At noon, the boys killed the fire in the kitchen stove. The room filled with smoke, but it was cold enough to make everyone's breath cloud, and that was all that mattered.

The parlour table was arranged at one end of the room, set with the long cool board that Lewis had brought in from the barn. Bessie had ironed the cotton sheet to lay over it, and Mary Jane drew the rainwater from the cistern herself, the liquid bearing a spicy scent from the leaves in the gutters. With thanks to winter's blessed cold, they would need little else to prepare Zona's features. To make her lovely for the After Life.

The big scissors left a clean edge on the white linen, and a small stack of light cloths waited beside the pewter basin of water. It would not be long now. The riders who had come ahead of Trout said that he was due within the hour.

Women were arriving, all dressed in their weeds, crows rustling and shuffling into the kitchen. Ann Power, who had brought Zona's little girl into the world, was amongst them, steady with the quiet and comforting authority of those women skilled in both birthing and the laying-out of the dead. The time for quiet and pragmatism was already upon them, and they moved about each other as planets around the sun, each in her own path, performing her own small task. A fresh corset was set aside just in case; the mirrors were covered; a smooth stick was left, discreet, on the dresser, ready to press one end upon the breastbone and brace the other against the jaw.

Margaret and Abigail, Zona's aunts, bore that expression which might be mistaken for impassivity, while her eldest cousins, Eulalia and Emily Dove, shook with the passions of the young and infrequently bereaved. The parlour was filling with family and neighbours seeking relief from the icy air, and some of the men were already huddling in the front yard, getting ready to form passage for Zona. The air was flat and even, playing no tricks to magnify or shrink the hills. Jacob stood out against this dull universe, hands idle by his sides. Lucy Frye was fixing a band of black crêpe around his hat, while he stared through the ground, into some place that no one else could see. Mary Jane watched him for a moment, and another of the bonds that had once been fastened between them came undone. Jacob struck her as unfamiliar, a thing forgotten, and which might have to be learned all over again.

The first sounds of horse and wagon came from the bottom of the hill, and a chestnut mare snorted her way up the earth road to the house, dragging Trout's flatbed behind her. He had engaged a sombre friend to take the reins so that he might sit on the back with the white pine box. His head and hands rested on the wood, and in his grief, he did not seem sensible of his surroundings. The small cavalcade following on horseback was made up mostly of strangers – from Livesay, perhaps – and as they paraded into the yard, Mary Jane's heart walloped as if closed inside a fist. This barren scene could not be squared with the vividness of her daughter; the burgeoning creature who used to sit in her lap on the rocking chair, spittle shining on the cool stick of coral that she had gummed to ease her teething.

She stepped down off the porch, willing the wagon to move faster. Rows of sad faces watched her, and she wished that they would disappear, leaving her alone with her child.

Save for the horse's laboured breathing, all was silent as the wagon drew up alongside Mary Jane. She touched the pale casket. The pine was rough, and felt almost warm. Where she had feared a type of alien disquiet, there was only the primal urge to take her daughter in her arms.

All six of their boys shuffled into line at the wagon's rear. The youngest two couldn't help with carrying their sister, yet they primed their little shoulders, ready to walk with her, new strength setting hard on their insides. Trout took his time lifting his head, seeming drunk on sorrow. When he did, there were tears shivering in his eyes. Mary Jane could not bring herself to soothe him, her head filling with unjust thoughts about how Zona might still be alive had he not stolen her away.

Only Jacob had the will to clutch his offered hand. The widower climbed down off the wagon, and her husband held him tight, absorbing a sudden outpouring of Trout's violent grief.

Mary Jane kept her hand on the casket until Armsted Harford moved in with a few other tactful men. There was the banging of bolts and slats as they set about dropping the sides of the wagon. They fed the casket along between them, each extending one thigh to give awkward support. Mary Jane's soul pitched as Zona's weight came off the wagon, and there was that special prelude, the counting, the coordination, before they lifted her onto their shoulders, each in partial genuflection. When they stood tall, and Zona ascended to that place of dignity afforded only to the dead, there could be no more denial, only the truth that her daughter was gone, and here was her shell.

Bessie caught her arm, and they followed the casket into the house, shepherding Zona's body home. Mary Jane's eyes adjusted to the dim as they passed through the narrow door to the parlour, and onward into the kitchen. When the flimsy box was set on the prepared table, Eulalia opened the back door and the windows, while Emily Dove lit the candles. Jacob and the boys went back into the parlour, high waters receding after a flood.

With her hand resting on the lid, Bessie nodded to Armsted. The moment had come to prise it open. Her husband stepped up, subtle as a shadow, claw hammer in his hand. But he hesitated when he saw that Trout was still in the room, fixated on the slender box.

'Darling,' Bessie said, trying to get Trout's attention. 'Sweetheart, you shouldn't be here now. Did you bring Zona's wedding dress? You give it to me, and I promise you, we'll look after the rest.'

She tried turning him gently toward the door, but the widower was unbiddable in his grief. There was no softness in his bearing, no willingness to lean on others.

'I have to see her,' he said, pale and insistent.

Mary Jane gritted her teeth, trying to abide him as she might any small irritation, until he grabbed the hammer from Armsted.

'That's enough,' she barked. 'Go on, Trout. Get out of here.' She reached for the tool, but already her son-in-law was setting about the iron head of a proud nail. 'Armsted?' she said, hoping that her placid friend might stop him. Instead, his eyes begged her to let the widower's outburst run its course.

The soft pine cracked as Trout levered each spike from its socket, the scent of resin rising. When the lid was loose, and ready to move, he wiped his running nose with his wrist, and looked to Armsted for help. He was that choked with sadness, Eulalia and Emily Dove clung to each other, gasping to see a strong man so reduced by his suffering.

All of this would have been bad enough. But then Armsted eased the wood away. And beneath was an obscene surprise.

7 | LUCY FRYE

Meadow Bluff

January 24, 1897

There was a crack, a great smashing sound in the kitchen, that put Lucy in mind of a fractured skull. Certain to draw disapproving glances from Zona's cousins – the ones who considered themselves to be the closest thing she'd ever had to a sister – she decided that intruding upon the kitchen could make little difference, now, with the sacred air of the room already so violently disturbed.

Jacob stayed where she had propped him against the mantel, his lips drawn into an exasperated line, as if all along he'd been expecting Mary Jane to cause some kind of trouble. Lucy weaved through the stunned silence in the parlour, stepping over those fragments of cream-coloured pottery that had skidded along the hallway; three pieces, much like big teeth bashed from a great head. Jacob's brother, Johnston Heaster, was holding Trout by the shoulders, steering him out the kitchen door before Mary Jane could launch anything else at him. Once they had jostled past, there, at last, was Zona, surrounded by women in ink-black dresses, each standing in her own static pose of shock.

There might have been a wire fastened to Lucy's stomach, and a pulley wrenching her forward, because all at once she was standing by the casket. And what she saw, as she gazed down upon Zona, made no sense at all. Her friend should have been draped in soft provisional clothing, waiting to be dressed. But instead of a nightgown, or a chemise, or even a loose wrapping of clean cotton, Trout had buttoned Zona into her wedding dress, the silk right up to her neck. A gauzy, white scarf veiled her face, the fabric plucked carefully upward to stand proud of her features.

Mary Jane's angry and baffled frown was fixed on Zona where she lay, marble-white, with not one inch of her skin on show except for her pale fingers, which were knitted below her breast. 'You had no right,' she hissed.

Trout was edging back into the kitchen, shrugging Johnston off. His chest rose and fell, the self-righteous panting of a man who thinks he's been wronged.

'Madge,' he said, daring to use the terrible nickname that Lucy knew Mary Jane despised. 'Come on, now. Don't be like that.'

His bad taste was in keeping with the worst details of Zona's attire. He had tied the scarf in big loops beneath her chin, the bow large enough to have an air of glamour. It lacked the plainness – the purity and honesty – preferred by the dead when meeting their Maker.

There was the unmistakable sound of scissors being dragged across wood, a flash of metal as Mary Jane turned from the dresser with the twin blades splayed, ready to snip open the veil.

'Easy,' Bessie said, staying her friend's arm with a strong grip.

She was right, Lucy supposed, to try to avoid an even bigger scene. With friends and neighbours looking on, a nick in the pristine fabric could be as distressing as a scalpel on skin.

The scissors grew heavy in Mary Jane's hand, and Lucy hurried to ease the metal from her cold fingers. She allowed her touch to linger; a quiet way of saying that she understood, even if Trout did not.

'Doesn't she look beautiful?' he said, seeking praise for his efforts. When the only reply was raging silence, he looked forlorn, seeming oblivious to the fact that by laying out his wife, he had cheated her mother.

Lucy could smell the crushed rosemary that Mary Jane had used to perfume a deep bowl of water. Broken sprigs floated in the pewter, their scent green and woody and camphorous. But there would be no running of clean soaked linen over Zona's body now. No crucial act of acceptance as Mary Jane washed her daughter's mottled skin, feeling the looseness of her muscles. The coyness of the veil was more desolating yet, allowing none of that frank gazing which permits the living to finally let go of the dead.

'You've done your best, Trout, darling.' Bessie stepped forward, with all of her usual warmth. 'Won't it be nice, now that she's home, to take off the veil?'

She made it sound simple; like the polite removal of a hat, or a pair of muddy boots. Trout wouldn't refuse her, Lucy thought. Nobody in Meadow Bluff could. But as she glanced at Bessie's face, there was none of her usual tranquil character. Instead, her cheeks were burning, as if with shame, causing Lucy's heart to stutter.

'Let Mary Jane see her daughter's face for the last time,' Bessie said, her mouth dry. 'I know better than anyone what it means to miss that final moment.'

She pressed a lock of her dark hair behind her ear, chin dimpled with humility, seeming to confirm the painful rumours that everyone had heard. She was giving them licence to picture her just as she had been on that mournful Easter Sunday when Ruth had died. Lucy was free to imagine her fleeing her daughter's side, unable to look upon the sallow flesh that had blackened like overripe plums, leaving Mary Jane and Zona to do all the washing and dressing and the closing of the casket. It was Zona who had told her about it, how she had found the distraught Bessie sitting on the dung-matted straw of the cattle crib, babbling about her cowardice. Which meant that Trout had heard all about it, too.

Bessie seemed to battle her instinct to hide, now, standing with her shoulders back, a worn goddess on the prow of a ship.

The widower pushed his hands deep into his pockets. 'Mrs Harford,' he said, and he bit his lip so that he might look hesitant, 'I don't think you're being fair. That's Zona's favourite scarf. You're asking me to ignore her wishes.'

Lucy felt the rumble of Mary Jane's anger, the detonation of a buried magazine, as Jacob came hobbling into the room. He stalled his tobacco-chewing on the threshold, the last traces of colour draining from his complexion. Eyes round, he saw his daughter in all of her stately whiteness, and it seemed to Lucy that he was a planet tilting away from the sun, spinning into his own winter. Spring might come again to Greenbrier County, but Jacob's sap would not rise along with that of the sugar trees.

'What have you done, Trout?' He looked baffled, and broken. 'Why didn't you leave the women to their work? I don't know how you do things up on Droop Mountain, but that's how it goes here in Meadow Bluff.'

'The same in Droop,' Trout said, seeming wounded that anyone might suggest otherwise. 'But, Father,' he said, 'a man who loved his wife as much as I do mine would never leave it to others.'

He glided to Zona's side, like an ardent groom who had been neglecting his bride. He rested his hand on the pale weave of her fingers, looking for all the world as if he might try to rock her awake. And Emily Dove's face brightened.

'All professional undertakers are men,' she said in her crisp voice. 'Remember last summer? How the funeral parlour in Bowling Green took care of Great-Aunt Flora? Start to finish.' Her finger traced an arc through the air, a barometer needle moving from *Stormy* to *Fair*. 'We're living in the future,' she said. 'Might as well get used to it.'

'You think a man does a better job,' Mary Jane said, 'if you pay him for the work a woman does for free? I suppose men are better cooks, Emily? Better tailors? Better midwives?'

'Aunt Mary Jane.' Eulalia rested a gloved hand on Trout's shoulder. 'I think money is beside the point.' There was no deference in her gaze. Newly married, her hair in a pompadour, she had an imperious air, and Lucy watched as the balance of power seemed to teeter between the two generations. 'Don't forget,' she said, 'Trout is Zona's husband.'

She waited for her aunt to fill the rest in for herself. *The wife does not have authority over her own body, but the husband does.*

'Him?' Mary Jane said. 'He hardly knew her.'

She was railing against sacred vows, now. Against the Bible itself. And just like that, Lucy saw that Mary Jane was being cast as the offender. Trout, with an expression of mild forbearance, pulled a stool up to the casket, the rest of their little congregation ignoring Zona's mother where she stood wild-eyed. Jacob staggered in the direction of his whisky barrel. And amidst the hum of rising conversation, Sam Withrow's hard voice piped up in the hallway. The others joined in the hymn, his low register forcing the women to sing a shrill octave higher. *Some day the silver cord will break, And I no more as now shall sing.*

Silent and shivering, Mary Jane was a ghost at her own daughter's funeral, watching Trout from some strange cusp of life. But there was something about her mood – her resistance to his big show of devotion – that chimed with Lucy, a bell ringing and ringing though she could not put words on the feeling.

'Eulalia,' Trout said, urgent, 'my Zona's not comfortable. Go get her a pillow.' Obliging, Eula lifted a sun-bleached pad of feathers from a kitchen chair. 'Quick.' He snatched it and screwed it up small, pushing it into the space above his wife's right shoulder. 'That's better,' he said, pressing down on the bolster. 'Isn't that much better? Doesn't she seem more comfortable?' He pulled his fingers back through his hair with what seemed like genuine relief.

'Don't let him rile you,' Lucy whispered, moving closer to Mary Jane.

Zona's mother turned to the dresser, trying to quell her temper with industry. As she lifted the sprigs of rosemary from the pewter bowl, Lucy saw her freeze, the greenery dropping from her fingers. Something in the water had caught her eye, and she was fixed on it, equal parts charmed and fearful.

'What is it?' Lucy said.

Mourners were inching around the casket, now, friends and neighbours condoling with the widower. But the procession stalled as Mary Jane's voice came very low and clear.

'Trout didn't cover the mirrors,' she said. 'There's a looking glass above the mantel in Zona's house – isn't there, Lucy?'

'Yes,' Lucy replied. Now that she thought of it, she had seen a hand mirror there, dangling haphazard on a chain. 'A small one.'

Mary Jane made a circle with forefinger and thumb, and pressed the little hoop to her eye. 'Look in through one mirror, see out through another.'

Her son-in-law tried hard to ignore her as she walked toward him, her gait stiff. 'Emily Dove,' he said, brusque. 'Get me that sheet.' Zona's cousin moved to the place on the dresser where he had spied the clean linen. 'My poor darling, she can't get comfortable.' Emily pulled the corner of the sheet, and its folds opened, an avalanche of white diamonds tumbling to the floor. Trout squatted to meet the spill, ravelling the fabric into a tight ball, great effort showing on his face as he squeezed it into the small space above Zona's left shoulder. 'Much better,' he said, primping her veil with affection. 'Isn't it, my darling? You're so beautiful.'

'Why didn't you drape the mirror?' Mary Jane said, nearly upon him. Her smooth cheeks had wrinkled like the skin on scalded milk, the sharpness of her shoulder blades ghastly where her black-fringed shawl had slipped.

Trout smirked, encouraging the others to laugh at his mother-in-law. 'That's a silly old superstition, Ma.'

'It was good enough for Lincoln,' she said. 'They hung yard after yard of mourning cloth for that man in the East Room. White silk, black silk, crêpe on every window. You wouldn't do it for my Zona. Didn't cover even one little mirror. But I'll tell you what you're right about.' Her eyes glittered with warning. 'My girl has no comfort. I saw her. Wandering.'

Trout gave a troubled sneer, as if she were crowning her own disgrace. Still, he was riveted to her progress as she straggled back toward the pewter bowl. With grim anticipation, she seized its metal sides, and peered into the water. Not seeming to find what she was looking for, she reached in, fingers tentative, breaking the shining surface of the liquid. And with this, some part of her was released back to the world.

'Lucy,' she said, quietly frantic, 'pray for her. Pray for Zona to come tell me why she's restless.' She began to spill the water to the floor in a careful trickle, casting back over her shoulder toward the casket. 'She shouldn't see what's happening here,' she said. 'It will only break her heart.'

Lucy watched the rope of liquid, listened to its bright splash, and as Trout sat defiant, a terrible idea was crystallising. One so ugly that there was no clean, soft water on earth that might ever rinse it away.

8 | MARY JANE HEASTER

Hughart

February 8, 1897

'Mind the step. Foot up high . . . right up high, Mary Jane.'

Bessie was treating her like she was infirm, or convalescent. In a way, perhaps she was both. 'I've still got my wits, Bessie,' she said. 'I know this threshold as well as my own.'

'You sure?'

Mary Jane took a long breath before admitting, 'No. Can't say I'm sure of anything any more.'

There had been too many times, this last couple of weeks, when she had seen a face hovering at the corner of her eye. It disappeared each time she tried to look straight at it, melting into the grey shade of the springhouse, or the weak sunlight on the porch, or the branches of the apple trees where Lenny's buckets of fermenting wheat were still hanging, though it was far too cold, now, to breed maggots for his fishing hooks.

Even in her sheepskin coat, there was a chill patch on her breast, where her caul used to be pinned. The perilous little thing was pressed back inside the pages of her Bible, where it might have less influence. She had prayed, hard, for supernatural intrusions, that could not be denied. But with Zona gone, they had come on too strong, and with the buzz of terror.

Breathless, she covered the short stretch to the kitchen table, boots scratching stone.

'What's wrong with your feet?' Bessie said, taking the broom to scrub out the marks that she was leaving in her wake.

'I'm sorry, Bessie.' Mary Jane groaned, letting her weight fall onto the nearest bench, and she stretched her legs out to display the soles of her shoes. 'Jacob's new ice grips.' She plucked off her mittens and set about the brass buckles on the leather straps that Jacob had used to lash a pair of rasps to her feet. 'Look.' She released the first of them, and dangled the steam-moulded pine in the air. It was studded all over with metal, the sort of toothy instrument that she might have used to scale a fish. 'This is my reputation now. Someone who might fall over at any time.'

She gave a shrug of defeat. It had been easier to let Jacob fuss than to argue with him. When he had dropped to his knees to fasten the grips, it had been an act not of love, but of discipline. Since the funeral, she had grown smaller, while he grew bigger, as if to fill the emptying space. And he had seemed oblivious to her pain, pulling her this way and that, leaving her amazed by his parched and freckled skin; how it didn't welt or scald when he collided with the terrible force of her grief.

There was a flash of brass, the second buckle springing loose. Mary Jane could see Bessie stealing furtive glances at her, making quiet assessment of the weather in her soul. She threw aside the last ice grip and rubbed her sore knees.

'I'm not so bad, Bessie,' she said, trying to settle her friend's concern. 'I'm here. And I'm breathing.'

Bessie caught the kettle just as it came up to a whistle, poured the bubbling water into the tall coffee jug. 'I suppose that's good enough.'

I understand, she seemed to be saying, *the feeling that every bone is broken and none will heal.* What she could not possibly understand was Mary Jane's sudden sense that a silvery figure was moving about in the room right above them. Whispering its feet across the boards, it was abiding in that simple chamber where Ruth had died, and where Zona had given birth. As it seemed to pass above her head, the metal of Zona's wedding hoop grew very hot on her little finger.

Already the ring had chafed her skin, turning it hard and red. 'Would you credit,' she said, 'that Trout used this to make his vows to Zona.' She shimmied the band off and held it out to Bessie. 'Imagine that sealing holy matrimony.' She gave a mirthless laugh. 'I've never seen such a sorry piece of scrap.' The dull circle was nothing more than the wide end of a silver thimble, the dome hacked off in coarse fashion. 'Trout gave it to me in the graveyard, and I knew I recognised it from somewhere,' she said. 'I looked inside for a hallmark, and there it was. A little leopard . . . a crown . . . King George's head. All worn flat. Bessie, this was my mother's thimble – the one she left to Zona. And I don't reckon Trout Shue asked permission to saw it up.'

'Of all things.' Bessie, holding two mugs, made haste to bang them down on the table. 'Why would he part with that?'

Mary Jane offered the ring, and Bessie accepted it on her open palm, watching it in the same delicate manner as she might a damselfly. Mary Jane wondered if she could feel it, too, the wrongness in the metal.

'We were standing by the grave,' she said. 'And I heard myself saying to Trout, *Bring Zona's things over to the house. I'll deal with them.* After the way he dressed her for the wake, I knew he hadn't the first idea what to do with a woman's things. *Don't forget her ring*, I said.'

'You meant the chalcedony?'

'What else could I mean? I didn't want him getting any ideas about keeping it.' Set into silver, the stone was lighter than wheat, milky and polished, and had been big enough to cover one of her daughter's long fingers from knuckle to joint. 'I remember teasing Zona about it when that windbag Snow found it washed up in the creek. I'd no idea what she saw in that rough old thing, no lustre at all. Jacob asked William Frye to buff it up, set it in that claw.' When it reappeared in its velvet box, she hadn't liked to admit how lovely the pattern was, wheeling across the gem – blooms of old coral scattered through the oval like quiet memories of exploding stars. 'Does Trout really think I'd ask for his wife's wedding band? What kind of man would give it? He fished it out of his pocket, Bessie, handed it over with balls of lint.'

Bessie shook the band gently onto the table. 'A man leaving the past behind him,' she said. She lifted a fork and gave their jug of coffee a languid stir. And there they were, in the silent aftermath. The green blades of their lives had been cut to the quick, the emptiness astonishing.

'I saw her,' Mary Jane said. She had planned to make this

announcement in a calm and steady way, but it came out frayed and nervous. 'In your pewter bowl, in the water. I saw Zona.'

Bessie tapped her fork on the edge of the jug and set it down very precisely on a saucer. Then she drew up a little stool and gripped Mary Jane's hands, examining her expression just as a doctor might.

'Now.' Bessie's demeanour was patient as she looked into her friend's eyes, but her lips moved subtly, as if to shape the words of retraction that she wanted Mary Jane to echo. *I didn't mean it. I spoke out of turn. It's the grief talking.*

'It wasn't very clear,' Mary Jane said. 'The reflection, I mean. But I know it was Zona.' She squeezed Bessie's fingers, willing her to accept the truth. 'I'm calling it a reflection, but it was more like looking through a window. And she was there, Bessie . . . a bit hazy, but looking tall in that way that she always did. There was a stair behind her, light coming in at the top, her hair shining, flowing over her shoulders. And I said to myself, this is her house in Livesay, and my girl isn't at rest.'

Bessie dropped her head with a tormented sigh, her breath hot on Mary Jane's skin. 'Zona was a good woman,' she said. 'There's no reason why she wouldn't be at peace.'

'I've been praying on it,' Mary Jane said. 'I know something's wrong. But the messages I've been getting, they're not very clear.'

'Mary Jane Heaster.' Bessie squared her backside on the stool. 'Your daughter is resting easy by the Lord's side, same as my Ruth.'

'I have reasons, Bessie – real ones – to be worried about Zona's eternity.'

'You're not yourself. The same as there were many times

when I was not my own self. I'll wager you're not eating.' She looked as if she were about to clutch Mary Jane around her middle and guess her weight, the same as she might a stringy hen that wasn't laying eggs. 'The shock you had, well, it won't ease for a long time.'

'There were footprints in the ashes yesterday.' Mary Jane had waited to hear herself say this out loud, and now that it was done, she felt relief. 'Yes. Yes, Bessie, there were. Very neat. A size four, I would say. Right on the porch where Lewis left a spill. And this morning, in the snow, I saw them again. All the way over to the stable.'

'You're reading too much into things,' Bessie said. 'Why not ask the doctor to give you something comforting. A draught to help you sleep.'

'Not for me,' Mary Jane said. 'No. I have to stay sharp.'

Perhaps her friend didn't remember much about those strange days after Ruth died. How she had sighed and sobbed on her bed, her breath bitter and spicy with opium and cinnamon and clove. The soles of her boots had often been thick with mud, the ferrous soil gathered during her dreamlike wanders on the slopes of Miller Mountain; those determined but fruitless walks that she had taken, hoping to shake her grief off in a ditch, or snag some harrowing part of it in a hedge, leaving it behind like so much discarded wool.

Mary Jane couldn't stand the idea of Zona's spirit finding her listless, drinking down yet another murky spoon of Manus Dei. 'There's something you need to see,' she said. Her fingers fluttered and trembled as she tried to open the worn satchel that was slung across her body. Her ledger was inside, and she slid the book out, now, smoothing the blue-marbled paper of the cover where it was lifting from the cardboard. She flipped through sheets of her own neat arithmetic until she came upon the remarkable page.

'There.'

Bessie's face tightened with worry. She didn't dare to touch the strange writing, but brought her fingertips very close. 'Reminds me of the war,' she said.

'Yes . . . like they were trying to save paper.' The slim rations during those terrible years had forced Mary Jane to cross-hatch the sentences in her own letters and diaries in exactly this same way; collecting ink on the heel of her hand, running words both across and down the page.

'What do you mean? They were saving paper?' Her friend looked so unsettled that Mary Jane supposed she had already guessed the truth.

'I was holding the pencil, but I wasn't the writer, Bessie. It was more like I was just watching.' She traced the words lightly with her finger, felt the imprint of the letters – those energetic loops and points that broke the faintly ruled lines of the page. 'It's so neat, you wouldn't know the words came fast. Very fast.' It was this urgency that had frightened her; the way that the pencil had pressed harder than she would have chosen, until the whole page was embroidered.

'What does it say?' Bessie seemed spellbound by its uncanniness.

Mary Jane offered the book, and her friend stood up to hold it in the same noble posture as she did her Book of Common Prayer. Composing herself, she read aloud.

'*When I was a girl, I was a girl, I was only a girl. When I was a . . .*'

She stopped and looked at Mary Jane. 'This is nonsense.

The same thing over and over.' She laid the journal flat beside Zona's wedding ring, and changed the angle so that she might set about reading the vertical writing.

'*Six thick thistle sticks . . .* ' she said, tripping over the words, '*six thick thistle sticks six thick* . . . Mary Jane, this just goes on and on,' she said with a shudder of disquiet.

'I was in the parlour. Trying to write something to Zona,' Mary Jane said. 'I didn't know what, because I wasn't sure what to ask her. Here's the pencil,' she said, reaching into the satchel to pull out one of those bright yellow Koh-i-Noor types that Jacob liked so much, and that Zona had liked, too. 'I couldn't find a pen, and someone had left this sticking out of the match safe.' More than one half of its bright barrel had already been pared away, and there were tooth marks on the ferrule where it had been squeezed very flat. Her husband had never chewed a pencil in his life. Only her daughter had been in this habit. 'Look how the writing goes outside the lines. You don't think those big loops are familiar? The curls on the *W*, the way it all slants left?'

'Mary Jane, why didn't you tell me you were ailing?' Bessie said. 'If you had a fever, Jacob could've sent one of the boys, and I'd have been right over.'

'The only fever I've got is from reading this journal,' Mary Jane said. 'Anyone can see this writing is more like Zona's than mine.' There was no denying the similarities between this script and the wilful left-handed writing that Zona had never been cured of, not even after all those months of her offending hand being strapped to the back of her school chair. 'It felt like she was close to me, exactly as if someone was trying to talk over me, boss me around the same way she used to. And I went along with it because, even though it scared me, I thought she might be telling me what's wrong.' She held up the little pencil, squinted at its knife-sharpened point, weighing it eagerly, now, for any lasting signs of possession. 'Bessie, I need your help. I don't know what it means. What am I supposed to do?'

She despised seeking counsel, but better this feeling of exposure than the hot revulsion that spread through her belly when she thought about Zona going unheard. 'Is it something to do with the child?' she said. 'Her little girl? Or was she carrying some debt over from Watchnight. I tried, I warned her not to. What if she's trying to tell me something, and I'm too stupid or frightened to hear it?'

'This isn't Zona,' Bessie said, edging onto the bench beside her. 'I won't believe it. And the pastor won't either. What you need is time, and rest, and . . . '

Her words swilled inside Mary Jane, and her stomach rebelled with a lurch, palms and forehead clammier than if she'd taken a dose of antimony. 'Find a new page,' she said, trying to quell her nausea.

Pins and needles bloomed across her shoulders, down her spine. And a special kind of gravity turned her body toward the journal. It was not her dominant hand that seized the pencil, but her left hand, seizing it in a claw-like grip, clamped between her thumb and three twisting fingers. It twitched, as if with impatience, and a startled Bessie turned the page just in time. Mary Jane saw her own hand move miraculously across the paper, the pencil pressing down very hard, the soft lead making glistening marks.

Tell Pa
Tell Pa
Will you tell
You tell
Tell

The tip jumped clean from the page as there was a sudden and terrible noise. Bessie had slithered away in fright, and sent their jug of coffee crashing. A lake of steaming liquid and grounds dripped onto her lap where she sat clutching the corner of the table, breath heaving with alarm. Only then did Mary Jane feel the metal against her teeth, her molars pressed tight on the brass ferrule. The pencil returned just as quickly to the paper, moving swift and easy.

The lead was swept in two deft rounds, matching ovals appearing, large and almond-like. The sharpened point began shading inside them, with short, deliberate strokes, until Mary Jane recognised a pair of glimmering eyes. Simple as the drawing was, it held some essence of Zona, the same shocked and disbelieving cast she had had on that day when the Wylie woman had come to take her girl.

'Tell me,' Mary Jane whispered. 'Tell your ma what happened.'

A series of heavier strokes, now, each one forming a single lash. When both eyes were fringed with long, deep lines, the pencil shifted to scratch final words onto the page.

little man
little man
the little man

Mary Jane heard herself uttering a cry of dismay, and she threw the pencil aside as if it had burned her. There was a fiery creep of acid in her throat as she looked into those panicked eyes. Each large pupil held a small white void – more than a fleeting suggestion of what Zona had seen in her last moments. Here was the shape of a person. The warped outline of a broad-shouldered man.

'Bessie,' she said, reaching a desperate hand out to her friend. 'Bessie. Do you see him?'

Her friend covered her mouth and huddled by her side. And Mary Jane's breath was shallow and fast, something monstrous coming into resolve.

9 | LUCY FRYE

Meadow Bluff

February 15, 1897

Her stepfather had called her to his study to deliver the news.

'A ghost?' Lucy said. 'What do you mean?'

'You know. A spectre. An apparition.' With his usual lack of tact, William made a haunting *woo* sound, and wiggled his fingers in the air to suggest a shivering phantom. 'Your mother thought you should know. Apparently Mrs Heaster is telling anyone who'll listen that Zona Shue's ghost is wandering around Meadow Bluff. And her spirit is very troubled and unhappy indeed. No perpetual light shining upon her.'

It seemed too cruel, even for Mary Jane, to persist with the lie that Zona was a dark wretch, still roaming the earth. And yet this embellished story took root very easily in her mind. She pictured Zona, lost and desperate. And as she tried to draw closer, her friend made a snare of her arms and elbows, hiding her waxen face.

A sharp, mournful note broke her reverie as William ran a wetted finger about the rim of his brandy snifter. She watched him, hoping for a bout of his wheezing laughter, because nothing, from the ridiculous to the obscene, was sacred to her stepfather. But his face, for once, seemed a mirror of her own dark shock.

The ring of William's glass had pierced her; was still humming in her bones, now, as she pushed open the Heasters' back door, stiff on its hinges. She barged through the dim of the deserted kitchen, and onward into the jumbled house. In the winter drab, she turned the handles onto several empty rooms, before continuing her search along another of the short and peculiar hallways. The house was quiet as an abandoned ship. Until she came to the little windowless room that Jacob usually reserved for himself and his corn whisky. From inside came the low rumble of conversation. Each muffled sentence had a slow, insistent rhythm, their patterns telling her that there were negotiations under way here. High stakes, and acts of persuasion.

She steeled herself, and lifted the black iron ring that served for a handle. The heavy wood traced an arc on the floor, and a measure of smoke caught in her cold lungs. Inside, a scribble of black rose from a lamp that had been left burning too high, its light falling on a clutch of startled faces. There was Ann Power, the corners of her mouth curved down like a fish's. Bessie Harford sat with one finger in the air, the digit no more than six inches from the midwife's face. And there was Jacob

Heaster himself, looking just as disappointed to see Lucy as he was surprised. On the other side of the crooked room, sitting in a neat row, were Zona's uncle and aunt, Johnston and Abigail Heaster, along with their youngest boy, the studious and bespectacled Thomas, who, it appeared, had been taking notes. But there was no sign of Mary Jane.

This was the kind of private assembly that any family might call were an outrage looming. And Lucy knew, all of a sudden, exactly what her presence signalled to them. That it was too late, now, to prevent their embarrassment.

'I'm sorry.' She shrugged. 'William says it's all over town.'

Jacob sighed, and reached into the bag of clove drops that he had perched on the tap of his whisky keg. Gone was the soaring optimism and ready cheer he used to share with Emory Snow in this little room. As he placed a red lozenge on top of his aching wisdom tooth, he might have been wishing for it to extinguish his even greater agonies.

'Wipe your face,' he said, pulling a large handkerchief from his pocket.

She touched a finger to her cheek to find that her mask of pig fat had melted. She scraped the edges of her lips with her thumbnail, trying to stop the taste of pork belly from creeping in. 'Nobody tells you how tough it is bicycling in a Greenbrier winter,' she said, snatching the big square of white cotton where Jacob fluttered it in the air. She swept it through the grease, and, hoping to ease the tense atmosphere, twisted one corner into a little plug and swabbed inside her nostrils.

'What did you hear?' said Ann Power, her usually musical Galway accent taking on a shrewd tone.

'I heard that Mary Jane saw Zona's ghost,' she said. 'I know she's been worried Zona isn't at peace, but it's just a rumour, right? Somebody got the story wrong?'

Ann threw her hard grey eyes up to heaven. 'If only.'

'Why would Mrs Heaster say such a thing?' Lucy said. Ever since Trout had wedged those sheets into Zona's casket, a queasy feeling had been lodged in her ribcage, squat as a bull-frog. It stirred as she realised that Mary Jane, too, might have the lingering sense that something was gravely amiss.

'Lucy, darling,' Bessie said, her eyes red-rimmed with exhaustion, 'Mary Jane's been praying on this, asking Zona to come back. And yesterday, well . . . '

'Well nothing,' Jacob barked. 'Knapp needs to get over here. Write me a letter that puts her in the Trans-Allegheny asylum before she can wreak any more havoc.'

Any time that Zona had described her father's temper, Lucy had been unable to imagine the mellow Jacob Heaster in a rage. Now, his face was white as the moon, and almost as brilliant with anger, his jaws squeezed shut tighter than a mussel shell.

'She's grieving, Mr Heaster,' she said, trying to bring calm. 'If she needs help from anyone, it's the pastor.'

'After all your complaining about the weather,' he said, 'you know it'll be weeks before Pastor Bailey's back.' He turned to Bessie, cold and accusatory. 'I'm not waiting around while my wife spreads stories about my Zona, saying she hasn't been redeemed. What if Armsted told you Ruth hadn't found her salvation, and the whole of Lewisburg was talking about it? Stop encouraging her, Bessie Harford.' He gave her one of those looks meant to shrink a person to half their normal size.

'She's talking trash about the cause of death. If she keeps this up, she'll ruin a man's life.'

Lucy's heart was so loud in her ears that she thought the others must hear it racing. 'What man?' she said. 'What's Mrs Heaster been saying?'

Bessie and Ann exchanged sour glances, neither woman willing to let the other offer her version of events. Having the same nervous tic, Abigail and young Thomas set about examining their fingernails. Only Johnston Heaster seemed able to speak.

'Best you ask Mary Jane yourself,' he said, dispassionate. 'Go on into the parlour, Lucy. You'll get the measure of it fast enough.'

Jacob stood, hands clenched at his hips. 'She'll do no such thing.'

'Brother.' Johnston spoke this word as if it were an incantation, capable of dissolving Jacob's frustration. 'Mary Jane won't let this go,' he said. 'There's no way to stop it getting out. The faster you let it run its course, the better.'

'Oh, Lucy.' Bessie brightened, and made a little shooing gesture with her fingers. 'Yes, do go and see her.'

Before Jacob could raise any objection, Lucy was taking quiet footsteps along the hall, dizzy with trepidation. *Cause of death.* Mary Jane was questioning Knapp's verdict. A little varnished table had been arranged outside the parlour with a wide enamel basin, a jug of water, clean white flannels, and a bottle of smelling salts. These were the trappings of the sick-room – of something contagious on the other side of the door.

Mary Jane was settled on her wingback chair, her face the same pale yellow as whipped butter. Lucy forgot the loose floorboard beneath the rug, and it groaned underfoot. But Mrs Heaster didn't seem to hear a thing, turning neither head nor eyes toward her.

'Hello?' Lucy said, softly. Then, firmer, 'Mrs Heaster. It's me. Lucy.'

She strode to the mantelpiece and waved her fingers in front of the lamp. Little shadows fluttered above Mary Jane's eyes, but still her trance was unblinking. Lucy followed the path of her gaze toward the chair opposite, and the hairs along her spine lifted. Mrs Heaster's lips were moving, as if she were in silent conversation, her pupils very large and black. After another moment, she seemed to fall to rapturous listening, face filled with curiosity and amazement.

The empty haircloth chair had bleak grace. For Zona's sake – for Mary Jane's, too – Lucy wished that her friend really was sitting in the old wingback, come to tell her mother about the After Life, along with any secrets that she might have been keeping about the life that came before. There was such terrible sweetness to it, Mary Jane's face very bright with the kind of love and interest that Zona had so yearned for when she was alive. But the static in the air was not some signal breaking through from the Other Side, Lucy thought. It was the telegraphing of Mary Jane's pain, grown too vast for her to contain or understand.

She wriggled off her jacket and pushed up the sleeves of her bicycling sweater. Kneeling, she brought one hand to rest on Mrs Heaster's hands where they were clutched in her lap. Her short eyelashes were glistening, and her eyelids were purpled, her body almost as lean and bony as a newly hatched chick's. In her fingers, there was a twist of fabric. Pink as a carnation, it trailed from the bloom in Mary Jane's hand, down off her narrow thighs, and on past the yellowed edges of her bare feet to flow behind her chair in a blushing river.

Mrs Heaster would never cut bed linens in this impractical hue. She only used white cloth, sun-bleaching it in summer and freezing it clean in the winter. Lucy brushed a petal of cotton with her fingertips, and the atmosphere in the room changed, as if something long since suspended had suddenly been let go. Even the log fire settled in the grate, exhaling a cloud of sparks.

The smell of singeing rose quickly, and Lucy snatched the fabric from Mary Jane, in dread of a blaze. She found the little smouldering hole and stamped out the kindled fibres with her heel. Zona's mother gazed right at her then, eyes swimming into focus as if she had woken from a fever.

'Mrs Heaster,' Lucy said, urgent, 'are you all right? Bessie says that Zona's been coming to you. Has she told you anything important?' Finally, she forced herself to speak her fears aloud. 'Did she tell you something terrible about Trout?'

'Good girl, Lucy.' Mary Jane lifted a weak hand to dry the shining corners of her mouth. 'Soon as you came in, Zona told me you'd guessed. You were always so clever. She forgives you for everything, you know, because you were right about Trout. Only thing she wishes is that you hadn't said all those things about him at Christmas. He stored up his bad mood, and she had to pay for it later. That's what you were seeing when she got mad at you. She was afraid, and it would've been worse if she hadn't asked you to go.'

The pain and regret that seized Lucy was complete. Throughout the autumn and winter, her own selfishness and naivety had made for a perilous mix, making it unsafe for Zona to tell her the awful truth.

'How did you know?' Mary Jane narrowed her eyes. 'You saw something, didn't you?'

'Last time I was alone with Zona,' she said, 'we were up at Oakhurst.' Hands on hips, she tried to firm up the truth. 'She came after midnight. In secret. Because Trout didn't want her going out. When I look back, I see that she was afraid of him. Of going against him. He must've found out about her leaving the house that night, and made her stay home every day after, because I never saw her again, except at Christmas.'

'Yes . . . yes . . . ' Mary Jane said, giving subtle encouragement. 'He kept her family away too. I blamed Zona. I should have known that it wasn't like her, not for all her stubbornness.' She paused, then, seeming to notice the confession sizzling on Lucy's tongue.

Out it came, a scalding acid. 'That last night at my house . . . she'd been hurt.' Lucy slid her hand up behind her ear. 'There was a cut, right here, on her scalp. Zona told me she fell and took a lamp down with her. I had a feeling – I just knew – that Trout had something to do with it. But I didn't follow through. Didn't push her on it when I had the chance.'

She supposed that Mary Jane would tell her how reckless she had been. Instead, she gave her a bitter smile, as if every diabolical word had brought her both new terror and fresh relief. 'You already know what she told me,' she said. Lucy nodded, eager for her to put words on it. 'You're right. It was Trout. He killed her that morning, with his own two hands.'

They stared at one another, each waiting for the other to

dismiss the notion. Instead, it took on ghastly momentum, maturing, in an instant, from seed to grotesque flower.

'There's no evidence,' Lucy said. 'How can we prove it? I saw the way Zona was lying on the floor, how her neck looked all wrong. The penny dropped when I saw him putting those sheets inside the casket, but I was too frightened to let it land. I'm sorry to say this, Mrs Heaster, but I think he was trying to stop her head from moving around.'

'That's it,' Mary Jane said, her mouth pulling into a terrible grimace. 'Zona told me everything about it . . . how her neck was broken.' She had to clear her throat to find her voice again, and when she did, it wobbled with anger. 'I have all the proof I need.' With a scrawny hand, she brandished a corner of the pink cotton sheet. 'It's from Zona's casket,' she said. 'I went to wash it clean, and when I stirred the tub, the sheet turned red. Stained the water with blood.'

Something wild and greedy was creeping into her eyes. Lucy gave a nervous laugh.

'Mrs Heaster, someone's played a trick on you,' she said. 'Lenny? Maybe Lewis? I'll bet they poured the water from the beets in with the washing. That's how my aunt dyes her poodle. It doesn't prove anything.'

'It'll make those Lewisburg lawyers ask some big questions about Trout.' Mary Jane was setting her jaw against her, showing more signs of fraud, now, than of any derangement.

'You're wrong. No court will accept that sheet as evidence against him. He won't be charged unless we find real proof he did it.'

Mary Jane eyed her with thinly veiled fury. 'My daughter's word is more than enough. The evidence you're talking about is buried in the grave, where no one will see it. Why else would Zona be going to such trouble? She's been writing to me. Bessie will show you.' She waved toward the door, as if she'd had enough of her feeble reasoning.

Small as Lucy felt, her shame hot and crippling, she wasn't going to let her friend down again. Mary Jane had to see reason.

'The problem,' she said, 'is that if you keep on like this, Trout will hear about it. And he'll hide anything that might prove him guilty. *Real* evidence,' she added, 'that could put him in jail.'

'I've already promised Zona,' Mary Jane said. 'And I can't break a promise like that. I'm going to the courthouse tomorrow. Bringing this bloody sheet, and all the words that my girl's been writing and saying to me, and I won't leave until I've seen the prosecutor.'

'Please, don't do it,' Lucy said, feeling powerless to stop the headstrong Mary Jane. But then she saw it in her mind's eye – a sudden image of her own fingers, reaching out to turn the handle on Trout's door. So bright and clear, it was as if she were already standing on his porch. She grabbed her jacket and wriggled into its tight sleeves. 'I'm sorry, Mrs Heaster,' she said, 'I have to go.' After the many times she had failed Zona, there was only one way to make things right now. 'Thank you.' She squeezed Mary Jane's hands, taking inspiration from the ruthless way she followed her instinct.

Her blood felt very thin as she walked fast through the dim of the hallway. She wanted to escape to her bicycle, but hesitated outside Jacob's little whisky chamber, where six worn-out faces turned to stare at her.

Mr Heaster crossed his legs, as if expecting unsavoury news.

'I promise you,' she said, her jaw stiff, 'no one will hear a word of this from me.'

Her pretend shock, and disbelief of Mary Jane's story, must have been very convincing, because both Jacob and Ann Power gave her deep nods of approval. Bessie looked at her with such hurt and disappointment that Lucy wanted to blurt out her plan; but she would not risk being talked out of it.

She clattered through the house until she burst out into the fresh air. In the freeze of the yard, she pinched her tin of lard from her pocket, the fat whitening as she screwed off the lid. Two fingerfuls, smeared onto her face, were enough for a fresh mask. Her skin grew tight, and with fogging breath, she pushed off, sailing back toward Livesay.

She had not seen Zona's ghost; not as Mary Jane had. Yet as she departed, her friend was alive again, in an electric way that she could not explain. And she would not leave until Lucy had secured her redemption.

10 | MARY JANE HEASTER

Greenbrier County
Courthouse, Lewisburg

February 16, 1897

'One more minute,' Johnston said in the same infallible tone he shared with his brother Jacob.

His height made him more insufferable yet, as he looked down Court Street, right over Mary Jane's head, hat and all, expelling her from view. The pocket watch in his palm reflected the chasing clouds, meaning that she had to squint to make out its face. It was only a matter of seconds until 3.15 – the rather precise time that Johnston claimed was best for waylaying the County Prosecutor.

Her brother-in-law might understand the mechanics of the situation, but he cared little about the difficult business of managing her courage. She watched her breath rising in a white fog, and imagined that this vapour was a portion of her spirit, trying to make good an escape. The only tonic for this feeling was Thomas, solid and radiant beside her. It wasn't the black of his coat that made him look indelible on the sidewalk, nor the jet hairs of his glossy brows, which twitched as he sniffed in the cold. It was his spectacles that made him vital, firm on the bridge of his nose, and the journal that he carried with its waxed-leather cover. The boy had the best handwriting in Meadow Bluff, and when the time had come to transcribe the details of her conversations with Zona, her daughter had deserved nothing less.

He and Johnston settled, two crows on a branch, staring in earnest, now, at the courthouse where it loomed across the street. Its four tall pillars were rendered in grey, the sturdy trunks shouldering a great triangular pediment jutting upward into sunlight. It was a simple but imposing affair – just big enough to make the soul quake, rattle the guilt out of any man.

Johnston stowed his watch, and raised a gloved hand in the air. 'And . . . now.' His arm fell, as if he were dropping the flag at a horse race.

They fixed on the double doors of the courthouse – and there was a sense of energy building, a hive ready to swarm. The big wood and glass panels swung open, a wave of men emptying onto the street. It struck Mary Jane that they were all in their Sunday best; as respectful to the justice served by men as to that served by the Lord. They moved in a slow explosion, some thrown free at once, hurrying about their business, while a tangle of jurors and witnesses and spectators lingered in conversation.

'Quick.' Johnston gripped her elbow and pulled her across the street, causing a fast rider on a black mare to swerve.

Through all this sudden noise and movement came a glistening peak of resolve, slicing brightly through her anxiety, carrying her forward. They pushed through the small crowd, and she searched for anyone who might recognise her; who might spread the word that Mary Jane Heaster had come to seek justice for her daughter.

All three strode into the lobby, and they bunched together under the amber light of a crystal electrolier. A young woman of about Zona's age swept past, a line of pearl-white scalp at her centre parting.

'Goodbye, Mr Gilmer,' she said in a polite but firm tone to the man at the foot of the mahogany stair, who gave her an exaggerated salute.

'Until tomorrow, Miss Grose,' he said.

Mary Jane could see why she might all but run from this fellow and his studied dishevelment. The middle button of his vest was open; or perhaps missing, repelled by its owner. The straggled collar of his shirt was limp with heat and sweat, his tie askew, the knot pulled too small and tight, and the fine cashmere of his jacket was very creased. He had a contrary and self-satisfied air, a whiff of groping about his attitude. Here was a creature who might miss nothing with his prying eyes. They were not the sort that stole furtive glances, but were filled with challenge, waiting for a person's belief in themselves to collapse beneath his gaze.

These fervid organs turned on the three of them, and he approached, grinning like a ringmaster who had found freaks to employ in his circus.

'Good afternoon.'

He made no effort to veil his amusement at their

unsophisticated appearance. It was the first time since Mary Jane had thrown off her corsets that any man had dared to make so free in staring at her. Most looked away in confusion or disappointment, or even anger, but Gilmer concealed nothing of his interest, his exploration just as thorough as if he had laid his hands on her.

'Mr Henry Gilmer.' Johnston ignored the man's lewdness, speaking his name as if it were exalted by history. 'Sir, I'm Johnston Heaster. Mary Jane,' he said, 'Mr Gilmer here is the Assistant County Prosecutor.'

Gilmer shook Johnston's proffered hand, though he seemed to bristle at the word *assistant*.

'I've heard about you,' Mary Jane said, smirking. Jacob had mentioned this fellow when begging her not to make a show of herself at the courthouse. This was the Henry Gilmer who had lost the recent ballot for County Prosecutor, and instead of swallowing his pride, and pretending to be happy playing second fiddle, he was choking on it.

Johnston took his boy by the shoulders and pushed him forward. 'My son, Thomas.'

Gilmer lit up, as some folks do around a child's innocence. 'Hello there.' He lifted a hand to tousle Thomas's curls. But seeing the boy's hair stiff with grease and dried sweat, his fingers cramped in the air. 'You taking an interest in the law, son?' His nose lifted, and he scanned all three of them, his thoughts legible; *clodhoppers*, that was what he was calling them.

Mary Jane gave her nephew's crown an affectionate pat. 'Thomas is here to help me get justice for his cousin.'

'Justice.' Gilmer's eyes widened, as if this were very big

talk. He was expecting her to speak of some minor crime, no doubt, like trespass or larceny. 'Sounds like you need the constable,' he said. 'Not a lawyer.'

'I need the County Prosecutor,' she said, unabashed. 'Tell the Honourable John Preston that Mary Jane Heaster has come to speak with him about her daughter.'

Gilmer clapped his hands together, and cast about the lobby as if searching for a marshal who might remove them all by the scruff. But as he glanced up the polished stairway, a better idea seemed to float into his head.

'You know what?' he said. 'Follow me. All of you.' His smile insisted as he carved sudden passage with his short arm. 'Come along now, let's find the Honourable John Preston and make sure he has enough work to do.'

Mary Jane lifted her skirts. 'You go first, Thomas.' The order of procession felt important, and the obedient child led the way, holding the solemn journal a little out in front.

On the second landing, a burnished panelled door announced the COUNTY PROSECUTOR in neat golden letters. Below this, the name HONOURABLE JOHN ALFRED PRESTON was scribed in newer and shinier gold leaf. Gilmer knocked on the mammoth wood, and turned the handle without waiting for an answer.

'You've got visitors, John,' he said, grinning.

He swept the door open to reveal an astonished man, seated at a table so large it was deep enough for two people. But he had it all to himself, the wood bright with French polish.

Mary Jane was gladder than ever that the boy was with her, a foil for this grandeur, as she walked behind him, removing her tight gloves.

'I wasn't expecting anyone, Henry,' Preston said, watching Thomas slide the journal onto his desk. He set down his pen, the boy's ardour seeming to deliver him a reserve of patience. 'Who do I have here?' he asked his colleague with more than a little of the politeness and fairness that Jacob had told her to expect of this well-liked man.

'This is Mrs . . . Easter, wasn't it?' Gilmer said, directing her to one of the two gilded fauteuils facing Preston's desk.

'Heaster,' she said, her full breath behind the *H*, as she sank onto the brocade cushion. 'Mary Jane Heaster from Meadow Bluff. I believe you know it well, Mr Preston.' After all, he owned half of Sewell Mountain, with all its forests and its small measure of coal. 'This is my brother-in-law, Johnston Heaster. And his youngest, Thomas.'

Now that she was sitting, with her coat buckling and sticking in all the wrong places, Preston seemed to note the coarseness of her shape with enquiry and alarm.

Gilmer angled another chair for Johnston. 'I'll let you all get down to business,' he said. With that, he patted his stomach and turned on his heel for the door, as if he had pulled off a great joke.

Preston's eye lingered on Gilmer's back, perhaps harbouring futile hope that he might one day reform. 'Where were we, Mrs Heaster?' he said. 'You have something to tell me?' He placed one inquisitive finger on the cover of the journal.

'Yes. Something very serious,' she said, resolving not to prattle in the way that a man like Henry Gilmer might expect. 'It's about a murder,' she said, bringing her hands to rest on her velvet lap.

Gilmer's shoes squeaked on the wooden floor behind her.

Not only had he been eavesdropping – a childish pastime – but he was striding back across the room, eager to face her.

'Have you come to report a crime?' he said, very grave. 'Or to confess one?' He had the look of a man about to enjoy a porterhouse steak, a fellow who found his job toothsome.

'Sir,' she said, 'it is my daughter who is dead. Buried these four weeks up at Little Sewell. You don't think me capable of killing her?'

Preston gave a quiet gasp of imagined pain. 'Your own child, Mrs Heaster,' he said. 'My very deepest condolences.'

The loss of a young one was a wound shared by both attorneys; Johnston had told her as much. But Gilmer did little more than draw his mouth into a line of watery sympathy before rolling up his mental sleeves.

'You say she's been gone a month?'

'Four weeks this Saturday.'

'And how old was your daughter?'

'Twenty-odd. Married to a man ten years older.'

'You do see the problem, Mrs Heaster?' He shook his head in a way that suggested she was even more stupid than she looked. 'It's usual for foul play to be suspected at the time of death. For one of our county coroners to hold an inquisition. Was there any inquisition?'

'No.'

'And did you bury your girl after the normal fashion?'

'Yes. That is . . . mostly. Her husband, Trout Shue, dressed her for the wake. I don't think anyone around these parts would call that normal.'

'And was there suspicion of murder at that time?' Preston frowned, attempting genuine understanding.

Johnston squirmed, grown too uncomfortable to hold his wind any longer. 'No,' he said. 'No, no. There was no question of it. Mary Jane only got worked up after.'

She felt her gut twist at this betrayal. And before she knew it, she barked, 'Trout Shue did it. Zona's own husband. He's the one who killed her.'

Gilmer's gaze was cold. 'What have you got against this Shue?' he said. 'Are you holding a grudge? There's no point trying to fool us, Mrs Heaster.'

'You would abide a man who killed your child?' she said, trembling.

Johnston cleared his throat. 'Listen,' he said, as if it were his job to bring calm, 'Mr Gilmer, everyone knows that Mary Jane hates Trout for the way he handled the funeral. But the family – me and her husband – we're begging you, please let her put her case to you, or this will never end.'

Mary Jane felt an oncoming wave of embarrassment, but she resisted it, knowing that Jacob and Johnston had set her up, and that she must endeavour, now, to reverse the effects of their treachery.

'Do you believe in the After Life, Mr Preston?' she said. 'That your own children, the good Lord rest their souls, will be waiting for you in heaven? Do you talk to them when you pray?' Her appeal was urgent, for this was the very meat of it all; the unbreakable connection with a departed child.

'I do,' the prosecutor said.

'And do you ever believe they answer?'

Preston steepled his fingers. 'In their own way,' he admitted.

'You'll understand, then, that Zona answered my prayers.

Open the journal, Thomas.' She patted his knee where he had settled on the arm of his father's chair.

Sober, the boy opened the book to the first page, and smoothed the cover back along that line where it met with the binding. Mary Jane's heart leaped to see Zona's words there in strong ink, set with such an amount of powder that the paper had turned silky with pounce.

'The last time Aunt Mary Jane came out of her trance,' Thomas said, 'I took down every word, just how she told it.'

'Her trance?' Preston gave the boy a puzzled look as he lifted a pair of spectacles from his pocket and hooked them over his large ears to read Thomas's script aloud. '*This is the Testimony of the Ghost of Zona Heaster Shue.*' He fell silent, scanning the rest of the page with an air of disappointment, eyebrows lifting as he saw, for the first time, the terrible message that Zona had brought from the Other Side. He read aloud again, in a flat tone that did not convey the terror of her daughter's words as she had spoken them. '*He complained that there was no meat for dinner, and he got very angry, saying that I treated him like he was less than he was. And when I argued, he choked me and he broke my neck.*'

Mary Jane waited for the prosecutors to be moved by her daughter's restless plight. Instead, that blowhard Henry Gilmer interrupted.

'You speak with the dead.' He threw his hands up and rolled his eyes. 'Will your daughter's ghost be joining us to confirm this supposed testimony? No? How convenient for you.' A dark pool of disgust seemed to well inside him.

'I'm not a liar, Mr Gilmer,' she said, 'if that's what you're saying. I would rather die than use my daughter's name for dishonest cause. Four nights in a row she came to me. It says it right there, Mr Preston, does it not? Thomas has it marked. I saw her yesterday, right after the lamps were lit. There was no stopping her from coming. Not until I promised that I'd find you and tell on him.'

Preston removed his glasses and closed the book, eyes twinkling with a fresh helping of disbelief. 'Did any of our coroners attend your daughter – pronounce her dead?'

'It doesn't matter what Dr Knapp said.' Where there should have been the relief of imminent justice, there was only desperation. 'Zona told me what happened. You have to listen to her.'

Johnston sighed. 'Truth is,' he said, 'Dr Knapp went to Zona's house on the morning she died, and it was all very straightforward. The cause was everlasting faint.'

'The girl's heart gave out,' Gilmer said with a sickening note of triumph. 'Mrs Heaster, I think we're done here. The next time you invent a story, at least try to make it believable. Not even a layman could miss a broken neck, never mind Dr Knapp. Take your things and go. Unless,' he added, turning to the prosecutor, 'you want to press charges for making a false statement.' He poked the child's journal. 'One that she forced an innocent boy to record. What do you think, Thomas? Did your aunt see your cousin's ghost?'

He fixed on the boy in an encouraging way, and Thomas wriggled with the same eager-to-please attitude that so many of the Heaster children had; that desire to impress. 'Pa says Aunt Mary Jane is confused because she had a dream that seemed very real,' he said. Then, thinking better of passing off second-hand information, along came another, more original salvo to devastate her. 'Even if ghosts were real, I wouldn't believe her.'

The boy had the happy defiance of any child with newly discovered power, seduced by the thrilling moment, ignorant of the ruin that it might bring to themselves and others.

'All of you, tidy your souls up, now,' Mary Jane said, a scolding, righteous tone taking over. 'What would John Wesley make of you?' With her handkerchief, she dabbed the spittle from her lips. 'The very father of our church believed in apparitions, and why would he not? The testimony of the ages confirms it. You must accept,' she said, 'that there are ghosts. Wesley didn't deny it when the beds of his childhood home quaked under the power of a boggart – a terror – on Christmas Day itself, groaning and sawing and slamming in the rafters. And didn't his family come to call this haunting "Old Jeffrey" – putting a name on him, because maybe such a christening brings a lost soul closer to God? Well, you may be sure that my Zona is not the same kind of deaf and dumb devil as that. She came to me just as she was in life, and spoke the truth about that evil man.' She stalled, trying to conceal her upset at recalling her daughter's spectral appearance. How distant she had seemed, repeating the same words over and over, as if stuck in a moment from which she could not progress. 'Arrest Trout Shue,' she said. 'He must be questioned.'

'Mrs Heaster.' Preston used a cool tone, stamping out any spark that she might have set before she could bring her bellows to it again. 'My own dear Lillie has an ulcer. It often brings her bad dreams. They're no less upsetting for being dreams, but the key is to see them for what they are.'

She looked down, making vague register of her fists in her lap, and her eyes fell on Johnston's canvas bag where it rested limp on the floor. The sheet from Zona's casket was inside, stained all over with blood. She had folded it, very neat, as if this act could contain even a little of its horror. God's truth was not one yard from her ankle, and yet were she to hold it up, these men would deny and despise it.

She was trapped, body and soul; just as Zona was captive on the threshold of the Other Side. Black panic spread inside her, terrible pressure building. But in spite of this evident distress, the conversation continued around her.

'Who is the dead woman's husband?' Preston talked across her. 'Would I know him?'

'He's a blacksmith, at the forge in Livesay,' Johnston said. 'A good one, too.' If his tone were to be believed, Trout's skill was enough to put him beyond suspicion.

'Oh, Cruikshanks' place. Yes. An excellent farrier.' Preston said this with a kind of delighted surprise. 'Saved my Arion from going lame last winter.'

'Is that so?' Gilmer said.

The talk was casual now, working toward a polite winding-up.

'Thank you.' Johnston brushed his pants as he rose to standing. 'There's nothing astray here but a mother's grief. A boil that needed lancing. It will all settle now.'

'You hear that, John?' Gilmer said. 'We're as good as any alienists up at the asylum.'

Preston shook Johnston's hand. 'Anything for the good folk of Greenbrier County. You take good care of Mrs Heaster.'

'Please,' Mary Jane said. Her vision darkened, as if her thwarted promise to Zona were stealing all light and colour from the world. 'He did it with his bare hands.'

Preston was looking at her with the wrong kind of pity.

And at Gilmer's urging, Thomas took her arm to help her up, designating him the small, rational man who must lead the demented woman to the door.

'Good boy,' the assistant prosecutor said. 'And keep in touch if you'd like to study the law.' He took a cigarette from the tin on Preston's desk, slamming the lid shut as if to close all official business. A match flared, and Mary Jane heard him mutter with amusement, 'Wait till Knapp hears about this one.'

11 | LUCY FRYE

Livesay

February 17, 1897

At last, Anderson's silhouette came into view beyond the stained glass of the kitchen door, and Lucy rushed to open it.

'Morning,' she said, lifting the basket of eggs from his arm. 'Did you come from Mr Shue's house? Has he gone to the forge already?'

'I didn't see him, Miss Lucy,' he said. The boy had grown more serious since discovering Zona's body, his soul seeming to have aged. 'I never see Mr Trout before school.' He fidgeted, as if eager to be on his way.

'Thank you,' she said. And with a fresh surge of anger at the blacksmith, she watched Andy depart.

Zona's house was empty, that much was clear. All she had to do was make her excuses and go. Her anticipation was shrill as she left the basket of pink Silkie eggs on the nearest chair.

On the stair to the dining room, every window seemed too bright, and the dark in every corner too deep, and as she eased onto her usual chair at the table, the acrid scent of tarnish and polish rose from the silverware.

'You look like I feel after reading the Siegel-Cooper bill this morning.' William regarded her with a puzzled frown, and stabbed another of his tinned oysters where they sat, grim and grey, in a china bowl. 'Too much wine last night?'

'If you're really interested,' she said, 'I hardly slept.'

From the moment she had left Mary Jane's side, she had been in a state of vigilance, anticipating her trespass into Zona's house. And this feeling soured as William pitched a green-tinged mollusc into his mouth, while her mother's slippers patted the wooden floor, the fabric of her train whispering closer with each step.

'Lucy?' she said. 'What's wrong with you?' Her tone was two parts disgust to one part concern. The tips of her white fingers flickered, too repulsed by her daughter's sweating brow to check for any fever.

'Nothing a little air won't cure,' Lucy replied. 'I think I'll ride Sugar into town. Maybe see how far this silly ghost story has spread.' She smiled as widely as she could, pretending that this would make for great sport.

'What a lovely idea.' Her mother brightened. 'Wear the new cheviot,' she purred, as if this might be a real treat.

'I'll try it with the blush shirtwaist.' As it happened, Lucy had already decided on the crisp riding habit, because there was something about the day that demanded orthodoxy. 'I suppose Trout will have heard all the rumours by now.' Trying to sound breezy, she looked to William. He always had the latest gossip, delivered by the customers browsing his sparkling vitrines.

'I know Anna wrote her aunt in Kentucky all about it,' he said. The handsome hard-boiled brunette from Wheeling was his best store girl, known for parlaying the sale of cheap garnets into fat rubies. 'At that rate, the news has made it to the forge.' Seeing her nervous expression, he pressed a starched napkin to his bristly moustache. 'Don't you worry about Trout,' he said. 'That man won't spend more than a minute scratching his head about it before laughing it all off.'

'I suppose.' She grimaced, as if deploring it all on Trout's behalf.

'The way folks are talking, you'd think Zona was in ten places at once,' William said. 'Homer Hepler says he saw her standing beside her own grave up at Little Sewell, mud on the hem of her wedding dress, black roses tangled in her hair. Jeremy Callison's been talking about a silent woman in a white dress down by Beaver Creek, one he didn't recognise as Zona until she was slipping down into the water. Libby Miller had the earliest sighting of all: a white face looking in her window on the morning Zona died, eyes very hungry, gazing at her baby girl.'

'Heavens,' Lucy said, feeling sick. 'Word gets out fast.' It was a type of madness, people who barely knew her departed friend talking about her in this way. Or maybe it was a type of blind knowledge, buried deep inside their bones, that her friend's death had been corrupt. 'If you'll excuse me, I'd better make the best of the morning.'

She adjusted the cheval for the first time in many months, the mirror creaking on its screws. Her skirt, the tight-laced corset, the shirtwaist, her straight, cooperative hair in a neat low bun, the tan silk riding hat: all of it looked as normal as possible, and would inflame the least contempt should Trout catch her in the house. It would matter very little what she was wearing, of course, if she was found rifling every drawer. Still, it felt like an act of protection.

Kneeling, she stretched one arm under the bed frame and gripped the silk pouch that she had hidden the night before. Inside was a tin of Trout's favourite liquorice candy, a sachet of dried lavender onto which she had hastily embroidered the letters *TS*, and a squat candlestick in solid brass, in case of . . .

There was little point in thinking any further about it, except to say that she must be prepared. At the dressing table, she took a plain piece of paper and rolled it into the carriage of her Remington. With something less than her usual fervour, she struck the necessary keys.

```
I have gone to search Zona's house.
   If I am not home before supper, ask
Trout Shue where to find me.
```

The time when it might be safe to visit Zona's house was an ever-narrowing window – it might even be closed if Mary Jane had already been to see John Preston. Trout might laugh at stories about a silent and powerless wraith, but his manner would surely change once Zona's mother had seen an attorney and given her voice. He would be nothing like the easy-going man of yesterday, who had ignored Lucy as she bicycled past the forge, time after time, trying to get the measure of his routine. He'd acted as if she were invisible, meaning that her beady eye had been free to rove wherever it liked. She had winced to see him greeting customers with those same strong hands that were capable of taking a life; to see that he suffered no trace of natural grief or anxiety, not even when he was alone, replenishing the water in the slack tub, or murmuring to one of the reluctant horses.

Trout Shue was hale and happy, down in the glow and amity of the forge. With any luck, he would be there until noon, while Zona's house stood empty under the sky's chill glare.

Fear rusted her joints as she rapped on one of the little window panes in Zona's front door, her mouth dry, heart at a steady gallop. When there was no answer, she knocked again, loud enough this time to wake the dead. There was no sign of any movement, save for her own shadow, as she reached out to try the latch.

The knob squeaked around, but the door was locked with a bolt. A new one by the look of it, raw pine showing where the edge had been chiselled. Trout didn't want any neighbours fetching up without notice, walking right in with hopes of good coffee and conversation. The brass candlestick bounced off her hip as she hurried around the side of the house, sliding on the hard frost as she scrambled up the steps to the back door.

It, too, was locked, her breath billowing white as she leaned in close to the window. A plaid gingham drape obscured her view, finished in Zona's uneven stitching, and the hem was resting on the door key. Her fingers grasped the contours of the candlestick through soft silk, and she crashed the brass butt through the window pane.

Fangs of glass stood proud in the frame, and she jabbed at them until they were no more than sharp glints in a putty gum. She gripped the key, but the lock was very slow to shift.

Only after a great contortion of her wrist did it turn with a loud *clack*. Trout had the skill to make the bolt run smooth, but he had chosen to leave this trap for Zona – insurance that she could never again steal away unnoticed. The hinges, too, announced Lucy's entry with a violent creak.

She might have been walking into one of those silent galleries at the National Museum in DC, because every object felt significant. Her heart swelled to see how well Zona had laid everything out. This kitchen was similar, in many of its practicalities, to Mary Jane's. There was the same steel shelf fixed above a coal oil lamp in the corner, for proving bread. On the table, a plaid cloth had been folded back on itself, leaving a space clear for kneading and chopping. Beside the stove, there was the same basket of salvaged wax paper, scrunched into loose balls, ready for polishing the stovetop.

It was a strange comfort to see. Sometimes Zona had tried so hard to be different from Mary Jane that she had forgotten to be herself. But here, she had made concessions to her mother's sensible ways of doing things, letting them sit alongside other marvellous arrangements that Mrs Heaster would never tolerate. Beside the gable window, where the western sky showed high and wide, there was a makeshift easel. A number of little white ceramic bowls were scattered beside it, the inside of each holding a dry wash of paint.

Lucy pressed a finger to a matte streak of yellow; a precious trace of her friend. There were brushes, too, standing in a clay pot, their soft bristles in the air. One was round and slender-tipped. Another was flat with a squashed ferrule. A third was very plush and fat as a squirrel's tail. At a glance, the collection seemed to admit to Zona's talents. It suggested freedom, even a small measure of indulgence. Until she saw the box of water-colours where it had been flung onto the dresser.

It lay on its side, the little cakes of paint expelled, as if by force. The baked lozenges were cracked and broken, the pigments splintered and powdered across the dresser's walnut top. It was Trout, surely, who had done this, and she could not bear the explosion of crimson and cobalt and viridian, how it looked so vivid and thrilling. As she smeared the colours with her gloved hand, destroying their joyous appeal, a fat tube of paper caught her eye. In tight behind the iron weighing scales on a high shelf, it looked as if it had been hidden in a fit of spite.

She pulled it down with one shrewd tug before smoothing the pages flat on the table. Cockled by dried watercolours, the leaves dimpled and sprang beneath her fingers. These paintings were more muted than Zona's usual style. An image of a bobwhite quail, hanging from a hook, eyes sunken, breast spangled in black and ochre. A rendering of an owl pellet, scaled up so that the tiny ribs and femurs trapped inside the grey matted fur looked almost as big as her own.

The last of the paintings shocked her into stillness. Limned half in shadow, half in light, was Zona's face. The likeness was striking, the features very immediate. A stroke of white indicated the rounded bridge of her nose, dense black brows vaulting her wide-set eyes. There was no flattery here. Circles of fatigue were showing, and her old chickenpox scar, in all its silvery whiteness, was a puckered dent in her temple. Her expression was open, the invitation to observe her so candid that Lucy could barely look.

The picture's mood — its weariness and stubborn strength — seemed to possess her as she folded it, hastily, and pushed it to the bottom of her silk pouch. The rest of the paintings she curled back into one another, before looking through the open door to the parlour; that place where she had first seen Zona lying. A patch of sunlight was shining right on the mark, as if trying to bleach away any lingering fear, or pain. She peeled off her paint-smudged glove, walked to the foot of the stair and pressed her fingers tenderly to the spot where Zona's head had been resting. All at once, it felt too convenient to be true that, after the violence, she should have been found here, in such a peaceful pose.

She grasped the rails on either side of the staircase, hoisting herself upward, stirred by the dreadful urge to know where Trout had really killed her. To the front of the house was the newly-weds' bedroom, southerly light catching specks of lint in a lazy waltz above the bed. The blankets were accordioned down the mattress, as if Trout had pressed them away with his feet that morning during some satisfied stretch. The sheet, which should have been pulled taut, was lying in heavy rumples, its starch long since relaxed.

Lucy was doubtful the linens had been changed since Zona had last slept in them. An impression made stronger by several pairs of pants that were pooled beside the bed, right where Trout had stepped out of them. Shirts were spilled where he had shrugged their sleeves off, union suits abandoned with discoloured insides on show. The man of this house was more careless in private. If Trout was only interested in appearances, there was a chance that he might reveal himself in this backstage place where he scrubbed himself dishonestly clean and rehearsed his fake charms.

The smell of him – his sweat, oil, dander – was strong as she examined the leather trunk at the foot of the bed. Zona's new initials, *ZHS*, adorned the lid in neat black calligraphy, each corner inked with swags in the same modern pattern as the fuchsia trembler brooch that her friend had once admired at the jewellery store. Lucy heaved the lid open. But there was nothing inside, save for a sachet of cedarwood chips. In disbelief, she moved to the narrow dressing table, where she found one drawer after another empty of corsets and pantalettes and hairbrushes and talc and every other small necessary that should have been stored there.

While she had been dandling Zona's memory, Trout had been busy erasing her. She imagined him pouring kerosene over her belongings in the firepit, smiling when the wind came to take their ashes. Or perhaps he had travelled to a dark pool in the New River to heave in armfuls of dresses and boots and stockings, leaving them to wash up on a distant bank where the particular shape of her foot, worn into the leather of her shoe, might never be recognised. The cruelty of it brought a fresh jolt of fear, the room seeming to conspire with Trout, giving up no evidence of his wrongdoing.

Defiant, she kicked his union suits aside, and saw that he had a whisky jar tucked in by one leg of the headboard. A little shake of the bottle told her that it was almost empty. And amidst the dust under the bed frame, she saw the glint of steel. It was the bluing of a revolver, shining even in the shadows. She seized the grip on the small gun, the mark of Smith & Wesson impressed on the plastic. Holding it firm, she pressed down on the short barrel to reveal a fully loaded cylinder, the dimpled ends of five golden cartridges. A wound from one of these .32s might not be fatal, might not even need a doctor if the man shooting it kept one cold eye on the basics of anatomy.

This little belly gun was for torture, not for killing. By the look of it, Trout had never felt the need to fire it, its threat, perhaps, being enough.

But then Zona had always been good at hiding all traces of rebellion. The more overbearing her mother became, the more selfless Jacob expected her to be, the more her army of brothers teased and provoked and crowded her, the greater her determination had become to secrete away little parts of her life. Her dime novels from the Sweetheart Series; her love letters; her caricatures of Mary Jane, drawn as if she were a coarse slum kid from a New York comic strip. With ribbon and glue, Zona had made little stows on the undersides of her chiffonier drawers. Lattices strong enough to hold her books and letters and drawings very firmly in place.

Lucy jerked open the middle drawer of the dressing table and eased a hand underneath, her thumb grazing what felt like a taut line of ribbon and, perhaps, the edges of folded paper. With the drawer pulled free, she could see the black criss-cross on its reverse. Zona had tied reef knots in the silk, glued and pinned the netting to the wood, leaving the neat pocket open at one end.

Inside were four envelopes. Lucy could already see the ghost of Zona's handwriting through the topmost letter. With the parched sound of falling leaves, they slid out onto the floor. Three were numbered, addressed to Elisabeth. If Lucy wasn't mistaken, one of these held the crisp outline of a small star. Almost like a pencil rubbing. And it gladdened her heart to realise that here was the enamel pendant she had made for her friend.

She felt no pain as her knees hit the boards, gathering the letters greedily to herself, hungry for Zona's words. But the final envelope was not quite like the others. It was a bigger rectangle, in durable cream paper, the corners very weathered. She opened it and scanned what announced itself to be a *Certificate of Death*. The words swam.

Hannah Shue

22 yrs

Married

Housewife

Diphtheria

She read it again and again, cold stones seeming to pile high in her chest. Until she heard a key rattling in the lock of the front door. The bolt opened with a great crack. There was a pause before Trout's footsteps started into the house, heavy and loud and fast. The back door was slammed shut on its groaning hinges, and the snowy crunch and tinkle of glass told her that he was on the move again.

The stair creaked, step after step depressing and lifting, and she seized the drawer, trying to fumble it back into position. It was barely closed flush in the dresser when Trout was on the landing, his big frame seeming to fill the space. Too late to bag the documents, she used her foot to drag each one beneath the big umbrella pleats of her skirt. She took a deep breath for his arrival, and turned to the door.

'Trout!' she said, as soon as she saw him. 'Oh Lord, how you scared me.' She pressed a hand to her chest, heart walloping. Agitated as he was, Trout stood very still beside her. He was regarding her with more confusion than anger, although the latter clearly boiled in his veins. He had heard the news about Mary Jane – she was sure of it. 'I've never been so frightened,' she continued. 'I thought you were a burglar.' She made a show of deflating down into her wide skirts, head bowed in faux relief. 'I came to see how you were, and when I saw the window broken in the back door, well, I didn't know what to think, except that you might have been beaten up or robbed. But here you are, all in one piece.' She exhaled in that way that sounded grateful and pleased. 'Help me up, would you?'

He was already underestimating her, believing she had come here to check on his welfare. He offered a reluctant hand, and she gripped his dry, hot skin. Soot shone on every polished contour of his face, as if he'd been fire-scaled in the hob of hell. She made him take all her weight, before springing to her feet in an artless way, confirming his opinion of her as stupid and unattractive.

'What's that?' he said, craning to see the letters.

'Oh,' she said, ditsy, letting her skirt trail over the envelopes, 'I got such a fright when I heard you, I dropped Ma's orders for Montgomery Ward.' She collected the papers from the floor, knowing all at once what she must do with them, the risk making her feel sick with dread. 'Look,' she said, offering them excitedly. 'Pa's getting a new surrey, and I'm getting a new White Star bicycle, and I wondered if you might like to come and try it for yourself when it arrives, because I'm not sure you've ever ridden a bicycle, and I'd love for you to—'

'Go home,' he said. He stood back, clearing a way to the door. His character was vain and weak enough to suppose that she held a flame for him; that all along she had really been jealous of Zona.

'All right,' she said. Feigning a sulk, she shoved the envelopes carelessly into the pouch, feeling the welcome graze of the candlestick. 'I know you're grieving. But if you're ever lonely and need someone to talk to . . . ' She gave a flirtatious shrug.

'Lucy,' he barked, as if disgusted that a girl like her might have feelings for him. 'Go home.'

'You take care,' she said, summoning a hurt tone. 'I hope you find whoever broke your glass. And you might as well have these.' She fished inside the bag for the lavender sachet, and threw it onto the bed. Dipping in again, she drew out the tin of liquorice candies. She rattled them at him, and when he wouldn't take them, she flung them onto the mattress with the lavender.

He stayed in the bedroom as she escaped down the stairs, her feet barely touching the treads. She had the sense that his rage was dilating behind her, expanding through the house, seething at Mary Jane's accusation of murder.

She stumbled across the yard to where Sugar was tied. Only when the horse was swaying beneath her did she steal a glance up the sloping roof of the porch. Trout was standing with his back to the bedroom sash, his fingers buried in his long hair. It was not the pose of an innocent man. And with the grace of God, Zona's letters would prove as much.

Reins in one hand, she gripped the pouch with the other. It had been a strange and terrible way to discover that she, Lucy Frye, had all the mettle and determination that it might take to be a good reporter; all the backbone needed to discover a connection between Zona's death and the demise of young Hannah Shue.

Dear Elisabeth,

In case you hadn't guessed – this is your mother's
handwriting. I feel very much like talking to you tonight
and I cannot be with Lucy so I will risk writing you and
putting a little of my ignorance on show. I am slower
with words than I am with pictures but maybe you can
understand that and forgive my mispellings and my
grammar which is not all that it should be. Thats what
they told me up at the Newell School anyway. They
didnt like me writing with my left hand either. But I
have decided that all of this is okay and doing no harm
to anyone. Also I believe that I can do many other things
worth just as much as proper reading and writing.

That sounds kind of big-headed I know. But Beth I have
to set an example if I want you to have confidence too.

<u>Confidence means trusting yourself</u>

Doing your best with what you've got is good enough,
my darling girl. There will always be those who say
otherwise. But when this happens listen to your consciense
and try to be strong.

There was a time when I was foolish and believed that

trusting other people was a virtue. I thought that the harder it was for me to have faith in somebody, the better I was for placing all my stock in them, the same as I throw everything in with the Lord. The truth is that you should only trust those people you can really depend on. The ones who have earned it. Otherwise, you can end up throwing good money after bad, so to speak, until finally you reach a type of ruin.

It will be Christmas soon enough and Thanksgivings not long gone, though you will have been too little to remember it. It was my first as a married woman and I gave thanks for many things. I thanked God for you despite the distance between us. And I thanked Him for my home in Livesay that I hope you will come to see now that you're grown. Its not a beauty to look at yet but will be finished by the time you visit. The walls will be papered with prints from Harpers Weekly and Scientific American and The Century and American Gardening and maybe a few pictures of the wonderful inventions that your grandpa Jacob Heaster has come up with for his farm. We will paint the furniture all in bright colours and I'm going to make a story quilt for your bed with a special patch for each year that I have had to miss you.

I know that I promised you a portrait – a photograph from the studio in Lewisburg. I am sorry I have not been able to get into town yet. I am sending you a painting of me instead. One by my own hand. I do not know what you will think of it. You will see one thing where I might see another. And my husband, Trout, might see another thing again. By now you will have heard of Mr Whistler and his famous picture of his mother. His oil paint depicts nothing except the shape of his mamma and the way that the light and shade were falling when she was sitting in that chair. Even so, many people say wonderful things about her character, describing virtues that the artist did not hint at with his brush. And, dearest Beth, I do not think that it is right to judge another by their appearance in this way.

<u>We must take the time to learn their true heart.</u>

If one day God allows me the joy of meeting you, I promise to be patient and curious in getting to know you, just as you are. Maybe you are like your grandma Mary Jane who thrives on notice. If you have more in common with me then you would rather disperse to the four winds than have all eyes on you. Trout is different again. He seems able to reserve certain parts of himself and push others to the front depending on who is looking. And I do not believe that he ever feels exposed.

It is possible that we will meet quite soon after you read this letter. Strange to think that by then a kind of eternity will have passed for its writer. As I sit here, you are too young to ever wonder about me though I imagine you very often. Perhaps you are speaking a little and have small square teeth that are very white. Last time I saw your dark hair I figured you would grow into an infant with dark curls around her forehead. I would give anything to hear the sound of you. Or to have a picture of you – a photograph or a painting of a girl with sunlight streaming yellow into her little nursery – some sign that your life in Virginia is just as blessed as any mother could hope.

I have only to think of you alive on the other side of the mountains and it brings me strength and calm. I will write again soon lovely Beth. Until then,

I will remain,

Yours ever truly,
Zona Heaster Shue

from:

THE TRIAL OF TROUT SHUE

A TRUE STORY
CONTAINING HITHERTO
SUPPRESSED FACTS

by Lucia C. Frye

Justice Joseph McWhorter proved to be mel-
lower on the porch of his red-brick home
than on the bench of the circuit court –
comfortable enough to bring out his fine
black silk robe for inspection, explaining how he feels 'fully possessed' by his
'scholarship of the law' when the cloth is
on his back.

McWhorter's mild squint – a result of boy-
hood measles – is more noticeable when he
smiles. Of course, most of those who meet
with the judge do not find him in complai-
sant mood. He is known as the 'Old Wolf' of

the circuit court, attorneys and defendants alike fearing both his bark and his terrible bite. But, elaborating on an 'unlikely-seeming event' that took place on Friday, February 19, 1897, a relaxed McWhorter seemed to let his gaze stretch far into the past.

Four months before the trial of Trout Shue began, the judge received a letter over breakfast. That it should be from the County Prosecutor, the Honourable John Alfred Preston, was no surprise. With professional affection, McWhorter describes the attorney as an 'energetic communicator' known to send several missives to the McWhorter household per day when court is not in session. But Preston's written request for an emergency sitting of the court was out of the ordinary.

McWhorter remembers how Preston mentioned an 'irregularity' in the register of deaths for Greenbrier County. 'The letter didn't mention a mistake in the record,' he emphasised. 'A mistake could have waited. This suggested something more serious.'

The judge met Preston at the courthouse, a little after sunrise. There, the prosecutor opened the county death register to the only entry recorded for January 23. The original cause of death listed for a 'Mrs Shue, Livesay's Mill' was 'everlasting faint'. And McWhorter remembers how these words had been 'crossed out, and replaced with an alternative verdict – "childbirth"'.

John Alfred Preston has confirmed the facts of the day as the judge remembers them. His well-appointed office, furnished with an ormolu clock and a pair of gold-leaf fauteuils, is on the first floor of the courthouse. And when asked if Mary Jane Heaster's now notorious visit to this chamber on February 16, 1897 had been his motivation for investigating the record of deaths, he declined any discussion of the allegedly supernatural elements of the case. 'The law does not, and never can, make provision for a ghost,' he said. 'The real issue was the importance of due process.'

'Knapp had some acquaintance with the deceased and her husband,' he explained, George Wesley Knapp being the doctor who not only registered the cause of Zona Shue's death but later requested its alteration. 'The medic's position is easy to understand,' Preston said. 'Faced with the extreme grief of the widower, and with no reason to suspect foul play, his care for the living overtook his ministrations to the dead. While the exam confirming Mrs Shue's death was minimal, the doctor was confident in his verdict of heart failure.

It was only days later, when he happened upon Mrs Shue's medical notes, that he recognised the more likely cause – the complications of pregnancy – and, quite rightly, had the clerk amend the record.'

'The problem was Zona Shue's mother,' Preston said, diverting attention from the coroner's failure to conduct a thorough report, along with all rumours of the doctor being a closet drunk. 'Mary Jane Heaster undermined confidence in our physicians – trying to make the people of Greenbrier County doubt the coroner's ability to uphold the law. Under the circumstances, we couldn't afford to conceal any discrepancy in the [death] register, no matter how minor. The only way to ensure faith in due process was to follow due process.'

It was at Preston's urging that Judge McWhorter made the order for Zona Shue's body to be exhumed at first light on the following Monday, February 22, 1897 for the purpose of a coroner's inquest. 'There must be dozens of times, lost to posterity, when doctors have used similar discretion,' the judge said from the comfort of his porch. 'None of it worth investigating. It seemed like the most incredibly bad luck, this administrative hiccup coinciding with Mrs Heaster's ravings.'

12 | MARY JANE HEASTER

Little Sewell

February 22, 1897

The moon was a gold-tinged eye, only half open, where it gazed down on the cemetery at Little Sewell. Mary Jane had arrived long before Sheriff Nickell, wrapped in her heaviest sheepskin coat and mittens and fur-lined boots. Her oil lamp had been the only glimmer of unnatural light in the black of the graveyard then, resting against the small makeshift cross that Lenny had painted with Zona's name. She could not allow her daughter to be alone when it all began, and she had come to tell her that her grave was soon to be opened, her body carried through the ice-flecked air.

Nickell had strung the cemetery with glaring lamps. A few were shining on Zona's grave, setting the rugged clay glittering, while the rest marked the short path to the Newell School. Its doors had been thrown wide open, ready to accept the exhumed casket, and the building's illuminated insides glowed with a near-festive atmosphere, at grim odds with the horror of the morning's task. She could not believe that it had come to this; that her greatest need and the thing she most feared and abhorred were one and the same.

Jacob rode up alongside the chapel, and she lifted her head to see dawn's cold fire behind the hill. Riley's hooves beat the earth in slow rhythm, a caravan of wagons following behind, lanterns swaying, people arriving as if they were about to attend chapel, when really they had come for the spectacle of a reverse kind of funeral.

'I'm here, Zona,' she said, pressing her hand to the clay of the grave, wishing that she were lying beneath the ground, holding her daughter in the darkness. 'Don't be afraid, darling. No matter what.'

She stood up, then, to meet her husband, Nickell's lamps revealing the full of his anger and distaste as he came strolling across the grass. He leaned in close enough that she could smell the liquor on his breath.

'The bread you get by deceit might taste very sweet, Mary Jane,' he said. 'But afterward, your mouth will be filled with gravel.'

His every word had been vicious since hearing that the grave was to be opened.

'I haven't lied about anything, Jacob,' she said.

He shrugged. 'Nothing can excuse what you're doing to our girl.'

'You always choose the easy road,' she said, trying to keep the sadness from her voice. 'But the right path and the painless one, they're not always the same. You think I want to be right about this? That I want to think Zona was murdered? Believe me, I'd give anything to be wrong.'

She did not admit to him that fear circled her heart, chill as the moon's halo. If Knapp's verdict had been right all along, she'd be restrained in the Trans-Allegheny asylum before nightfall. Whatever happened today, she was going to lose.

She watched the sheriff as he hailed the gravediggers. They straggled into the cemetery with their picks and shovels, and he beckoned them to the bright door of the schoolhouse, delivering a white packet to each of the three. They were hesitant as they pushed the money into their pockets, as if there were no compensation that might remedy the burden of raising a Christian woman from that soil where she had been committed to God for eternity.

Nickell had said the outcome would not go in her favour. When he had arrived to the house, a little before sunset, he told her that the whole inquest was an *unfortunate formality*. The coroners – for there would be three of them – would be swift in confirming Knapp's diagnosis. *TUBAL PREGNANCY*. She had asked to read these two words for herself where he had printed them in capital letters in his notebook. There was a swirl of talk, then, about *an infant gone astray in the body*; a *rupture*; the *hopeless resignation* that must attend every woman diagnosed with the fatal condition.

The sheriff was leading the gravediggers toward her, now, his expression sour. 'Move back.' He forced his way between her and the grave. 'You stay behind that line,' he said, pointing to a thick rope cordon that he had raised more than a yard away. 'Go on,' he added, waiting for her to retreat behind it. Given half a chance, he would arrest her, she thought – charge her with wasting state money, because she was to make no mistake about how many dollars were being thrown away on this wicked folly.

Stern, Jacob lifted the hemp so that she might duck beneath it.

'I'm right here, Zona,' she said, unable to bear their separation. 'The doctors, they're going to look after you now. It'll be over before you even know it.'

At this, Jacob and Nickell exchanged a glance so severe that she pictured her own body laid out in the schoolhouse, skin bared, a series of sharp and polished instruments lined up ready to take a look inside, yards of muslin and silk ties waiting to receive the excised bloody evidence of her deficiencies.

'The pastor's not coming, Nickell,' Jacob said. He dug the toes of his boots into the slope to gain a better footing by the head of the grave, and took his Bible from his pocket. 'Someone has to pray over Zona.'

'All right,' the sheriff said with a patient look. 'But only you. Everyone else stays back.'

The way her boys were gathering along the rope – their nearness to Jacob – suggested allegiance to their father. The Millers and the Stuarts, the Neals and the Hollidays all shuffled forward, waiting for the indecent prising of Zona from the ground. Every neighbour avoided her eye, as if expecting the day to end in her disgrace. Three men flanked the opposing side of the grave, picks and shovels at the ready, their coats thrown off as they waited for Nickell's signal. Jacob let the Bible yawn open at the marked page. And just as dawn was bleaching out the light from the lamps, Nickell gave the nod.

Two pickaxes took their first bites from the snow-kissed grave.

'*Fear thou not,*' Jacob read stoutly, '*for I am with thee. Be not dismayed, for I am thy God.*' With trembling authority, he held fast, the metal falling beside him in steady rhythm.

Mary Jane's shrinking heart floated upward to her throat. She could not sense Zona's spirit, not anywhere close. Her daughter had retreated to that place where she might neither see nor feel the disturbance of her casket. Making her mother's loneliness pin-sharp.

'Mary Jane.' Bessie's voice was soft and low behind her.

Two heads of glinting steel swung in great arcs, their impacts thudding in her chest, as she allowed her friend to lead her a little way along the cordon. They stalled in front of the schoolhouse, its walls lined with dozens of kerosene lamps, ready to illuminate any secrets that had been committed to darkness. And Bessie delivered her to a clutch of women who were all huddled in their weeds. Eulalia reached an arm out from this dark mass, and it might have been a wing stretching from a crow. At once, Mary Jane was gathered into its breast, and the great bird divided into its smaller parts: Eulalia and Abigail and Emily Dove and Ann Power. Even Lucy Frye hovered behind them, ashen, in a smart mauve riding habit, her lips parted as if in terrified expectation.

'No going back now, Aunt Mary Jane,' Eulalia said. She had meant to be kind, perhaps, but her tone was filled with gentle reproof; the suggestion that she had brought all this suffering upon herself.

She let her gaze drift to the schoolhouse, where Sheriff Nickell was bivouacking a surgery. Already he had lifted a board onto several bales of hay to form a table steady enough to hold a casket. With a few yards of starched cloth gathered in his arms, he climbed onto a little stool and pegged the fabric to one of the washing lines he'd strung across the ceiling, raising her hopes that the smallest measure of Zona's modesty might yet be preserved.

A sweet, tarry scent filled her nostrils, strong and volatile. The large wooden chest outside the door had a row of red-brown bottles arranged on top. Each was labelled in large, clear letters: ACID. CARBOLIC. LIQUEF. There was a small heap of rags alongside, all stained the same deep pink. The sight caused her stomach to twist. But then again, if the doctors used the acid to coat their hands, and instruments, and even the coarse table that Nickell had improvised, it might protect her daughter from the worst of their touches.

What she had not expected was for Knapp, with his gouty hands and bloodshot eyes, to be one of Zona's examiners. Yet here he was, emerging from the back of the schoolroom. A caustic fountain of loathing sprang up inside her, the sound of the relentless pickaxes driving into her heart.

'Doctors don't get paid for inquiries, Aunt Mary Jane.' Emily Dove was observing her with a critical eye. 'Not if it turns out the death wasn't suspicious.' She had a dogmatic tone, and a habit of hoisting professionals onto pedestals. 'Imagine if Knapp had called a jury for Zona. He would've ended up paying for it out of his own pocket. And that wouldn't be fair.'

Bessie pressed in close, her warmth a balance for Emily's coldness. And instead of railing at her nieces, Mary Jane hooked her friend's arm, remembering those earlier days when they, too, had been naive; unable to conceive of any betrayal so great that it might cost a woman her life.

'Look,' Bessie said. 'There's Rupert. And McClung.'

Sure enough, the Greenbrier elders Mary Jane had been praying to see were striding up to the door of the schoolhouse. They stopped to soak rags with carbolic, and wiped their hands right up to the wrists, the strengthening of the hard morning light seeming to drain the colour from everything, except for the knot of Preston's scarlet cravat as he hurried to join their company. It was frightening, the sheer number of eyes and hands that were waiting to inspect her daughter.

More unsettling yet was the rattle of an approaching wagon. Trout Shue was sitting proud up front, giving Mary Jane a thin, sick feeling, because she could not believe that he would dare to show his face. But when she saw that his driver was none other than Constable Shawver, she supposed that the blacksmith had not been given a choice. Men tipped their hats to the widower, and women waved their gloved hands, Trout replying with grateful smiles as they drew up by the schoolhouse. Henry Gilmer came riding behind on his black mare, chewing an ivory toothpick.

'Nickell,' he roared, dropping from the saddle. 'Get out here.' He let his reins fall and sauntered over to Trout. When the sheriff emerged, Gilmer gave the widower a little shove toward him. 'Get him inside,' he said. 'And make sure he has a good view.'

Trout smoothed his black coat, and walked into the schoolhouse with a proprietary air, as if all these doctors and lawyers had been gathered in his service. A white sheet soon obscured him, shifting in the breeze.

There was the sound of sharp metal on soft wood; a muffled

thud from the blind fathom where Zona was buried. The drone of Jacob's voice stopped. A gravedigger uncoiled two great straps of leather, and Mary Jane might have been sinking to the bottom of the sea, drifting down and down to a place where she could rock in numbing currents. The straps were threaded beneath the casket, and when they were pulled taut, there were cries of anticipation across the churchyard. The wood shifted, and Mary Jane felt the same great shock as when a tooth is pulled from the socket. Then, with one last terrible wrench, Zona was pulled free of the ground.

'On three,' Nickell called.

After the count, there was the weight of her daughter, balanced across the shoulders of four men. They crossed the frozen grass, entering the schoolhouse, many lamps illuminating the soiled and splintered wood. With his usual bold manner, Gilmer closed the doors. And Zona was gone, with these strangers, into the smoke and the light.

They might have come inside to escape the fresh skiff of snow blowing down from the mountain, but to Mary Jane, the chapel felt even colder. Bessie gave her a slug of medicinal brandy from a silvered hip flask, and she swallowed, racked with chills.

The constable maintained a patrol, checking on her every now and again, as if she were in his custody. Trembling on the pew nearest the back, she waited for Truth, in human form, to appear at the church door. Already they had been here far longer than the hour that Shawver had estimated, and agitation was growing amongst those neighbours and friends who had taken shelter inside.

Most tried to disguise it by bowing their heads in even harder prayer. Only Lucy stalked the aisles, blowing her cheeks out, brandishing the little notebook and pencil that she always carried in her breast pocket. Mary Jane considered the Frye girl's queer-duck facade, and wondered what malice might be glinting behind it. Hadn't she been bruised when Zona chose Trout above her? Wasn't it possible that they had done nothing more than egg one another on in their suspicions of Shue, making each other's hearts beat a little blacker?

The girl was tense as she perched on the chancel rail opposite Jacob. He had chosen to sit alone in the pew nearest the pulpit, but she didn't hesitate to pester him with questions. She listened carefully to his curt answers before scratching down words. But her pencil soon dropped from her hand, a shadow appearing at the chapel door.

Mary Jane shot to standing as she saw the vivid knot of Preston's cravat, conspicuous through the window. He had no hat in his possession, yet approached her as if holding a stiff derby to his chest.

'Mrs Heaster,' he said. Unable to read his expression, she felt stretched tighter than gut on a violin. 'If I could speak with you. And your husband.'

Jacob was walking toward them, a certain steel and confidence to his stride. Together they followed the prosecutor into the vaulted porch. She should not have been surprised, she supposed, to find Dr Knapp waiting there, the medic in shirtsleeves, his black suspenders straining from waistband to shoulder. The heavy scent of carbolic made her stomach flip, the truth so ripe on the man's tongue that she might have plucked it out with her fingertips.

'Get it over with,' she said. 'Whatever it is, just say it.'

'The first thing when conducting a full autopsy,' Knapp said, probing his shallow watch pocket with his finger, 'is to check for poisoning. We found no haemorrhage or congestion in the stomach ... no odour of volatile substance, alkaline burns, et cetera.'

He was trying to baffle her, she thought, flaunting his knowledge so that he might draw attention to her ignorance. But his cheeks tightened with emotion, then, and he huffed, long and hard.

'More surprising,' he said, hoarse, 'is that we found no evidence that Mrs Shue was with child. It was in the area of the neck, in fact, that we discovered the injury. Just here.' He touched his hand to the base of his skull. 'There is a dislocation,' he said, 'between the first and second vertebrae. And the ligaments are torn. The windpipe ... well ... the evidence is very clear that your daughter was choked.'

In the sudden silence, with all doubt gone, Mary Jane felt that she might blow into dust. Beside her, Jacob's soul fizzled into some waiting darkness.

'Mr Shue has been arrested,' Preston said. 'Sheriff Nickell has already taken him to the jail, in case blood runs high when the news travels.' He nodded toward the chapel, where, no doubt, the mood would soon take a violent shift. 'Constable Shawver will hold him in custody. And charges will be brought against him this afternoon.' The prosecutor regarded them both, as if checking for understanding.

'It could have been a vagrant,' Jacob said, his tone high and desperate. 'Or a pedlar. The Midland Trail is crawling with them.'

'We have to look closer to home,' Preston said. 'Everything points to Mr Shue. And we must do all we can, now, to secure his conviction.'

Harrowed, Jacob rounded on Mary Jane where she stood cold and heavy as iron.

'Don't think you've fooled me,' he spat. 'There was no ghost. You knew something was wrong and did nothing to help my poor Zona.' He swiped his cap from his head, crushed it between his hands.

'You accuse me?' she said. 'When my girl should have been able to count on you, her own father, to see that man's badness. All you cared about was your steam wagon.'

Jacob gave a pant of disbelief, turning to Knapp and Preston as if asking them to bear witness to what he had to suffer. 'Our daughter's body is lying in that schoolhouse, and she still has time to be jealous of a machine? I hope you're happy, Mary Jane. You finally got all the attention you wanted – the misfit psychic, making a circus out of her own daughter's murder.'

He had spoken the terrible word, leaving the air scorched. Knapp hung his head. But Preston had new energy, pressing onward.

'Mrs Heaster,' he said, 'you may not like what I'm about to say, but you must stop telling this story about your daughter's ghost. Shue says you made it up to turn people against him. Do you want the defence to claim unfair prejudice?'

'What prejudice?' she said, baffled. 'Zona told the truth. How can he say I made it up when three doctors confirmed it?'

'Mrs Heaster,' he said, 'when Trout is arraigned, it will not be because of any ghost. Only the results of this inquiry will be considered. And the evidence that we have found is circumstantial, meaning that it does not directly prove the facts.' He fixed on her with savage determination, face white above his red cravat. 'There is a great burden on me, now, to tie Mr Shue to this crime beyond all reasonable doubt. As Trout was leaving with Sheriff Nickell, he spoke to Mr Gilmer in what I can only describe as a jeering tone, saying that we can't prove he did it. We must hope, very strongly, that he is wrong. And you, Mrs Heaster, must stay quiet, and avoid any chance of being called as a witness for the defence. You are not credible. Make no mistake, if you take the stand, we will lose this case.'

Part Three

1897

Solstice to Sirius Rising

from:

THE TRIAL OF TROUT SHUE

A TRUE STORY
CONTAINING HITHERTO
SUPPRESSED FACTS

---

by Lucia C. Frye

On the first day of the trial, when opening
arguments were concluded, disappointment awaited all those in the gallery who
had hoped to see the infamous Mary Jane
Heaster take the stand. She had pressed for
the exhumation of her daughter, after all,
and the evidence found was exactly as she
had predicted. Surely, many assumed, the
case for the prosecution would rely on the
testimony of Zona's ghost?

These onlookers did not realise that
a spirit can have no legal standing in
a court of law, as ruled by the Supreme

Court of Nebraska in the case of McClary v. Stull, 1895. The case concerned the will of a certain Elizabeth Handley, deceased, who had seen fit to disinherit her husband's youngest living children; that is, two sons and one daughter who had been born to his second 'plural' wife according to the tenets and rites of the Mormon church. Cut off without a cent, this second family desired that Handley's will be declared void. Elizabeth had been insane at the time of its writing, they said, believing herself to be acting under the instruction of their dead father's spirit.

In life, Elizabeth had made no secret of her alleged communications with her long-dead husband by means of that popular parlour toy, the planchette. But the court upheld her will, accepting all evidence given by her executors that she had been compos mentis. With regard to the departed father, while the judge allowed that spirits cannot be denied the right to speak to their 'friends who are still in the flesh', he ruled that 'spirit wills are too celestial for cognisance by earthly tribunals'. No 'undue influence', nor any potential attempt by the late Mr Handley to 'prejudice the interests of persons still within our jurisdiction', was recognised.

The law, in short, concerns itself with the living – with morality, reason and order on earth. And the court could not entertain any possible attempt by the departed Zona Heaster to meddle in the legal affairs of her friends, or indeed enemies, who remained on this plane.

The larger of the two courtrooms at the Greenbrier County courthouse is designed to allow those corporeal beings who practise the law to conduct trials in a fair manner. The judge's bench sits, impartial, in the centre, while both the defence and the jury are positioned to the right of the presiding justice. The demeanour of the accused is, therefore, visible to the jurors at all times. The prosecution takes its place on the same side as the judge's heart, likewise the witness box, which faces the jury across the well. The court reporter sits directly in front of the bench, hands to her stenotype machine, a neutral party recording verbatim.

Witnesses are called, examined, cross-examined, re-cross-examined. The effect is one of order and scrupulous process. Yet several hitherto suppressed facts about the opening day of this trial will show that any court might fail in its attempts to be truly moral and reasonable.

County Coroner Dr George Knapp was the first witness called to the stand by the County Prosecutor. The doctor is known locally for having an efficient and busy manner that dissuades others from delaying him in conversation. But Knapp's mood appeared dull during the morning session, as the attorney, Mr John Preston, entered a 'medical skull and partial spine' into evidence for the prosecution. The doctor was invited to use this prop in detailing the fatal injuries sustained by the murder victim, Zona Heaster Shue.

The human skull, with a light patina of yellow, had several neck bones still attached. No edition of any newspaper has described how Knapp, with shaking hands, used the specimen to demonstrate the 'Atlas' bone to the jury. Sitting uppermost in the spine, this vertebra supports the globe of the head, much as the Greek Titan of the same name is reputed to hold up the sky. The coroner noted how, 'by a miracle of natural engineering', this bone sits into its neighbour, the 'Axis', the whole arrangement allowing the head to turn and pivot. Both the prosecution and the defence accepted the coroner's verdict that it was the separation of these bones, by extreme force, that caused Zona Shue's death.

Counsel for the defence chose not to take the witness, and Knapp was dismissed. What was not mentioned, or questioned, was the identity of the woman whose bones Knapp had articulated in demonstrating his evidence. Some weeks later, when interviewed in the comfortable panelled rooms of his medical practice in Lewisburg, the doctor declined to discuss their origins. He had no information about the woman's name, her nationality, the manner of her death, or whether or not consent had been given for her bones to be sold. And it might be argued that the court failed in its moral obligations by allowing the exploitation of one woman in the pursuit of justice for another.

The second witness called to the stand was the seamstress Mrs Martha Jones, of Livesay, Greenbrier County. Known to many as 'Aunt' Martha, she estimates that she was thirty years old when the trial began, her father and her mother being freed slaves from Monroe County, which shares a ragged border with Greenbrier. Slight in both frame and height, she has the strong reputation of being someone who likes to mind her own business, and for you to mind yours, too. But questioned by the County Prosecutor, she was patient in describing how her son Anderson had been the first to discover the victim's body.

He had found her, she said, 'lying at the bottom of the stair when he went to feed the hens and collect the eggs. He didn't touch her, or look too close. And came home so frightened I went straight to Livesay forge to find Mr Shue'.

Dr William Parks Rucker, for the defence, took the witness for cross-examination. With his long tobacco-stained beard, Rucker is famously mercurial. Assistant prosecutor Henry Gilmer describes him as being 'happiest when local sentiment is against him'. Even the discreet John Alfred Preston will admit that 'Rucker fought for the Union during the War, but only because it could buy him attention'. Whether or not this portrait captures Rucker's motivations as a man, it can be said that his history suggests no fear of adventure or controversy.

In his youth, Dr Rucker saw fit to marry into a wealthy slave-owning family, but since the war, he has been known for promoting the coloured vote. Choosing James P. D. Gardner as his assistant – making him the first coloured attorney to represent a white man in a Greenbrier court – was further in keeping with this reformed image. Still, Rucker elected to cross-examine Mrs Martha Jones.

CROSS-EXAMINATION
By Dr Rucker: -

*Q: All right, Mrs Jones. Your state-
ment says that your son, Andy, found
the deceased, Mrs Shue, at around
nine o'clock on the morning of
January 23rd.*
A: Yes. The Shue house is ten minutes
away. By my reckoning, he left there
about nine.

*Q: And can you tell the court, Mrs
Jones, the exact time that Mrs
Shue died?*
A: I don't know, sir. I never
touched the body.

*Q: Mr Shue's sworn statement says that
he departed the house at eight o'clock
that morning, leaving his wife fit
and well. Which means, Mrs Jones, that
she passed away between the hours
of eight and nine o'clock. Can you
tell the court where you were during
this time?*
A: Where was I when Mrs Shue died?

Q: Yes, Mrs Jones. Can you give an account?
A: I was at home. Stitching button-holes on a new shirtwaister for Mrs Gabriel Johnson.

Q: And is there anyone who can confirm this story?
A: That I was home?

Q: Yes. Is there anybody who will swear that you remained in your house for the duration of that hour?
A: Well, people are not in the habit of calling to my house, sir. I call to them – my customers, I mean – after noon, most days.

Q: Is the answer yes or no, Mrs Jones? Can anyone confirm your story?
A: No.

Q: Would you say that you knew the routine of the Shue household? In other words, given all the information that your son, Anderson, must have passed on to you, did you know that Zona Shue was likely to be alone in the house once her husband left for work at eight o'clock?

A: I suppose so.

Q: *Can you speak loudly for the jury, please?*
A: Yes. I might've guessed she was home alone.

Q: *No further questions, Mrs Jones. Let the record show that Mr Shue was not the only person with access to the house that morning. And that if Mrs Jones had knowledge of the victim's routine, the information that Mrs Shue was alone, and vulnerable, may have been abroad in the wider community.*

By the end of his cross-examination, the jury, who had seemed so open and curious at the beginning of the day, had acquired the harder set of men harbouring reasonable doubts. Rucker had been canny to introduce the idea of a well-apprised intruder entering the Shue house on the morning of Zona's death.

In August, several weeks after the final verdict, Dr Rucker was exuberant as he reflected on the trial, his blue cashmere suit matching the surrounding walls of the dining room at the Old White hotel. When he hired his assistant, Gardner, he explained, it was because the attorney, from the east of the county, was 'very talented and qualified, the best man for the job', adding that he holds 'all people, black and white, in equal regard'.

However, when asked about his shrewd examination of Mrs Jones, Dr Rucker grew very distracted. Under sudden and immense pressure to 'attend a meeting back in Lewisburg', he had the waiter deliver his satchel from the cloakroom, and abandoned the hotel.

This means that important questions have gone unanswered. Did Rucker deserve his growing reputation as a friend to the coloured community? Or was it his intention to appeal to known bigots on the jury, attacking this black woman's credibility, character and associations, knowing that the jury would award the benefit of any doubt to Trout Shue – a white man?

13 | LUCY FRYE

Greenbrier County
Courthouse/Livesay

June 24, 1897

Lucy stretched her legs into the aisle, fanning herself, to little
avail, with the *Greenbrier Independent*. The ink from the flaccid
broadsheet smeared onto her damp fingers, the headlines and
small print blurring. But the damage little mattered, given the
poor quality of the reporting.

George Stanley, the man responsible for the feeble jour-
nalism, was sitting very upright on the other side of the
gallery, cartridge pen already uncapped, with the alert air of
a person who believes their presence to be crucial. Lucy was
prone, on any given day, to chiding and bashing his work, but
his article about the opening day of trial was, by any measure, too lazy and short, the text covering less than an inch,

concluding that *Little evidence was heard before yesterday's court was adjourned.*

'Stanley,' she called, lifting the paper into the air as if it were something she had found on the bottom of her shoe. 'Nothing about Knapp? Nothing strange about Rucker and Martha Jones?'

His jaw slackened, and though he seemed to contemplate an answer, he settled on the same derisive look that everyone over at the *Independent*, from the editor to the message boy, seemed to reserve for her. He had glued his few strands of reddish hair across his tanned pate with thick pomade, and now, as if worried about the effects of the heat, he set to smoothing them.

His detachment was hard to believe, as if yesterday's hearing had neither moved nor excited him, while Lucy had been left with a kind of purling nausea. It was embarrassing to think how foolish she had been in the spring, spending the brightening days looking forward to the trial. Trout's conviction had seemed inevitable, nectar-sweet on the horizon, and she had pictured him buckled by shame and remorse, the judge pronouncing a life sentence. But as Minnie Grose emerged through a door at the back of the court, she knew how uncertain this outcome was. Already the trial records were filled with defiance and lies and tasteless accusations; every dirty trick that might be played to free the accused.

Minnie pulled her chair up to her small desk in front of the judge's bench. She was dressed head to toe in navy cotton, all very plain save for a few pleats at the back of her walking skirt and one red button at her throat. Her expression was set to neutral, her mind already cleared so that she might channel the day's testimonies. It seemed a miracle that when she set her hands to romping over those few keys on her stenotype machine, she was able to record every word spoken in the room. Yesterday, as the roll of paper had spilled toward the floor, working its way into a series of fat loops, it had been a grand surprise to learn that truth and knowledge are not the same thing. As if it were all a type of game, Rucker had been bold in picking and choosing from the facts in the same way that Lucy might browse the wall of coloured ribbons at the Bunger Store. He had selected only those samples that served his purpose, weaving them into ghastly fabrics. Minnie had recorded it all for posterity, even as Martha Jones had leaned forward, fingers grasping, as if trying to pinch the attorney's false hints and implications from the air.

Henry Gilmer launched himself in through the double doors at the back of the gallery, the assistant prosecutor moving at such a pace that Lucy hadn't the time to sit up straight before saying, 'Mr Gilmer,' by way of hello.

He grunted, and gave her one of those same knowing looks that had made her so furious in the graveyard all those months back. Gilmer could not have forgotten her mood on that day, the way it had been so raw and wild after the exhumation. Her memory was of hollow steps on frozen turf as she pulled him around the side of the schoolhouse by his lapel with something like a sense of triumph. When she had pressed her typed-up copies of Zona's letter into his strong, fat hands, he had read them with joyless contempt, and refused to surrender them again. *Writing to her misbegotten child?* he had said. *Only a damned idiot would show these to the court. They should be burned, Miss Frye.*

It was excruciating, now, to realise that every word on every page she had found in Zona's house could prove to be more dangerous than useful. She imagined how Rucker might slice the letters with his mental scissors, rearrange them to make some hideous and blame-filled découpage. He would paint little Elisabeth as a bastard child, and dismiss the many signs of Zona's unhappiness. She remembered, too, how Gilmer had balled up the death certificate and shoved it into his pocket. This had left her so wary of interfering that she had cancelled her ride to Pocahontas County the next day, too worried to search the records for the identity of *Hannah Shue, 22 yrs, Married.*

She pressed her fingers to Zona's emerald-green pendant where it was hidden by the high neck of her cotton shirt-waister, and as she burned to ask Trout about the deceased woman, Zona's mother seemed to sail, rather than walk, up the aisle. Her forehead glistened and black bombazine clung in tight wavelets to the damp of her armpits. The best that could be said of her was that her body, having grown very small, no longer strained at her clothes. Her hair was piled, thick and listless, on top of her head, as if the effort of tying on a bonnet were too much for her. She swerved very close to Lucy, an impatient Jacob striding behind.

He was gripping a battered pillow, the bags beneath his eyes as sallow and creased as its murky green cover. When he threw the tired pad onto the bench nearest Gilmer, Mary Jane lowered herself onto it, and the three eldest Heaster boys, Alfred, James and Joseph, filed into the row behind their parents, wearing starched collars and black crêpe armbands. Their show of solemn unity had no calming effect on Mary Jane and Jacob. Husband and wife seemed to repel and attract each other in equal measure, the affinity of their shared suffering holding them in perfect tension.

Counsellor Rucker came sweeping from chambers, Gardner in his wake. Preston, too, came striding out, paying no attention to Mary Jane where she sat, chin raised in expectation, willing him to give her any small detail about the case. The prosecutor had labelled her *a hazard*, many months since, and it seemed that there was to be no softening of his attitude as he smoothed his dyed black hair and straightened his cream linen jacket.

No sooner was he settled beside Gilmer than a wandering knot of twelve bodies emerged from the jury room. They untangled, in slow fashion, until each man had taken his place on one of the twelve ladderback chairs that had been arranged on a low dais. Sheriff Nickell fussed over them, making sure that every juror had a tumbler of water, along with a notebook and a small pencil pared to a dangerous point. It reminded Lucy to fetch her own journal from her satchel, and as she turned it to a new page, she noted how the men of the jury had a tired and seasoned look about them, as if the grave evidence of the previous day had left them altered.

Trout was next to make his entrance, tilting his face as if toward an imagined spotlight. Perhaps it was Shawver's wife who had starched and pressed his immaculate linen suit, while the constable himself escorted the prisoner, handcuffs dangling at his belt when they should have been fixed about Trout's wrists.

'All rise for Mr Justice McWhorter,' Sheriff Nickell called.

A panel swung open onto the judge's bench. Here was McWhorter, throwing his gaze out over the gallery, broad and sweeping as the beam of a lighthouse. His hair was wet, the water stretching his elastic locks down almost to his shoulders in an effort, Lucy supposed, to keep cool. The gavel that he never used was gripped in his right hand, its silver head shining. George Stanley had told her about this specially commissioned hammer. *The faces are polished so he can see his reflection*, he said. *Means he can check that he's working without any emotion or bias.* And, sure enough, McWhorter took a solemn look into one flat end before resting it on its block.

'Sit down. Sit.' The judge patted the air, as if it had been a nuisance to find them all vertical, and muttered with satisfaction as young Thomas Heaster sidled out onto the bench behind him.

The boy was holding a big palm-leaf fan, wider than his body. Having seen something of himself in the child, Henry Gilmer had secured Mary Jane's nephew the job of agitating the soupy air beside the justice. Thomas set the fan in motion, its flickering and sawing bringing an uneasy edge to proceedings.

'Mr Preston,' McWhorter said, 'please resume.'

'Your honour.' Preston gathered his papers. 'The prosecution calls Mr Patrick Jesper Shue.'

Toward the front of the gallery, a man with dull black hair rose from his seat, causing Lucy's pulse to chirp loudly in her ears. His sinuous gait was very similar to Trout's, as if each muscle were wound just a little too tight. He was a man from the same mould as Trout, but finished to a lesser degree of perfection, the tanned nose misaligned, the eyes watery pale and the lashes sparse.

'What is your name?' Preston said.

'Patrick Shue.' His voice was that loud, he might have been

talking over a brass band at the State Fair. Preston would have no need to ask this particular witness to speak up.

'Can you tell the court where you live?'

'Droop Mountain,' he blared. 'Pocahontas County.'

'Thank you. And can you tell the court what your relationship is to the defendant, Edward Shue?

'You mean Trout? He's my big brother.' Patrick gave a familiar nod to the accused, one more suggestive of affection than estrangement. 'We grew up together on Droop.'

'And you maintain a close family relationship?'

'We don't write each other every week, but yes, sir – a brother is a brother for ever.'

'Mr Shue, to the best of your knowledge, how long did the defendant live up on Droop Mountain?'

'All his life. Until last summer – that's when he set out for Greenbrier.'

'I see. And while your brother was living up on Droop Mountain, how many times was he married?'

Lucy pressed her pen to the page, her blood feeling bright and sharp. Preston was sending a shaft of light down the dark well of Trout's past, and here, at last, a clammy secret had caught in its path.

'Twice,' Patrick said, as if revealing some great virtue about his brother. 'He was married twice, and he doted on both them girls.'

Two marriages, Lucy wrote, every letter shaky. Zona couldn't have known. Worse still, perhaps her friend had discovered the whole truth but had been too afraid to tell her, unwilling to risk another blundering and dangerous reaction.

Preston wetted his thumb and turned to the next page of his

notes. 'Mr Shue, the defendant's first wife was Alice Estelline Shue of Droop Mountain – is that correct?

'Estie? Yes. Tall woman,' Patrick boomed, holding one flat hand a little above his own head. 'Very shy. Lovely singer.'

'And how did Mr Shue's marriage to this timid and musical woman end?'

'Well, Estie divorced Trout,' Patrick said. 'He didn't want that to be the way of things. Not at all.' He lifted a qualifying finger. 'He wanted to stay together.'

'Please tell the court, where was your brother when the divorce took place?'

'You mean . . . are you talking about Moundsville, sir?'

'Answer the question, please, Mr Shue. Where was your brother at the time of the divorce?'

'Well, I suppose he was in prison around that time.'

Lucy's fingers cramped around the barrel of her pen, scrawling *Moundsville prison* in black ink, trembling to think that Trout had sheltered his colossal secrets with such ease.

'What was your brother's crime?' Preston asked.

Patrick gave Trout a sympathetic look. 'They say he stole a horse.' His voice was a fraction quieter than before. 'One not even fit for glue.'

'The crime you describe is grand larceny, Mr Shue.'

'That old nag belonged to Nathan, that coloured man down in the valley. But Nathan, he—'

'Isn't it true that this man Nathan had worked for decades to afford the animal? That it was a callous crime – the sort that might ruin the victim's life?'

Gardner piped up, as if in astonishment. 'Your honour,' he said, 'the defendant's record is not relevant to this case.'

Lucy's pen hovered, waiting for McWhorter to bestow one of his disparaging looks. But it was Preston he reproached in place of Gardner.

'Counsellor, get to the point,' he said. 'If you have one.'

'Let's talk about the defendant's second wife,' Preston said. 'Mr Shue, can you tell us her name, please?'

'You're talking about Hannah, now. One of the Tritts from over in Locust.'

All at once, Lucy was back in Zona's house, breathing the overripe scent of the bedroom as she unfolded that dog-eared certificate. If she wasn't mistaken, Henry Gilmer turned his head a little in her direction, an oblique admission of her part in this revelation.

'Hannah Tritt Shue,' Preston said. 'Thank you. Can you please tell the court how the defendant's marriage to Hannah ended?'

'Well, that was during the big storm in '95. Trout and Hannah were trapped in the house. The snow was that heavy, he had to dig his way out with his bare hands.'

'Please face the jury and answer the question. How did the marriage end?'

'I'm trying to tell you, sir. Hannah died, night of the storm. Trout had been saying how bad her throat was getting, how frail she was. He ended up grieving her so bad hc had to leave Droop Mountain altogether.'

'And what was the cause of Hannah's death?'

Patrick crossed his arms. 'Like I said, she had a bad throat.'

'Yes,' Preston said, clipped. 'In your brother's opinion. But what did the doctor say? Was it scarlet fever? Maybe diphtheria?'

'There was no doctor. The roads were snowed under.'

'Are you saying that no coroner visited the house to decide if there was foul play?'

'Your honour,' Rucker said, heaving himself to standing, 'there is no evidence to suggest Hannah Shue died of anything other than natural causes.'

McWhorter was nodding his assent, looking down at one polished face of his silver gavel.

Frantic, now, Patrick took the opportunity to blast, 'Trout was good to Hannah and her baby boy. You'd think the child was his own. My big brother is a good man, who—'

'On the contrary,' Preston interrupted. 'Your testimony shows that the accused is a liar and a convicted thief. And that two of his three wives died in suspicious circumstances.'

'All right,' McWhorter said, glowering at the jury, whose pencils were hurtling across their notepads. 'That's enough, Mr Preston.' The justice watched the twelve men where they sat in their box, his expression settling into one of patience with their efforts at civic duty. 'There is no evidence that the defendant is responsible for the death of his second wife,' he said. 'And the defendant's earlier crime does not prove that he has engaged in similar, or worse, behaviour at any later time. The allegations will be struck from the record, and you must put them out of your minds when you are deliberating. Discard any notes that you have taken. Is this understood?'

There was a moment of confusion, as if McWhorter were stupefying the jury with a magic trick. But then Lucy watched as pages were ripped from bindings, crumpled without ceremony.

Preston smiled in generous spirit, without a hint of defeat or regret. 'You may take the witness,' he said, returning to his desk.

Gardner tapped his pen on his thigh. 'The defence has no questions,' he said. But Trout nudged him, urgent, until the attorney added, 'Just a moment, your honour.'

Lucy strained to hear Trout's coarse whispering, but couldn't make out a single word. He spoke at length to his attorneys, with an occasional feverish gesture toward his brother. When he sat back in his chair, it was with an exaggerated shrug, as if to say, *Worth a shot.* Rucker lit up just the same as one of those electric bulbs in the ballroom at the Old White, and Gardner stood, adjusting his cuffs.

'Can you hear me quite well, Mr Shue?' he said, in loud sing-song tones that were not customary for him.

'Yes. Thank you.'

'You said you live up on Droop Mountain. Have you always lived there?'

'No. I lived in Brooklyn, New York, for many years. I moved back to Ma's house in the fall, on account of my hearing.'

'You have trouble with your hearing, Mr Shue?'

'Yes.' He looked a little ashamed to admit the defect. 'I was a riveter, at the navy shipyard. Doctor says it's the noise that did it.' He plugged a finger in one ear, as if trying to block out the din. 'Told me to live in a quiet place if I want to keep the little I've got.'

'Please, Mr Shue, can you tell the court about the character of the defendant? What sort of man is Trout Shue?'

Patrick turned to his brother, his bearing reflecting high esteem.

'Trout's good to his family. Loyal to his friends. Folks here in Lewisburg will know that already,' he said. 'He makes friends real easy.'

'And what about the father-in-law of the accused, Jacob Heaster? Does the father of the murdered woman hold your brother in high regard?'

Patrick flicked a covert look at Trout, and whatever he found in his brother's expression, he grew confident of Gardner's intended direction.

'Yes. Yes, I believe he thinks well of Trout. Even now.'

'What is your evidence for this?'

Lucy's brain buzzed; the crackle of another oncoming secret.

'Well, Mr Heaster, he wrote Trout a letter not too long ago, and asked if he would pass it on to me.'

'Would you be able to identify Jacob Heaster in this courtroom?'

'No,' Patrick said. 'I never met him. But I could guess well enough.'

He stared right at Jacob, the gaze of every juror moving to settle on him, too. And Lucy couldn't help wishing that he would colour, or flinch; revolt in some way. Anything except this brittle coolness.

'When was the letter written?' Gardner asked.

'Last month. I remember it arrived middle of May, when I was butchering the first hog of the season.'

Lucy noted the date with a fresh helping of despair.

'And what did Jacob Heaster say in this letter?'

'It was along the lines of wanting a riveter to work on some little invention of his. If you don't have good rivets, your boiler explodes, simple as that. Heaster was looking for advice, or maybe to get the names of some of the boys in Brooklyn.'

'Did you reply?' Gardner asked.

'No,' Patrick said, as if the idea were ridiculous. 'And not just because he was asking union men to break the rules. Trout's accused of hurting his girl. So why come asking his family for favours? No. That seemed wrong to me.'

'Wrong, Mr Shue?'

'Way I see it, if he's happy to use Trout that way, then he should be happy to speak up for him, too. His daughter was reckless and selfish and . . . ' He bowed his head. '. . . not wanting to speak ill of any woman, but she was of easy virtue. And Trout's getting the blame in place of whatever lover she took.'

Gardner left these lies dangling in the air where they might dazzle the jury. 'No further questions,' he said, returning to the counsel desk, rapping cheerfully on the wood.

'Mr Shue.' McWhorter waited for Patrick to shine his face up toward him. 'Am I to understand that you have this letter in your possession?'

'It's up home on Droop.'

'Can you furnish it to the court?'

'Yes, sir.'

'Mr Gardner, you will see that the letter is entered into evidence.'

Jacob turned a sickly grey as the jurors leaned back on their chairs, performing hideous calculations that would likely go in Trout's favour.

'Mr Preston, do you wish to re-examine?'

'No, your honour.' The prosecutor was rigid, eager for Patrick to be gone.

Lucy's heart went with the clean action of a piston as she watched Jacob rally, sitting with his chin level and eyes shining. There was no trace of guilt or remorse on his features. Even now, he looked prideful, still seeming to believe that the world owed him – including, and perhaps especially, his daughter's murderer. And he offered no word of comfort to Mary Jane where she rocked beside him, bent double with pain.

Oakhurst looked fresher and more beautiful than it had any right to, white columns gleaming as the late afternoon fell into a kind of delirium, the air shimmering and warping over field and tree. Lucy tied Sugar by the water trough, and climbed onto the porch, where her mother was half asleep behind a curtain of white silk netting.

'How'd it go?' she asked, opening her eyes wide with pretend interest.

'Not well. Morning session was a disaster. And McWhorter adjourned for the afternoon.'

'Listen,' her mother drawled, 'if Trout is innocent in the eyes of the law, you'll have to accept he didn't do it. You can't keep—'

The glass of the door rattled as Lucy slammed it behind her. The only place that she wanted to be was upstairs, at her Remington, writing the article that George Stanley never would. But as she pulled her chair up to the dressing table, shame prickled. Most folks thought of her as *harmless*; a special word reserved for the peculiar and the pitied. They might say different if they knew how callow and foolish she had been, lacking the sense to offer her friend any real help. With each strike on the typewriter, all she could do was wish for her words to punch their way into the past; for some earlier version of Zona to hear them and change her future.

'Lucy! Darling!' It was her stepfather's voice. 'Could you come down?' He was using that special tone he reserved for foisting his poorer customers onto junior clerks. 'Lucy, dear,' he said, firmer. 'You have a guest. It's Mr Gilmer for you.'

She ran down the first flight of stairs to peer around the banister. Sure enough, there was Gilmer, sparse hair wet from riding through the muggy air.

'How may I help you, Mr Gilmer?' she said, astonished. 'Go on through to the drawing room, won't you?'

'If it's about the case, I'll leave you to it.' William patted the deck of cards in his breast pocket, and went outside to play whist with his wife. In spite of his easy demeanour, Lucy knew that he would be stiff with rage at a local scandal visiting under his roof.

'What do you want?' she said.

The attorney reached into his jacket to pull out an envelope, its paper a little damp from the ride. 'I want you to read this aloud. You'll be sworn in first thing tomorrow. There's a whole load of practice to do. When you're examined, you'll need to have your answers straight.'

Lucy snatched the warped envelope from his fingers and plucked the folded pages from inside. Baffled, she saw that they were covered in her own neat typewriting. It was a copy of one of Zona's letters – the one marked *No. 4* – the most private of them all, confessing the name of Elisabeth's father.

'You can't be serious,' she said, raising an eyebrow at Gilmer. 'Don't you know the trouble this will cause? Nobody knows who the girl's father is – no one but Trout and me.'

The overwhelming pathetic irony of it all. She could still picture Zona, whey-faced, on that night when she had first written to her daughter. Newly betrothed, she had been bracing herself to tell the blacksmith all about it. *He's been so honest with me*, she'd said. *I can't live with myself unless I'm honest with him, too.*

'Why now, Mr Gilmer? They'll twist Zona's words, just like you said.'

'Rucker's found the man in Durham. And he's paying forty dollars to have him escorted all the way here, so he means business. We both know what Rucker wants, Miss Frye. To argue that Zona was promiscuous. Which means they're only a hop and skip from claiming she was adulterous, too. Killed by her lover.'

Stupefied, Lucy let her weight fall onto the sofa. She had been thick-headed not to see this trick up Trout's sleeve. 'Zona never told that idiotic man about the baby,' she said. 'Is Rucker going to tell him on the stand, make it look like she deceived him about their child?'

'Not if we get there first.' Gilmer nodded to the paper. 'That letter is our trump card. If McWhorter and Rucker admit it as evidence, you'll have tomorrow morning on the stand. Then, in the afternoon, we'll call on the father to close the case for the prosecution.'

Lucy couldn't understand his optimism. 'If I read this letter to the jury,' she said, 'they'll say that Zona was in the wrong, no matter what. Women are the keepers of all virtue, are they not?' She was alarmed, now, by her own frankness, while Gilmer's eye widened as if he were amused by her boldness. 'Any woman who says yes to a man threatens to drag him into sin and shame,' she continued. 'The men on that jury won't have sympathy for Zona. They'll think she deserved to be punished. And behind it all, you might even agree with them.'

She wanted the attorney to persuade her otherwise, but he did no more than part his lips in quiet amazement. He would like to scold her, she supposed, for speaking this truth. It was only the lustre of the Venetian chandelier above her head, the shining silks of the drawing room upholstery that made him bite his tongue. Were Zona here now, with her tanned skin, in her homespun linsey, she would not be given this latitude.

'Be smart about this, Miss Frye,' Gilmer said. 'We must use that letter to persuade the jury of Zona's good character. Her trusting romantic nature. You still have the original?'

'Of course. I swore to keep them all for Elisabeth.'

'Good. Read from it tomorrow so the jury has the intimacy of Zona's handwriting. Show them that she wanted nothing more than to be a family woman. Then, if the father comes along and says she was reckless – some common wagtail he soon forgot – he'll look callous. Cruel. That'll knock the wind out of Rucker.'

All at once, Lucy was a short girl in the tall grass at the Harfords' house, her hand meeting Zona's for the very first time on the velvet muzzle of Bessie's donkey. She imagined the soft fingers linking with her own, and could not believe that it was her task, now, to persuade others that this shining soul had every right to justice.

'Sit down,' she said, agitated. 'I'll read it through.'

He perched on the edge of the vast ottoman. 'Go on.'

'*Dear Beth*,' she began. Fraught, she stopped to check the carriage clock on the mantel, the squares of reflected light on the dome making it hard to read. 'You'll have to stop by the boarding house,' she said. 'Tell Mr and Mrs Heaster. You know they're staying at the Yellow Tansy.'

He gave a sharp *tut*, as if disappointed by her stupidity. 'Miss Frye, the State's case is none of that lying woman's business. Last thing we need is to set her off again. Now.' He gave one loud clap, and sat in readiness.

Lucy fixed on the page. *'I've been writing you about my hopes of meeting one day . . .'*

She was to spill Zona's past for the court, same as taking a knife to a fish's belly, letting the jury pick over the guts. In the middle of it all, Elisabeth's father would have free rein to jabber with his usual gilt-edged selfishness and lack of tact. A man larger than life, yet so small in spirit. The ghost of his scent was already in the room. He had always, somehow, smelled of wilted violets. And it seemed impossible, as she read on, that anyone's fate or happiness should be made to rest in the hands of the pampered Emory Snow.

14 | MARY JANE HEASTER

Livesay

June 24, 1897

There was the squeak of brakes, the sound of wheels crunching gravel, and Mary Jane looked up to see Lucy stopping her bicycle at the gate. Although she shrank from view, behind the window's casement, it was too late. She had already met Lucy's enquiring gaze.

The Frye girl was acting with an air of quiet emergency, now, concealing her bicycle in the black birch thicket before marching across Zona's yard, casting nervously over her shoulder with every high-step through the chickweed. When she pushed open the door of the musty parlour, it was with an expression of disbelief.

Mary Jane tightened her fingers about her beeswax candle and box of matches, defiant. 'This is what I get for checking if the coast is clear.'

'What are you thinking, Mrs Heaster?' Lucy whispered, as if trying not to alert the house to their presence. 'Coming here before the trial is over?'

'I'm thinking that in all this time, I've never seen the place where that devil killed my girl.' She moved to the foot of the stair, determined not to unsettle the calm atmosphere that she had been fostering for . . . what? A seance, she supposed, though she refused to say the word aloud to the sceptical Lucy. 'You heard that clever Mr Gardner this morning,' she said. 'The deceitful slant he put on Jacob's double-dealing letter. I should've asked Zona for more evidence when I had the chance. There's no telling what injustice is coming, Lucy. We need more proof. Something to stop Rucker dead in his tracks.'

'You won't find any here,' Lucy said, stalking across the empty parlour. 'You know Nickell searched the house after Trout was arrested. And Cruikshanks took what was left to cover the rent he lost.'

'You've no clue what we'll find,' Mary Jane said. 'The only person who knows where to look is Zona.' This was the most obvious thing in the world, and she could not cover her surprise at Lucy's inability to see it. 'If Preston won't let me give her testimony in the court, she has to lead us to something more . . . what did he call it . . . *material*. I've wasted too much time. If I'd called on her at the cemetery, when Trout was arrested, she might have shown herself to everyone – Preston and all – and there'd be no more lies or fighting about what happened.'

Instinct had called her here; a feeling, like thirst or hunger, demanding to be satisfied. It was drawing her to an invisible presence upon that spot where her daughter had been discovered lifeless. Were she to throw a cloak over it, she was certain the fabric would drape and fold to describe Zona's prone shape very exactly. She hunkered to graze the floorboards with her fingertips, trying to gather any lingering signals.

'Mrs Heaster,' Lucy said, her tone anxious, 'are you certain nobody else saw you come here? Because if anyone else knows ... '

Mary Jane settled onto a tread of the stair. 'If all you can do is fret,' she said, 'you won't be much help. Zona loved you, Lucy.' This was a fact that she could admit but not understand. 'And now you're here, well, I guess she's more likely to speak if both of us pray on it.'

The girl might have softened, and offered some invitation to Zona; lit the candle, or called to her friend with kind words in her familiar voice. Instead, she thumbed the buckle of her satchel. 'I'm not comfortable,' she said, 'troubling her rest. I was coming into town to find you, to put your mind at ease about tomorrow. But there won't be any more courtroom, not if anyone catches you here. You breathe another word about a ghost, and Rucker will call for a mistrial.'

Mary Jane struck a match, and as the candle wick lit, it was clear that for all her stern talk, Lucy hadn't the audacity to snuff it out. 'I know what I'm doing,' she said, flinty enough that the girl grew smaller, perhaps remembering whom she was talking to. 'The way I see it, the big risk is in not asking. Now get the pencil and paper from my bag.'

Lucy bent to open the clasp on the carpet bag. First she extracted the yellow pencil stub from which Zona's earlier messages had flowed. Next came the ledger, traced with ghostly handwriting. She riffled its pages, and the flame of the candle surged.

This gush of light seemed to bring all the static of the world to ground. Mary Jane squinted through the scalding blur, looking to that place where the flame caught in the mirror. There she was! A woman, stark and small, buoyed from a garland of changeful shadows. She floated in the glass, charging Mary Jane's heart to bursting. 'It's her,' she said. 'It's Zona.' The very same echo of her daughter that she had seen in the shining water of Bessie's pewter bowl.

'Where?' Lucy said.

'Can't you see?'

Lucy drew closer and matched her gaze. 'There's nothing there.'

'Take the candle. Quick.'

The exchange of burning wax for pencil and paper was fumbling, Lucy's fingers seeming stiff with fear. With the ledger open to a blank page, Mary Jane let it rest on her lap. Urgent, she twisted Zona's wedding band on her little finger, her daughter seeming to grow sharper and closer with every revolution.

'This isn't right,' Lucy said, backing away.

'There's no choice,' Mary Jane said. Pencil stub grasped in her left hand, its lead newly sharpened, she spoke gently to the shy phantom of her daughter. 'Zona. Darling, please. Come forward and talk to your ma.'

A message in her handwriting would do. But it would be better and sweeter were she to step from the mirror, right into the room, just as she had in Meadow Bluff. More sublime yet if she could take possession; use her mother's mouth and limbs to explain everything to Lucy.

'Stop it, Mrs Heaster,' Lucy said, her voice sounding tight with anguish. 'Why can't you leave her be?'

With that, the wedding band scorched, and Zona shimmered into clarity. Her dark eyes sent a bolt of shock through Mary Jane. Here was a look of recognition, and longing. And something more: distrust. Her daughter turned away, as if with alarm, a veil of black hair spilling over her shoulder.

All at once, she was gone.

'Lucy,' Mary Jane cried. 'What have you done?'

'Me?' Lucy said, as if in disbelief. 'It's been months since she came to you. If there was something else, she would have told you by now. You're bringing pain on yourself. On Zona, too.'

'You of all people want to lecture me about pain?' Mary Jane said, unable to quell her appetite for a fight. 'You saw that she was hurt – bleeding, you said, in your house. And what did you do about it? Nothing. Just aggravated him, all the time, letting him hurt her again.'

Lucy stood very still, biting her lip. 'I can tell you,' she said, 'I'm not proud of that. But at least I was close enough to suspect something bad was going on. I knew he was a rotten egg. How come you didn't know? You've never wondered why Zona didn't tell her own mother? You were hardly best friends. Especially after Elisabeth was born.'

There was a clear note of reason in Lucy's words, lighting Mary Jane's every nerve with panic. 'I did everything for Zona when that child came,' she said, loathing her own defensive tone. 'I gave her another chance at life. And if it wasn't for you, she might still be alive. You said you heard him talking down to her on the drive over at Christmas, such ugly thoughts. And you gave up so easily.' She could tell she was striking home, Lucy's devastation growing in the flickering candlelight.

'I'll regret it, always,' the girl said. 'But think about it, Mrs Heaster. How you helped with the baby but wouldn't let her forget it. Not for a moment. You were so busy blaming her for her own misfortunes, you even blamed her when Trout treated her bad.'

'No,' Mary Jane said, dread possessing her. 'If that was true, she'd never have returned to me. And she did come back and tell on him.'

'If Zona's ghost really appeared to you,' Lucy said, 'do you think it was out of love? Because I'd say it was desperation.'

'I don't have to listen to you, Lucy Frye.'

'Then listen to Zona. If you really believe you've summoned her here, ask her if this is what she wants.'

Before she could think, Mary Jane answered on a swallowed sob. 'No, Lucy.'

'Why not?'

'Because I can't bear to lose her for ever. I don't sleep at night, knowing how many things I could have done different.'

There was a harrowing silence, and Mary Jane felt a gentle force against her wrist. It brushed down her hand, releasing her fingers from the pencil. The painted wood rolled across the floor, a spark of yellow.

'Zona?' she said.

She looked to the mirror, which was turning milky. After a moment, the glass seemed shallow and ordinary. The air was empty of her daughter, the flat heat of the evening pressing against her skin. Her own face stared back from the mirror, exhausted, through the black lace of her veil.

The silence crackled between her and Lucy.

'We've got to put our trust in the court now.' Lucy sat beside her on the stair, a fellow in wretchedness.

'The court,' Mary Jane said. 'Where Zona's testimony will never be heard, and all those men who never knew her will have the final say.'

'I don't know about that.' Lucy's tone was conspiratorial, eyes flashing. But then, growing very severe, she said, 'Get up.' She was looking out the window, to that place on the road where a buggy had parked, lantern swinging as the driver unhitched it. 'It's Benjamin Harper. He's coming in.' She flushed with panic, but to Mary Jane's surprise, she refused to be mastered by it. 'He's a friend of Pa's,' Lucy said quietly. 'I want you to run. Get out the back, fast as you can. I'll handle him.'

Mary Jane rose from the stair, her body awkward with fright as she stumbled through the kitchen, the noisy latch releasing her into the suffocating air. Yellowthroats slurred in the beech trees as she pressed her back to the wall and slid down the rugged logs. Soon, she thought, the trial and all its theatre would be over, and there would be nothing to separate her from the void that was waiting – the vast, sombre distance that she had allowed to ripen between mother and daughter, where her grief would echo without cease.

'Hello, Mr Harper.' Lucy faked cheer in the parlour, raising her voice to warn that they were getting closer. 'Oh yes, I stop by most days. A comfort to see you here, too, checking on things. Especially after those break-ins. Strangers, so I heard, come looking for souvenirs . . . '

Mary Jane crawled, then ran, toward the pine trees on

the north slope, growing dizzy on the soft carpet of needles between the serried trunks. This was where he had kept her body, she thought; the night before her wake, Trout would have left her daughter out here in the frost, watched over by these towering sentinels. Her girl would never know of the remorse that travelled her bones with such violence that it threatened to crack them. 'I'm sorry, Zona,' she prayed, head pressed to rough bark. 'If you can hear me. Forgive me my spite. My impatience, and my temper.' She watched Lucy and Harper emerge through the back door, his lamp at arm's length in the falling light as he scanned the back yard for intruding vermin. While the girl kept him distracted, Mary Jane felt none of her usual mercy for herself. There was only her heart, torn open wide; the calm and unconditional harbour that should always have sheltered her child.

She would never close it, now, her soul a great lighthouse at its mouth, letting Zona know that she was welcome. And safe. And wanted. To blaze like this, for the rest of her days, would be small penance. And if her daughter could sense even the smallest part of this fire, she would understand that her testimony – her final precious words – was not to remain locked in a shallow drawer of Preston's office.

She was going to keep her holy covenant to reveal it.

15 | LUCY FRYE

Greenbrier County Courthouse

June 25, 1897

The rear entrance, Gilmer had said, *the one with the big oval window.* Still, as the massive door fell shut behind Lucy, she turned to check that she had found the right chamber.

'Miss Lucia Clementine Frye?' Minnie Grose was reading from her courthouse ledger.

'Yes,' she said, surprised to see the stenographer standing alone in another of her fresh navy shirtwaists with a red button at her throat.

Minnie used a sharpened pencil to strike through what Lucy supposed was a record of her name, her hair fixed in the usual simple bun, her small face very clean and bare, making nothing of her prettiness. 'Are you all right, Miss Frye?' she said.

Lucy leaned on the big mahogany table where the Bible had been left to rest on a small wooden stand. 'I'm fine,' she said when in fact her stomach was twisting at the prospect of sitting across from the man who had killed her friend while he sneered at her every word. By now, he was expecting Zona's letter to be read in court, and his contempt would be at its darkest.

'You've nothing to worry about.' Minnie had the efficient tone of someone who'd seen it all before. 'Your only job is to tell the truth. Nothing more, nothing less. Then you're all square with the Lord.' She glanced to the clock above the courtroom door, showing that it was already two minutes until ten. 'The defendant's gone in. Justice McWhorter won't be far behind, so let's get you ready.' The gist of her message was *pull yourself together*, and she made it sound so easy that Lucy wanted to believe her as she stood with the Bible balanced on her palm. 'One hand on top, please, Miss Frye.'

Lucy removed her glove. The cover was tacky as she pressed her palm to that same spot on the leather which had been so well oiled by every other promise that had come before hers. Her trembling set the book to wobbling in the stenographer's hand, strength leaving her when she needed it most.

'Do you promise to tell the truth?' Minnie said.

'I do.'

'That's it.' She peeled the book away. 'Thank you, Miss Frye. You may take a seat in the gallery. When he's ready, Mr Gilmer will call on you. Do you understand?'

'Miss Grose,' Lucy said, following her toward the double doors, 'what do you think? Can you tell which way the jury is leaning?' She felt herself frantic. It was one thing being Zona's best friend, but that did not mean she was confident or clever enough to secure her justice.

Minnie bridled at the enquiry. 'I'm sworn to make a faithful record of the evidence,' she said, 'same way you've sworn to tell the truth. It's not my place to have an opinion.'

'I understand,' Lucy said. 'But it seems to me that if everyone was telling the truth like they promised, the trial would be over in a day. Mustn't be a transcript in the world that isn't full of lies.'

The clerk looked down at her short fingers and flexed them, as if the residues of recent falsehoods might be lodged in their joints. 'There are so many sides to every story,' she said, 'it makes the lies very hard to see. But the truth will out. You go in there and make sure of it.' Although she was a woman forbidden any bias, she checked over Lucy's appearance as if hoping to guarantee its perfection. 'Wait,' she said. 'Your hem.'

Were it not for the fuss of putting on this morning dress, Lucy might have arrived a good deal earlier, and in less of a sweat. But her ma had insisted on turning her out like one of New York's famous Four Hundred, because no girl of Charlotte Frye's was going to *take the stand at the biggest trial in Greenbrier history looking like a rag-picker*. Minnie moved about her in a quick circle, plucking and smoothing the silk into place – the great expanse of cream with its blizzard of hand-painted cornflowers, the wide stripes of beige, painted with dark spills of poppy seed heads, the hidden pocket at her hip where Zona's pendant was stowed.

'Thank you,' Lucy said, mouth turning dry.

'After you.'

Minnie straightened up and pulled open not just one of the big oak doors, but the pair, so that Lucy was left standing in the wide frame, exposed to the many eyes of the crowded gallery. She tried to make her steps very bold and certain, though her tight-laced corset made her feel just as winded as if she'd been kicked by a horse. The fabric of her skirts whispered loudly as she walked, her cheeks flaming. She was here to be honest, but this dress was a huge lie. Vain and impractical, it was already buying her a rich woman's credibility as the chatter in the gallery resolved into what sounded like a quiet hum of admiration.

She swept past Gilmer, who opened his palms as if to say, *Finally*. Trout was a shifting blur, in silhouette near the window, as she made a beeline for Mary Jane. Swamped in her black percale, Mrs Heaster looked small and infirm in the front row of the gallery. Sad as this was, it was a relief, too, seeing her lack the energy to stir any more trouble. Alfred rose from his mother's side, eager to offer his seat, and his approving glances stung at Lucy's pride, seeming to suggest that she was a better person in this enormous frock than she had ever been at those times when she was free to wrestle and race.

'Mrs Heaster.' She slid up close, the seams of Mary Jane's black gloves creaking as she squeezed her hands into anxious fists. 'Listen to me,' she said, trying to hold her eyes. Their hollows had grown deeper overnight, and waxed the same sickly yellow-blue as the veins showing at her temples. 'Gilmer's summoned me as a witness this morning,' she said, 'and no matter what I say about Zona, you are not to give Trout the satisfaction of a response. Do you hear me? Do not let the jury see you angry or surprised or anything else.'

'You?' Mary Jane said. 'Why would he call on you?'

'Because . . . ' Lucy said, struggling to find the words that might hurt her least.

Behind them, Jacob sat apart from his wife, his jaw still set defiantly against the world. George Stanley hemmed him in, the journalist staring at Lucy, a lock of greasy hair sliding down onto his forehead as he dashed cryptic squiggles of shorthand in his notebook. He was eavesdropping, perhaps, more interested in scandal than truth. Amidst his scratching, the stiff door to the bench groaned open, and her heart ticked faster.

Mary Jane's officious little nephew, Thomas, appeared, with his big woven fan. Justice McWhorter ambled in his wake, grey hair and long beard holding the tracks of a wet comb. The wooden benches creaked as everyone stood to attention. 'Be seated,' he said, settling his polished gavel to one side.

Mary Jane was stiff with fright beside her, rigid arm inching toward her until the back of her glove brushed Lucy's painted organza, confirming that its quality was just as fine as she suspected. Her eyes held the glitter of panic, then, knowing that Lucy would only agree to such an impressive costume if the worst and most dangerous secrets were about to be spilled. She gave her a look of betrayal, her lips very thin and white.

'I have to.' Lucy squeezed Mary Jane's hand very hard.

'Silence,' McWhorter said.

Trout had pushed them to this. He had set them up to be examined, exposed, broken and judged, all in the name of justice that might never come.

'Mr Gilmer. You have a witness?'

With his usual surplus of energy, Gilmer rose and walked to the centre of the well, weaving an ivory toothpick between his fingers.

'The prosecution,' he said in his best baritone, 'calls Miss Lucia Clementine Frye.'

She could feel Jacob and Alfred's consternation as she pressed herself to standing. A narrow path to the witness stand seemed to glow bright as phosphor, everything else falling into shadow, and she might have collapsed into this shade were it not for Gilmer's hand seizing her own. With dire focus on the rippling pink trim of her skirt, she made it to her seat.

'Miss Frye, a glass of water,' the attorney said, lifting a fresh tumbler to her lips.

She took a reluctant sip, glancing at the men of the jury. Each was planted in the same seat as yesterday, but the mood amongst them seemed brighter, as if they were refreshed by her clean and sweet appearance. With that, she gave them an awkward smile, and angled her head so that the clear yellow stone of her hatpin sparkled.

The citrine light ghosted on the wall, and as she turned to face the gallery, it hovered, a jagged star, on the ceiling above Trout. His hands were knotted on the desk in front of him, where he sat calm as a barn cat with a full belly in the sun. As usual, he was not looking at Lucy as much as he was looking through her.

'Please tell the court your name,' Gilmer said.

'My name is Lucia Clementine Burns Frye,' she said, annoyed to hear the shake in her voice. 'And my home is in Livesay, Greenbrier County.'

'And what was the nature of your relationship with the deceased, Zona Shue?'

'She was a very dear friend of mine. From the time we were very young.'

Trout leaned back, as if sceptical of even this detail.

'Thank you, Miss Frye. The prosecution has asked you here today so that you might describe the character of the murdered woman for the jury. The defence has implied that Mrs Shue was the type of woman to court danger. To, perhaps, have a secret life behind her husband's back. Does this sound like the Mrs Shue that you knew and loved?' Gilmer lifted his eyebrows, waiting for her to deliver the rehearsed answer.

'No,' she said, finding it easy to affect a small laugh. 'Zona was a normal woman, living a normal life. She had everything she wanted, that is, a husband and her own household. A place to start a family. She was only three months married when she died, so as you can imagine, that time would've been very much occupied with setting up home.'

Trout sat up, chest inflating, and begged a sheet of paper from Gardner, on which he made a note with one of the court's small pencils.

'You wouldn't describe Mrs Shue as a wayward woman, then?' Gilmer said. 'I'm afraid we must address it head-on, this suggestion that the deceased was promiscuous, and perhaps entertaining another man. Or even men.'

'No,' Lucy said, fixing on the stricken Mary Jane. 'The fact is that Zona was honest and faithful and ordinary in the way that most people are. Ask anyone who knew her, and you'll get the same answer. She was happy and steady. A hard worker and a good friend.'

Trout was making another note, driving the pencil, a type of cold excitement creeping into his expression.

'Would you say, then, that your friend Zona was moral?'

'Yes. She was churchgoing and upright as the next person. But she had her troubles, sir – the same as any of God's creatures. In fact,' she continued, with forced confidence, 'a couple years back, she made what you might call an honest mistake.'

'A mistake, Miss Frye? Can you tell the court what happened?'

They had come upon the defining moment. Even Gilmer held his breath, while the jury sat as if spellbound. Her heart was very loose in her ribcage as she forced her gaze on Jacob, trying to pin him steady.

'Almost two years ago, Zona gave birth to a baby girl,' she said. 'To be clear, I'm saying she had a child out of wedlock.'

The shock of this release knocked a groan from Mary Jane, while the rest of the gallery sat in a kind of rumbling silence. Jacob's lips parted in disbelief, and he ignored Trout, who was leaning forward to look at him, a big scrubbed hand clamped over his mouth. The blacksmith was trying to disguise his enjoyment of Jacob's pain, the exposure of Zona's secrets giving his dark eyes a sheen of delight.

'Can you please tell the court about this special little girl?' Gilmer said. 'Face the jury, please, and speak up. What do you know about Zona Shue's child?'

Lucy felt as if she were balanced on a high, narrow ridge up at Seneca Rocks, the land sheering away. And her breath caught as she sensed just how far there was to fall.

'August, 1895,' she said, 'Zona's daughter arrived healthy. She was adopted by a well-heeled woman living in Richmond. Zona liked her, and believed that she would look after her little girl – who she called Elisabeth, by the way.' She paused, waiting for the jury to register this pleasant name; to think not of obdurate sin, but of a new babe in all her tenderness. 'You can hear the rest of the story in Zona's own words. You see, she wrote letters to her daughter very often. She wanted Elisabeth to read them when she was grown, to show that she was never forgotten.'

Jacob's expression curdled with anger and disgust. Alfred, too, was in the teeth of outrage, glaring at his mother, who was holding her head with uncomfortable knowing in place of surprise.

'Here is one of Mrs Shue's letters to her child.' Gilmer held up a sheet of folded paper, waiting for the jury to observe the small square. 'Written by the deceased not long before she died. Is it true, Miss Frye, that you provided this letter for the court? And if so, can you explain how you acquired it?'

'Zona had a secret hiding place in her dresser for her most special things,' she said. 'I called to the house one day, when Trout wasn't there, to see if she'd left anything important behind. That's when I found the letter.'

'Please read it aloud for the court.'

Gilmer set the paper into her outstretched hand, and Trout pushed his chair back, arms folded, giving her that same threatening and challenging look that he had always given her when setting her up to fail.

The two sheets of paper were covered on both sides by Zona's slanted and looped handwriting, and as she opened them out, she held them high enough for the jury to see the lively character of her deceased friend's hand.

'*Dear Beth*,' she began, faltering as she saw Mary Jane's expression soften. This grieving mother would have believed there was nothing left of her daughter's life to be discovered, that all its cinders had been raked and cooled. But here was a bright new snatch of her existence, delivering a peculiar kind of joy. '*Dear Beth*,' she repeated, projecting now, '*I have been writing you about my hopes of meeting one day. Things will be different when we are together. There will be more colour in the world.*

My food will have more flavour. And when I hear the sound of your voice — oh, if only it could break the quiet here now — it will be the sweet note that is missing from all other music. Without you, nothing is complete. But I can endure it all knowing that Eugenia Wylie is keeping you safe.'

'Eugenia Wylie,' Gilmer said. 'This is the adoptive mother?'

'That's right.'

'Continue, please.'

'I have been troubled since I last wrote, wondering what might happen if I died before I had told you everything. I would not be able to say, then, that I had done my best by you.'

'Pardon me, Miss Frye,' Gilmer interrupted. 'Can you tell the court the date on the letter please?'

'January twentieth.'

'Of this year — 1897?'

'Yes.'

'Zona Shue expressed concern for loss of her life just three days before her death occurred?'

'That's right,' Lucy said.

Rucker rose from his seat, belly nudging the desk. 'Your honour,' he said, 'Dr Knapp has testified that the deceased believed herself to be pregnant at the time this letter was written. And in danger of haemorrhage. She had every reason to fear for her life.'

'Except there was no child, was there?' Lucy said.

Gilmer gave her a warning look.

'You heard Knapp's testimony. He said he was treating Zona for pain.' Her tone begged the prosecutor to let her continue. 'In her shoulder, and her stomach. Maybe he thought she was pregnant back then, but the post-mortem said there was no baby. So why was she in pain? What if she'd called the doctor for help – to confide that Trout had been hurting her – but grew too frightened to say anything?'

Rucker stood up with a vexed smile. 'This is speculation.'

'Mr Gilmer,' McWhorter said, 'remind your witness that this is a court of law. Not a court of opinion.'

'But I have evidence,' Lucy blurted, 'that he's hurt her before.'

The justice chewed on his cheek. 'Go on, Miss Frye,' he said.

'Zona came to see me the week after she married Trout. There was a cut on her head. Just here, above her ear, deep enough to need a stitch, but she never called the doctor. She said she fell on a lamp. But when I asked her more about it, how she could've fallen over like that, well, she wasn't acting anything like herself. It didn't make sense, how defensive she got. I could tell she was covering for him, your honour. I'm certain of it.'

The gallery fizzed at this accusation, and Mary Jane gripped her wooden seat with her bony fingers, watching Trout for his reaction. A furnace seemed to light inside the defendant. He'd been letting himself exist far away from the truth, remote from his guilt. But there was a memory from his wedding night boiling up inside him now, Lucy was sure of it. It made him wriggle in his chair. And yet, ghoul that he was, he was quick to cover it with a smile. Eye teeth gleaming, he turned to Rucker, shaking his head in baffled denial.

'Your honour,' the defence attorney said, 'the witness has no proof.'

'Check the post-mortem,' Lucy said. 'I bet the doctors found a fresh scar, right where I'm saying.'

'Miss Frye,' the justice said, 'you will not speak in this court again unless it is in answer to a question. All mention of this accusation will be removed from the record.'

Minnie Grose's hands danced on the keys of her stenograph machine, working to erase the most important truth that had been spoken since the trial began. Lucy felt a howl of protest rising in her chest. The only thing to dampen it was Gilmer's obvious pleasure at her outburst.

'Miss Frye,' he said, with a sharp nod of approval, 'can you please read the next lines of Zona Shue's letter to the court.'

'Of course.' She tried to find her place, the paper trembling. *'Elisabeth,'* she said, *'it is easy to guess the question you might have for me now — who is your father? You might be very curious about him. Or you may never want to know. That is why I've written his name on the other side of this page. Only turn it over, Beth, if you are ready to hear about him.'*

Even little Thomas was distracted now, the sawing of his great fan coming to a halt. The paper rustled in the silence as Lucy flipped it over. Almost every face in the gallery had a dropped jaw or an open mouth, waiting to be fed some local gossip. Knowing what was coming, Trout leaned forward on the desk, as eager as if she were about to serve him a loin of venison, well seasoned. Only Mary Jane was pensive, confident of hearing George Woldridge's name. Yet it was she who was to have the biggest surprise of all.

'Your father,' Lucy said, slow and frank, *'is called Emory Snow. He is an inventor from North Carolina. He is clever and confident and quite well able to make his way in the world of patents and business.'*

'No. No, no,' Mary Jane muttered.

Lucy met her eye. *Is it not plain as day*, she wanted to say, *now that it is spoken aloud?* Zona had never lied about it, but had rather allowed her mother to believe what she wanted. Mary Jane had her own reasons, Lucy supposed, for explaining it all away; for not wanting to see what was happening under her nose.

Zona's mother cast over her shoulder at Jacob, tears of blame shivering. 'You did this,' she hissed, her burning rage meeting his hateful glare.

'Quiet in the courtroom, Mrs Heaster, or you will be removed,' McWhorter said, stony. 'Continue, please, Miss Frye.'

Trout pinched his nostrils closed, trying to cover the grin that dimpled his cheeks. Here was his smug judgement of Zona; the unvarnished contempt for his wife and her choices that he pretended not to feel.

Lucy looked down at the page, clearing her throat of any emotion. '*I think*,' she said, '*that Emory might have what your great-grandpa – my opa – called far-sickness. It turns out he doesn't like to settle in one place. Perhaps you, too, feel the pull of the foreign? If you ever wish to find him, you might ask at the summer school in Chapel Hill where he teaches. I think he would expect a lot from his students and would push them to work very hard. As far as family goes, he is the fifth of seven children, meaning that you have two living aunts and four living uncles on his side. He did not talk too much about his family except to say that his father was a dentist who trained in Baltimore, and because of this he always had one or two things to say about my teeth. Like "the front ones are good, but you need gold foil for those cavities at the back".*'

'If you could stop there,' Gilmer said, raising one finger. 'Miss Frye, this letter describes the child's father in rather caring and sympathetic detail. In other words, it doesn't sound as if Zona Shue's relationship with Mr Snow was a shallow dalliance. Can you tell the court, was it the kind of unsavoury and wanton flirtation that the defence claims to be at the very heart of her character?'

'No. It was never like that,' Lucy said. 'I don't think there was ever any flirtation; not in the way you mean. In the beginning, he was just a friend of Zona's pa. But after a few visits to Meadow Bluff, well, Mr Snow, he expressed his regard for her. Not just once. Many, many times. He was very persistent. After a point, she wondered if she should try to return his feelings.'

'She had no natural affection for him?'

'The best of us put duty before happiness,' Lucy said. 'A woman looks for a steady man who might support a family. A man looks for an able wife and mother. If you go by that measure, they could have been a good match. Zona thought it would make her parents proud, marrying a successful man. Jacob – I mean, Mr Heaster – in particular.'

'You're saying that the deceased wanted to marry this Emory Snow?'

'She would have agreed to marry him, yes.'

'And why did this marriage never take place?'

Lucy sighed away her rising fury with the inventor. 'The thing is, Mr Snow travels a lot for his work, and he used to send on copies of the newspapers from the bigger cities. He'd circle anything of interest to Mr Heaster, about patents or inventing. And just when Zona was expecting his proposal, the *New York Times* arrived with a big black circle drawn around a marriage announcement showing that Emory was betrothed to another woman.'

'How did Zona Shue feel about this?'

'Shocked,' Lucy said. 'Being thrown over like that, she never told him about the baby. She couldn't trust him. The betrayal was unbearable.'

'Does the deceased mention this betrayal in her letter,' Gilmer asked.

'Yes.' Lucy pulled the second page of Zona's letter to the fore. '*As I write*,' she said, '*your father is married to a young teacher in Durham whose name is Joanna Louise Farleigh Snow. There was a time when I was immature, and I believed that he would marry me.*' Lucy's voice grew tight, remembering how desperate and worthless the rejection had made Zona feel, believing that her parents would despise her for being a trusting fool. '*My head was spinning around and around back then, the same as any sunflower that turns to chase the light. But when the sunflower is all grown up, Beth, she gives up on whirling around. She stands facing east — toward the dawn — and she is rooted and steady with every new day. That is how I am now. Steady in my own counsel. Trust in your own judgement, little Beth. Especially when things are very confusing. You can do nothing in any moment except what you believe to be your very best. Take care, my darling. I will write you whenever I can. I pray so hard to the Lord every night that my words will reach you one day. Yours ever truly, Zona Heaster Shue.*'

These gentle sentiments brought a hush over the court-room, just the same as a fall of snow. In spite of their startled anger, both Mary Jane and Jacob looked hungry for more of their daughter's words, as if listening to their soft drift might keep them from the pain that was sure to bloom at their end.

'Miss Frye,' Gilmer said, 'what does this letter tell us about the character of its author? The woman you knew so well in life.'

'You can tell how naive she was. She felt stupid. And so embarrassed. The woman I knew,' Lucy said, brandishing the letter at the jury, 'was loyal and considerate and willing to make sacrifices for a steady home and happy family. Emory Snow took advantage of those virtues. And the loose and reckless behaviour that Patrick Shue accused her of yesterday, well, Zona was never interested in any of that.'

It was true. All of it. Gilmer took the letter and passed it to the jury, and as it was handed from one man to the next, she wished that each might feel the paper to be infused with her friend's sincerity, the words kindling their understanding and compassion.

'That will be all, Miss Frye,' Gilmer said. 'Thank you.' The attorney worked his ivory toothpick against his gum. And if she wasn't mistaken, both he and Preston had a renewed air of confidence.

McWhorter swiped a huge handkerchief across his sweating brow, prodding the astounded Thomas, who stood with his fan idle by his side. 'Does the defence wish to take the witness?' the judge said.

'One moment, your honour.'

Rucker conferred quietly with his colleague, and Lucy braced for merciless cross-examination. *They'll accuse you of lying*, Gilmer had promised. *They'll say that Emory Snow knew about the child all along – might even suggest that Snow killed Zona to keep her quiet. Keep to the tragic love story, Miss Frye, no matter what. You wait and see. Mr Snow will have an alibi that puts Trout back over the coals.*

Trout was silent between his whispering lawyers, eyeing her with faux patience. How many times, she wondered, had Zona seen this same look on his face? How often had she waited, in terror, for him to rise at her, to punish and berate and belittle her, when she had done no wrong? He looked down to his notes, retraced them with his pencil, slow and deliberate, as if he were whetting a blade. Then he wrote a new and insistent message; no more than four words, which he underlined very heavily before drawing Rucker and Gardner's attention to them.

Rucker stroked his beard as he read, looking impressed, then glanced at Gardner, seeming to ask, *What do you think?* The lawyer replied by tapping his pen on the desk, before giving one firm nod of agreement.

At once, all three men were in fine smiling form.

'No questions at this time, your honour,' Gardner said, squaring up his papers. 'The defence requests a recess.'

16 | MARY JANE HEASTER

Greenbrier County Courthouse

June 25, 1897

Mary Jane was grateful to both Miss Grose and the Lord for the shelter the court reporter had given her and Lucy during recess. It had allowed them to escape the very personal questions that the excited crowd in the gallery had started firing at them. But the clerk's comfortable, quiet and well-lighted chamber had also allowed Lucy to deliver yet more brutal news.

Emory Snow will be called to the stand today, she had said, while the tactful Minnie occupied herself at her typewriter. *That's why Gilmer had me read Zona's letter. We had to get there first, tell the jury the true story before Rucker has a chance to twist it.*

Lucy was swishing down the steps behind her, now, both making their way back to the courtroom. Mary Jane knew that the girl shared something of the towering malice she herself bore toward the inventor, but could know nothing of the struggle she would have to control it. It made her stall for breath on the first landing. And as she leaned on the rail, Lucy pressed a crush of green velvet ribbon into her palm.

'It's the pendant I made for Zona,' she said. 'I found it with her letters. I think you should have them all, Mrs Heaster. To keep for Elisabeth.'

Mary Jane pressed a thumb to one of the star's points before stowing it in the tiny pocket of her jacket. Lucy might believe that such relics could give her strength and hope. But today they served only to make Zona's absence sharper, harder to endure.

She carried this pain through the fizzing crowd, up the aisle of the gallery, into her usual seat at the front. Jacob was already in the second row, with George Stanley almost in his lap. Bad enough that her husband had refused to speak to her, or to meet her eye, when Miss Grose was leading her away. Worse still that he seemed nauseated, now, by the very sight of her.

'What right have you to fester?' she said, caring little what harm it might do to have Stanley overhear a few harsh words about her husband. 'I told you vanity brings nothing but ruin. You let Snow into our house, wanting to feel bigger than everyone else. Lord knows what he'll say when he gets on the stand.'

'I treated Zona like she was a good girl,' he said, trying to keep his whispering away from Stanley's ear. 'But that whole time . . . Lying lips are an abomination to the Lord. All of you, deceitful.'

'This from the man who thought Trout Shue's brother, of all people under God's sun, would feel obliged to help him with his invention. You're so stupid you're dangerous.'

Between them, it felt as if there was not one healthy inch of flesh left to be wounded. Exhausted, they fell into silence. And as Lucy arranged her skirts beside her, Mary Jane's fury with Emory took on new life. Here she was, denied a chance to give Zona's testimony, while the inventor was about to rest his smooth, fat hand on a Bible, buying himself his turn as a witness. She pictured his pompous face, and imagined the colossal sacrifice that Zona had been willing to make; how she would have allowed Emory to twist a wedding ring onto her hand, suffering his childish, greedy nature, putting aside any need for respect and love, all in hope of serving her father's ambitions. But the inventor had not wanted to be raised up by marrying a woman as good as Zona. His only desire had been the prestige of discarding her.

'Take it easy,' Lucy said. Her thoughts were clear to read, perhaps; the way she itched to let fly at the man. 'Snow might be gone before evening, and you'll never have to lay eyes on him again.'

'Unless Jacob's invited him to stay,' she said. 'Nothing would surprise me.' She pulled her shawl tight about her shoulders. *Mind your modesty*, Gilmer had gibed yesterday, slabs of teeth gleaming, reminding her that any glimpse of her natural figure might sway the jury for the worse.

Alfred, James and Joseph filed in beside their father, all in the same confused mood, just as the doors to the gallery were creaked shut on their big hinges. It was a signal that court would soon resume, but Preston and Gilmer were nowhere to be seen. Nor was the devious Rucker, or that conceited Gardner. Not until the door burst open, all four attorneys emerging in a snarl, Trout relaxed and beaming in their midst.

Preston and Gilmer sheered off toward their counsel desk, both scowling. The County Prosecutor ran one hand through his macassar-oiled hair and slapped open his leather folder to study a page of neat notes. Goosebumps lifted on Mary Jane's arms as the jury filed into their box. There was a taste of warning on her tongue, mineral and flinty, as McWhorter appeared behind the bench.

'Your honour,' the attorney said, stiff. 'The prosecution calls the defendant, Mr Edward Erasmus Shue.'

The sound of Trout's given name fixed Mary Jane to her seat. Her son-in-law took easy strides toward the stand, the room seeming to flare, cold and white.

'What's this?' she said, turning her questioning gaze on Lucy.

There were no answers in the girl's astonished face. It was she who had told her that this couldn't happen; who had explained that Trout's clever attorneys would never let him testify. Mary Jane had cursed Rucker for this counsel, wishing that the blacksmith might be hauled up with his guilt branded across his features. But something had changed – turned upside down – because here was Trout, bolder than brass, as if he could not wait for Preston to confront him.

The jurors seemed keyed up, their eyes out on sticks.

'Please tell the court your name,' Preston said.

Chin down, Trout raised his eyes to the court. They were brown and soft, kind and wise, deceptive as any of the fishing hooks that Jacob dressed in feathers and wool to disguise the barbs beneath. 'My name is Edward Erasmus Shue. Most folks know me as "Trout".'

His manner was cooperative and friendly, his soft tone and good diction seeming to ease the tension in the jury box.

'You're accused, Mr Shue, of murdering your wife,' Preston said, blunt. 'And you have pleaded not guilty to the charge of attacking her with such violence that you broke her neck with your bare hands. Mrs Shue's body was discovered in your marital home. Please tell the court, can you remember the morning that Dr George Knapp visited your house to determine Zona Shue's cause of death?'

'Of course.'

'The coroner has testified to this court that he did not complete a full examination because you would not allow him proper access to the deceased. Do you agree with his statement?'

'Yes,' Trout said, mild.

'Why did you prevent it?'

'Looking back, I suppose I was panicked. Part of me wanted Dr Knapp to leave, so I could go back to pretending it wasn't really happening.'

'You do not deny impeding the examination?'

'No,' he said, innocent.

Preston squinted at his notes. 'Your statement says that you brought Mrs Shue's body to her family home in Meadow Bluff the next morning. Is that correct?'

'Yes.'

'Before that journey, you spent more than twenty hours alone with your dead wife. What did you do during this time?'

'I took delivery of a casket from Handley's undertakers,' he said. 'Before I washed and dressed her.' He cleared his throat into his loose fist, as if to hold back his emotion. But with peculiar certainty, Mary Jane knew that there had been no passion or sadness in his half-hearted cleansing. 'It went very hard on me,' he lied, 'putting her in the same white frock she wore for our wedding.'

'Did you place the deceased in any other garment apart from this dress?'

'Do you mean the scarf?

'I mean any other garment or accessory, aside from the wedding dress.'

'I used her favourite scarf for her veil. Very fine, light silk, beautiful across her face.' He shifted in his chair, as if to stem his grief, when really he was gathering his patience.

'Was it tied in a large bow beneath the chin?'

'There was enough fabric for a knot. Yes.'

'The scarf, worn as you describe it, would have obscured the finger marks on your wife's neck. And the contusion on her cheek. Is that correct?'

'I suppose so. They were slight enough that I didn't see them.'

'You didn't see the livid bruise on her right cheek. Or the large marks where the strong fingers of a left hand had, perhaps, lifted her by her throat. Are you left-handed, Mr Shue?'

'I use my right hand, Mr Preston.'

'Have you favoured it since birth?'

'Yes,' he said, his lies fluent and natural as blackbird's song.

'Your wife's true cause of death,' Preston said, 'was the complete severing of her spine between two vertebrae. The post-mortem makes it very clear that this injury could not have been missed by anyone who disturbed her body. Can you tell us your recollection of this terrible effect – of your wife's head being loose from her neck?'

'Believe me, no man could forget a thing like that,' Trout said.

'When Dr Knapp left, I took my beautiful girl in my arms, and I couldn't hold her without cradling her neck with my elbow.'

He mimed the action, crooking his arm to one side, gazing down. And Mary Jane felt anger clamping about her heart. The final ripples of Zona's visiting spirit seemed to wash through her, and all at once she had a strong picture of Trout dragging her daughter by her feet toward the kitchen. The scene grew more powerful yet, until she had the sensation of sliding across the floor, the skin of her back burning.

'You had to make a special effort to stop her head from rolling about?' Preston asked, shattering Trout's romantic story.

'That's right.'

'Can you tell the court, please, did you embrace your dead wife at any time when there were other people present? For example, Charles Tabscott and Martha Jones were with you when you first saw the body. Did you take her in your arms in front of these witnesses?'

'No.'

'Why not?'

'I've told you, Mr Preston, I was in denial.' Trout paused, perhaps to settle the irritation creeping into his tone. 'Aunt Martha and Charlie, they tried to tell me she was dead. But I didn't believe them. And I didn't want to move her in case I made it worse.'

'Made what worse, Mr Shue?'

'Whatever injury she might have suffered.'

'According to Martha Jones and Charles Tabscott, you made no attempt to check her pulse or listen to her breathing. Nor would you allow them to check her for signs of life. Is that true?'

'Yes,' Trout said, seeming to resist the temptation to defend this choice.

'Let's revisit the moment when you finally held your wife in your arms.' Preston paused, as if to better lower his witness into the boiling stew. 'When you saw the extent of her shocking injuries, did you wonder what had caused them?'

'Not really,' Trout said. And in reply to Preston's sceptical glance, he added, 'Dr Knapp told me her heart gave out, all of a sudden. I figured she must've been on the stairs when it happened. Plenty of folks get ugly injuries from falling off horses and suchlike. You see that a lot in my trade. I wasn't surprised, but it was very upsetting, I can tell you. Seeing her so . . . changed.'

He made like a rope of grief was tugging his heart back to that mournful moment. And Mary Jane thought his palm should have been blistering and burning where he had rested it to swear on the Bible.

'As you know, Mr Shue, there was no fall from the stairs,' Preston said. 'Your wife, a young woman in perfect health, was murdered. The injuries to her windpipe, to her ligaments, show the terrible violence of the attack. Please tell the court, after you discovered that Zona's neck was not just broken, but entirely dislocated, whom did you tell?'

'No one,' Trout said, his voice tight with fake despair. 'When I thought about her family seeing her that way, well, it didn't seem right, putting them through more suffering.'

'You decided to conceal it?'

'Yes.'

'It's common practice in Greenbrier County,' Preston said, 'for the women in the family to lay out the dead. Did you know that this tradition was sacred to the Heaster family when you took it upon yourself to dress your wife for burial?'

'I did.'

'Did it occur to you that your extraordinary actions might seem cruel rather than helpful?'

'I had some idea that Mrs Heaster might be surprised. Maybe disappointed,' Trout said, speaking to the jury in a confidential tone. 'I didn't expect her to get so angry she'd throw crockery at my head.' His chin dimpled and trembled, as if he'd been scarred by the unfairness of this. 'If it wasn't for Mary Jane's friend Bessie talking her down, I don't know what would've happened.'

He turned toward Mary Jane, and fixed her with a sad and forgiving gaze, willing her to rail at the twisted claim that Bessie had been his protector. His lies felt sharp and dangerous as a blade pressed to her flesh. Seeing her stiffen, Preston made a point of walking between them, eclipsing Trout's noble expression.

'Your late wife, Hannah Shue,' the attorney said, 'did you also dress her for her funeral?'

Trout made as if he hadn't heard him, buying some time to think. 'Could you repeat that, sir?' he said.

'I'm asking if you also dressed your late wife, Hannah Shue, for her funeral.'

'Mr Preston, there was a snowstorm the night my Hannah died. Being trapped in the house, I had no choice but to dress her. It was a full two days before I could get even fifty yards from the door.'

The prosecutor nodded, pretending sympathy. 'It would be unusual,' he said, 'for any man to find himself in such a strange position. Alone with a deceased wife whom he has no choice but to dress for her funeral. The trouble is that you seem to make a habit of it, Mr Shue.'

Trout took on a wounded expression, a small measure of alarm in his eyes as he noticed that several members of the jury were taking notes. 'Most men,' he said, 'they haven't suffered my misfortune.'

'Misfortune.' Preston gazed into the light of the big southern window, giving the rapt jurors a little time to digest. 'Did you ever tell Zona Shue about your earlier misfortunes? In other words, did the murdered woman know that you were married not once, but twice before, and that your second wife was dead?'

Trout scratched the side of his nose. 'She knew. Same as any husband and wife, we knew plenty about each other that wasn't common knowledge,' he said, his untruths sending the prickle of pins and needles down Mary Jane's arms.

'After you brought the body of your third wife, Zona, to her parents' home in Meadow Bluff, did you at any time try to set things straight with Mrs Heaster? For example, did you explain to her why you had taken this peculiar step of dressing her daughter for burial?'

Trout shook his head. 'No.'

'You've told this court that she lost her temper when she saw what you'd done. That she was in great distress. Why didn't you speak with Zona's father, or her uncle, or any other person who could have explained things to Mrs Heaster? If upset was unavoidable, wouldn't it have been better for the truth to be told?'

'A man can't think straight at a time like that,' Trout said. 'I hadn't had a wink of sleep, and folks were queueing up to say goodbye to my beautiful girl.'

He dragged his fingers back through his hair, as if trying to dispel the fatigue of those miserable days. Yet another ghost-like memory quickened in the meat of Mary Jane's brain. She could hear Trout's boots, heavy on the narrow staircase, and had a strong sense of Zona lying in her casket, alone in the copse behind the house. She could almost smell the resin, feel the roughness of the wood, as she heard the harsh creak of the bed upstairs. Then came a subtle shift in atmosphere, just the same as when any soul surrenders to sleep.

The scent of pine was still fresh in her nose, cutting through the heat, as Preston checked his notes.

'According to several witnesses, you had the presence of mind to stuff the corners of your wife's casket with pillows and sheets to further conceal her injuries. You were also careful to patrol her body, making sure that no one else could touch the victim. Would you agree, Mr Shue, that far from being distracted by grief or exhaustion, you continued to be vigilant in your efforts to conceal your wife's condition?'

Trout bit his lip, shrugged. 'Seemed to me it had gone too far to turn back. Maybe I'd do different now. Like I say, I was just trying to protect the Heasters. It was hard, keeping it to myself.' He set his eyes to glittering with hurt. 'And I never asked for thanks.'

'Mr Shue, isn't it true that you were protecting nobody but yourself? That you were afraid of suspicion falling on you?'

'No.'

'And yet sworn statements from both Alfred and Mary Jane Heaster say that had they known the extent of Zona's injuries at the time, they would not have overlooked them – as you claim to have done – but would have called for an investigation. I attended your wife's autopsy, Mr Shue. Her body was very well preserved by the cold ground up at Little Sewell. I cannot imagine that any person who saw her brutal injuries would have dismissed them.'

'Your honour,' Rucker said, trying to seem composed, 'this is speculation. The personal opinions of the prosecutor are not relevant. The witness has explained the innocence of his behaviour.'

'Very well,' Preston said brightly. 'Let us summarise your testimony for the jury, Mr Shue. Make sure we have it all straight and fair. You would not allow the coroner, Dr Knapp, to examine your wife's body. Her true cause of death was a severed neck, and you kept this horrific injury a secret from everyone. You disguised it by covering the face and neck of the victim with copious fabric. And for the duration of the wake, you remained on tenterhooks, guarding Zona Shue's body, and bolstering her head so that nobody would see it moving about. But in spite of this calculated and devious behaviour, you expect this court to believe that you did not murder her?'

'You can't prove I did it.' Trout was quietly provocative, and Mary Jane saw Gardner wince, thumbnail pressed between his front teeth. 'Plenty of folks are willing to sit up here and speak for my character, while the man who killed her is still running free. How many women has that murdering mongrel hurt by now?' he said, bottom lip trembling with fake grief.

'That will be all,' Preston said, slapping closed his leather folder, cutting Trout off at the height of his performance.

Mary Jane saw the flicker of pencils across the jury box, a

dozen men recording the scornful exchange. Seeing Trout's expression turning sour, Rucker sprang to his feet, and McWhorter gave a loose wave of his hand. 'Your witness, Dr Rucker.'

The attorney approached his client as if some big moment had finally come, his obvious excitement unsettling.

'Mr Shue,' he said. 'You're right. The killer is still at large. Can you explain to the court, do you have any suspicions who this person might be?'

'I've worn out the floor thinking about it, going over and back, over and back. It could be that Emory Snow wanted to keep Zona quiet about their baby.'

'But Miss Frye has testified that Mr Snow knew nothing about the infant,' Rucker said, their conversation seeming well rehearsed.

'She was lying,' Trout said, squinting over at her. 'Zona told me he knew. That she tried to get Snow to leave his new wife to be with her and the child. You can see how fond she was of letter-writing. Wouldn't surprise me if she'd been asking him for money, too.'

Lucy was trying to hold her tongue, lips pressed just as tight together as if they'd been gummed. Mary Jane cast about the gallery, hoping to hear Emory give a dissenting sniff or cough, but there was no sign, yet, of the tedious inventor.

'Tell the jury,' Rucker said, 'was there any other man, besides Mr Snow, who had a motive to kill your wife?'

The attorney was throwing open a dangerous door for Trout. And he stepped back as if to let him pass through, the room seeming to bank and twist in a new and unwelcome direction.

'Listen,' the blacksmith said. His mouth puckered as if delivering difficult news. 'I loved Zona, but trust me when I tell you she wasn't the sweet girl that Lucy Frye told you about this morning. I saw another man up at my house on January tenth. He came striding around from the back door and climbed onto a bay horse. A mare I've never seen down at the forge. I wonder if he's the man who killed my Zona.'

'Who was this man?' Rucker said.

'I didn't see him up close. But he was wearing a scarf. The knitted sort, not woven. You could tell that from fifty yards. It had those same bright colours Sam Withrow wears. Purple and orange.'

'And who is Mr Sam Withrow?'

'A good friend of the Heasters.' Trout chewed his cheek, getting ready to unburden. 'Let me tell you,' he said, looking very directly at the jury, 'down at the forge, I do a lot of my work in darkness. I get to see how the metal glows, how willing it is to be worked. Well, I had some dark times with Zona, too. That's when I saw how cold and stubborn she was. I forgave her, again and again, for the way she neglected and . . . well . . . sometimes despised me,' he said. 'The thing is, Zona was fond of older men. Me, Mr Emory Snow and, I think, Mr Withrow, too. And what does a young woman want from an older man? Maybe money, or attention, or . . . I don't want to say. All I know is, when I got into the house that day, she flat-out denied I'd seen anyone. She had that way about her, of trying to make me feel crazy.'

Lucy tensed, her backside lifting from the seat. Mary Jane pressed her back down, whispering, 'Don't.' She pinned the girl's pink-gloved hand in her lap, shocked that the world was not tilting or flaming. It should have been shaking out of its place, pillars trembling, in answer to these wild accusations.

'Your honour.' Preston stood up, his confidence absolute. 'This is a waste of the court's time. Dr Rucker is well aware that Mr Samuel Withrow was more than twelve miles away, in Crawley, on January tenth.'

'It's not a waste of time,' Trout said, 'talking about evidence of my innocence. Why should Sam Withrow have been at my house the very morning Zona died? What if he was coming back to hide her body? I'm telling the truth after being made to listen to fairy stories – Lucy Frye telling the world that my wife was a wholesome woman, when she was nothing of the sort. They were birds of a feather, that Frye girl and Zona. Only reason Lucy is here today is to get me back for rejecting her.'

Mary Jane felt Lucy shivering in spite of the swampish heat, her face turning white.

'Mr Shue,' Rucker said, trying to sound astonished, 'are you suggesting that Miss Frye is taking some kind of revenge?'

'Mr Gilmer and Lucy, they've peddled a story about her searching my house for Zona's keepsakes. But they didn't tell you how I found her waiting for me in my bed that day.' Every eye in the gallery and jury turned to Lucy, who held one hand very close to her cheek, as if she'd been struck. 'Begging the pardon of any ladies present,' he said, 'but she was down to her silk chemise and pantalettes.'

'Do you have proof of her affection for you?' Rucker asked, giving Lucy a sidelong glance.

'Well, she was holding a lavender sachet,' Trout said. 'In her teeth.' He exposed his own and posed as if biting. 'She made it for me. Embroidered it with my initials.'

'Was it this sachet?' Rucker reached his hand out to accept a small object offered by Gardner's long fingers. It was a square of white linen, trimmed with lace, and he held it high so that the letters *TS* could be seen crudely stitched onto the fabric in rose-coloured thread. 'Is this the lavender bag that Miss Frye presented?'

Trout grasped it, inhaling its peppery scent. And Mary Jane felt the creep of dread through Lucy's blood; the terrible understanding that her reputation was running so far and fast from her grip that she might never have power over it again. It belonged to the gawping faces behind them, to the disappointed men of the jury.

'This is the same one she gave me,' Trout said, dangling the sachet for all to see. 'She threw it on the bed when I asked her to go, and threatened me, saying, *You'll be sorry.*'

Mary Jane met Lucy's frightened eyes, and as the girl whispered, 'It wasn't like that, Mrs Heaster. You have to believe me,' her heart began to drift downward, to that place where the light cannot reach.

'To be clear, Mr Shue,' Rucker said, leaning against his desk to allow the jury a clear view of the humiliated girl. 'In her testimony this morning, Miss Lucia Frye claimed that you were capable of killing Zona Shue. Are you telling the court that this very same young woman sought amorous congress with you after your wife's death, and was angry when you rejected her?'

Trout lowered his head, as if embarrassed. 'Yes. Me and my wife, we always thought Lucy was jealous of us being together. It got so bad at Christmas – Lucy's meddling, I mean – that Zona stopped talking to her. Then, soon as my wife was dead, she was trying to take her place.'

Twelve accusing glances settled on Lucy. In their credulity, the jury members were opening the way to a startling future. One in which Mary Jane might bump into Trout as a free man, somewhere in Lewisburg, perhaps, browsing the windows of William Frye, Watchmakers & Jewellers, with another young woman on his arm, while inside that secret skull of his, he would still be hiding the answers to all her questions. *Was Zona afraid? Did she fight you? Did you see it – the exact moment when you forced her soul to depart?* And all she would ever want to do was go back, back, back. To that moment when she might have taken her daughter's place; felt his hands about her own throat instead, and taken all her suffering.

As Rucker pushed his hands deep into his pockets, face creased with sham concern for Trout, Mary Jane could not believe that Emory Snow, one of the most selfish and arrogant and lazy and untrustworthy people she'd ever had the bad luck to meet, was to be Zona's best chance.

'Thank you for your honesty, Mr Shue,' Rucker said. With that, he smoothed his beard and swaggered to his desk. 'No further questions.'

'Mr Preston,' McWhorter said, sombre, 'do you wish to re-examine the witness?'

'Not at this time.' The attorney's voice held all its usual authority, despite his case standing in tatters. 'The prosecution would like to call a new witness.' He had an air of impatience as Trout moved from the stand, slow as a consumptive, milking the jury's pity. No sooner had he cleared the floor than Preston said, 'Your honour, the State calls Mr Emory Snow.'

With a mix of fury and hope, Mary Jane looked back down the gallery, where she saw a tall man in an immaculate suit of cream linen making his way toward the stand. The fit of his jacket, and the cut of the double vents, said that he could afford to keep the best tailors in his employ, and the stitching of his tan leather shoes was no doubt the handiwork of a fancy maker in the city. The overall effect was one of elegance and competence, his figure very neat, a glimpse of a purple pocket square lending some dash. Clean-shaven with a full head of hair, he had a healthy and pleasant appearance, although the lobes of his ears were glowing very red, as if he might be feeling worked up inside his pristine cotton shirt.

'What is your name, please, sir?' Preston asked.

'My name is Emory Elton Snow,' he replied, seeming to find the question tiresome.

Mary Jane blinked very fast. She had failed to bring him into focus, she supposed; did not recognise him as the short and doughy man she knew of old.

'And where do you live, Mr Snow.'

'In Durham, North Carolina.'

'Are you the Emory Snow who is married to Miss Joanna Louise Farleigh.'

'I am.'

'And was your father a travelling dentist?'

'He was.'

'Can you tell the court, Mr Snow, do you hold any original patents?'

'I have a patent for a bark-stripping machine. Called the "Snow Peeler". And before you ask, yes, I teach at the Chapel Hill summer school. And yes, I have two sisters and four brothers, all of them living.'

'In that case, Mr Snow, could you face the jury, please, and tell them whether or not you made false promises to the murdered woman, Zona Shue. Speak up, now.'

'Well, first of all, I'd like to offer my condolences to the family on the death of their daughter.' His voice was every bit as taut and loud as Preston might have hoped. 'But I must confirm that I never knew this woman, Zona Shue, nor any of her relatives or associates. In fact, this is my first visit to Greenbrier County.'

'Mr Snow,' Preston said, 'if you're attempting to be droll, a murder trial is hardly the right time or place. Your name and career are detailed in the correspondence of the deceased. And you live at the same address that you registered with the patent office. Further, the presentation of your United States passport has proved your identity to the court. Now, please tell the jury about the nature of your relationship with Zona Heaster Shue.'

'It's been interesting to hear how the private details of my life were so familiar to this woman,' Snow said, brittle. 'But . . . ' He paused, his eyes very blue and cold. 'I can only assume that another man has been impersonating me. I remember a morning in 1893 – it was June, I believe – when several of my trunks disappeared from the morning train for Chicago. My blueprints, my clothes, my family photographs, all of them missing. I believe you've been consorting with the robber,' he said, his gaze shuttling between Mary Jane and her husband. 'And I mean to discover who he is.'

Jacob floated to standing, as if weightless. He hovered behind Mary Jane, his face grey with the bleakness of his realisation. Perhaps his spirit wished to untether, just as hers did; yearning to leave this courtroom behind, along with the real Emory Snow. Then he might find the cruel man who had lied to them all. Gripping him by the collar, and drawing him very near, he might demand – what? A confession, an apology, financial amends? There was nothing of any value that they might wring from him. With Zona gone, there could never be any satisfaction. All he could do was stand there, swaying, exposed as a powerless fool.

'Sit down, Mr Heaster,' McWhorter said.

Trout leaned back in his chair, almost sliding off it with delight. Rucker frowned, seeming to warn him against giddiness. There was little point, not when even he and Gardner were struggling to suppress their knowing and victorious grins. They knew that Elisabeth's real father would never be found. He was a thief, and a fraud, and Mary Jane knew of old that he was sly and selfish, with a wild cat's instinct for self-preservation. He had used her girl, body and soul. Whoever he was, wherever he was, he would suffer no consequence.

'They've set us up,' Lucy said. 'Rucker's the one who brought Snow here. No more than a few words between them would have told him Beth's father was an imposter. How do we prove Zona's honesty now?' she asked, desperate. 'How do we prove mine?'

She shook on the bench beside Mary Jane, perhaps knowing that her life was taking an irreversible turn. Her reputation, now, would be as the low company that Zona had kept, and not even the Fryes' money would be able to save her from the shame and loneliness. As for Mary Jane herself, and her boys, thanks to Jacob they would all be dismissed as gullible fools, Zona being particularly witless.

'No more questions,' Preston said, walking back to his desk, as big and trusting an idiot as any of them.

Trout's expression was self-satisfied, and the jurors seemed to regard him with pity and understanding. As if the poor blacksmith had suffered a weak and shallow wife. One who could be readily exploited, even by strangers. And erased, finally, by her own misadventures.

'Don't go anywhere.' Mary Jane slid down off the wagon and moved out of the wobbling circle of light thrown by the driving lamp.

Armsted wrapped and rewrapped the reins about his hand. 'It's against my better judgement,' he said, squinting into the twilight. But he didn't budge the cart, knowing that Bessie would want him to stay.

His wife knew how injustice, and regretting earlier choices, could drive a woman, stinging at her like a whip. Despair, too, had found a restless home inside Mary Jane. A coiled spring that might have her do anything to secure Trout's conviction.

She slipped, velvety, up the gravel path of Rucker's house. On the front door, she saw the metal dome of the bell fixed on the crossbar, a big key protruding from it as if from a clockwork. Seizing its iron wings, she shattered the evening's silence, twisting it around and around, over and over, so that a shrill alarm echoed through the house. Even as Rucker's maid opened the latch, she did not release her grip, ratcheting the key for ruder and ruder intrusion.

Without any flicker of astonishment, the woman pulled the door free of her grasp. This suggested that Rucker's house was accustomed to violent disturbance, which in turn told her a lot about the man. The maid lifted her chin by way of quiet assessment. 'Name?' she said, guessing, correctly, that she had no visiting card.

'Mary Jane Heaster.'

The door closed. And despite the evening's heat, Mary Jane felt cold and clammy as any cheese in the springhouse. There was still time to walk away, she thought. But when the door opened again, and the maid said, 'Follow me,' she passed along the hallway, eyes fixed on the woman's flowing skirt and the flashing heels of her polished shoes.

A panelled door was opened on well-oiled hinges, and she was ushered into Rucker's library with its high white ceiling. The attorney looked up from what she supposed were his law books.

'Under cover of night?' he said. 'That's low-flung, even for you.' Without witnesses, it seemed he could not be bothered with pleasantries. There was no sign of the superficial charm that he brought into the courtroom, and had he been sitting in his flannel underclothes, the atmosphere could not have been more crudely intimate. 'You should've come to me at the courthouse if you had something to say. What are you, afraid of spooking Preston?'

He bit the stem of his pipe, leaving her to stand although she was close by a vacant chair. Given the heat of the night, he had only one oil lamp burning on his desk, and he pushed it toward her so that he might better inspect her.

'I want to go on the stand,' she said.

He huffed a quiet laugh. 'In case you've forgotten, I'm for the defendant,' he said. 'I'll do nothing to harm him.' Striking two matches, he circled their flames above his tobacco bowl.

'I can't think about this trial ending without Zona being

heard,' she said. 'She went through the agony of coming back to me, because she was so sick-hearted about what Trout had done, and I have to get up there and tell the truth for her.'

Rucker's look was one of hostile patience. 'Talking spirits aside, do you know the reason why Preston never called you to help his case?'

'I do. The prosecutor says I'm a liar. That I made up a story about my daughter's ghost, and now he doesn't trust anything I say. And since you only know me by reputation, Dr Rucker, I suppose you must think me a liar, too. Trout Shue has said as much, I'm sure. But let me tell you, I'm no such thing. And I can't go along with it any more. Being silenced, I mean.'

Rucker bobbed his head, sucked a cloud of smoke. 'Thing is, with a witness like you, Preston knows that the jury's feelings could go either way. Say he put you up there to talk about a ghost coming to your house. A juror might feel sympathy for your grief, thinking it had driven you demented. Or they might turn against you. I know I would,' he said, stabbing himself with one finger, 'if I heard your nonsense talk. No man likes a rumour-mongering, interfering woman. But if I put you up there for the defence, well, that would be different again. Even if the simplest man on that jury sees through your story, how would it look – the heartbroken mother of the deceased up on the stand with me savaging her testimony? I don't need you, Mrs Heaster. And I won't risk you gaining pity for outrageous behaviour. Go on home, now. Sarah will see you out.'

'Zona came to me, and I promised her,' Mary Jane said, feet suckering to the floorboards as if she were ivy. 'You don't understand. I made the sort of vow that can't be broken.' Her voice lit with a note of righteousness, and sensing this change, Rucker sat forward. He wore an expression that she knew of old: the bright attention of a man who had found some use for her. 'If Trout Shue walks free, without Zona having her say . . . ' Her stomach flipped just to think of it. 'I'm not sophisticated, Dr Rucker. But I'm not a stupid woman. I can see how the trial is going. I also know that whatever happens, my girl won't rest easy until she's heard. Her eternity is at stake, and I have to speak.'

The attorney's smile grew warmer. 'My dear Mrs Heaster,' he said. 'That old devil Preston, he never let on you really believed all of this.' He slapped the table, sipped on his pipe. 'I think you mean every word.'

'I do.'

He guffawed then, as if she were a small dog who had been trained to perform a delightful trick. 'All of it . . . Every word little Thomas wrote in that big journal?'

Mary Jane's teeth chattered with nervous fury. 'Yes.'

'My oh my.' He looked just as puffed up as Jacob had been that time he shot a fifteen-point buck, the antlers still in velvet. 'Well, dear Mrs Heaster, this is quite different.'

'I know you'll twist the truth,' she said. 'But that's no reason for me not to tell it.' She was trying to convince herself more than the attorney. 'I'm not going to lay down any more, let folks like you walk over me and Zona.'

Rucker nodded in earnest, as if egging her on. 'That's good. Excellent!' he said. 'By all means persevere. And remember, Mrs Heaster, the court doesn't twist things. It tests them, which is very different. Do you believe you're able for the test? It will be very short and sweet.'

'All I'm asking is to read from young Thomas's account. It's all there, in black and white, in Preston's office. Just the way Zona said it, word for word. The prosecutor will have to give it to you if you ask.'

'Oh, make no mistake,' Rucker said, twinkling, 'I've seen the pages you mean. I'll talk to McWhorter and Preston in the morning, try to get you on the stand first thing. Then we can tell the jury all about your daughter's ghost. Do we have a deal?'

She didn't like his soft speech; the way he was treating her as if she were disordered. The truth will set you free, that was what she had always been told. But this truth no longer felt clean or weightless or liberating. It had been pawed at and mauled, was bruised and clammy and tender from rejection. Nonetheless, it was time for its most dangerous exposure.

17 | LUCY FRYE

Lewisburg / Greenbrier County Courthouse

June 26, 1897

Lucy tied Sugar in the shade on Washington Street, and pressed her nose to the horse's shining mane, inhaling the scent of oil and root and leaf and grass. The mare had been rolling in the fields up at Oakhurst, where the hay had been cut and baled, and the bluegrass was down to stubble. There was no sign yet of new growth, but while the meadows would soon flush green, there would be no such pleasant recovery in Lucy's life if Trout were not convicted.

Keeping her eyes to the ground, she stepped into Burdette's drugstore. In the cooler air, toward the back of the room, Clara stood polishing the marble counter with a Turkish towel, her bright blonde hair tied in a practical braid. Lucy strode toward her, blue linen dress snapping smartly. It was a spruce get-up, if simpler than the one she had worn to give her testimony. But Clara's severe glance was enough to tell her that there was no frock, now, not in heaven or on earth, that could restore her honour.

'Egg phosphate, please,' she said.

Her old friend, whose life she had once saved from a firepit, refused to meet her eye, and wiped her hands down her apron as if she had touched something disgusting. Then she set about the cranks and spigots of the soda fountain with a certain fury. Crushed ice and tart phosphate were finished with an angry spurt of soda water, and she left the drink on the counter without a word.

Lucy watched Clara's back – the busyness of her shoulder blades as she washed down the already clean mirrors. This was the kind of disdain that would meet her for the rest of her life, she supposed. Sliding a shining dollar onto the counter, she took a sip of the slush, welcoming the freeze that streaked through her gut; the clean slice through her shame.

Worse was to come. Neither her stepfather nor her spoiled and brittle mother knew anything of her disgrace, because the subjects of gossip were often the last to know. But it wouldn't be long before she was packed off on the train to Lexington, made to live out her spinster years in the service of her maiden aunt, who had survived swallowing her false teeth but lost the better part of her voice.

She could hear her mother, lamenting that her plainest and chuffiest daughter had turned out to be desperate and loose; rejected by Trout even when she was bordering on naked. Now that she stood accused, she had even less understanding than before why it mattered which parts of a man's body might or might not have touched her own. How could it change her meaning in the world? – as if she were a book whose pages could be written and rewritten by the reader, while she was supposed to do nothing but yield to their ink.

'Miss Power,' she said, relieved to see the midwife's tall silhouette against the glare of the window.

'Miss Frye.' Ann was matter-of-fact, finessing a paper-wrapped parcel into her mysterious bag that held all the secrets of the birthing room.

'You're still talking to me?' Surely Ann would not judge her, one way or the other. Nobody knew the women of Greenbrier County the way Miss Power did. She had seen them at their best, and their very worst, and knew that in spite of their mistakes, they were held close by God and loved by Him.

But Miss Power gave her a quizzical look. 'If I stopped talking to everyone who disappoints me, Lucy,' she said drily, 'I'd be very lonesome indeed.'

The midwife bustled out onto the sidewalk, skirt trailing in the dust, and heaved her clattering burden onto her old buggy. Lucy followed.

'You know I didn't do it . . . what Trout said.' She was surprised to hear how thin and unconvincing her voice was, how it grew quieter as Ann's face took an ugly twist toward righteousness. Then all at once, instead of trying to appease the midwife, she pulled open the fussy ribbon of her bonnet, and yanked the blue confection from her head. 'You know what? Even if I was guilty,' she said, 'I still wouldn't be sorry. What about *your* sins, Miss Power? You don't think it's a vice to feast on other women's shame?'

Cool and superior, the midwife lifted her eyebrows. 'Speaking of shame,' she said, 'isn't that Mary Jane Heaster?' Her gaze spilled toward the next corner, where Zona's mother was walking with Sheriff Nickell. She looked frail and parched as moth wings where he was supporting her elbow. 'Seems like justice might finally be done,' Ann said with malice. 'If there's one testimony that can set that poor man free, it's Mary Jane's.'

Nickell and Mary Jane didn't turn for the front of the courthouse. Instead, they crossed over to Randolph Street, the sheriff easing her down the steep slope. They were heading toward the dim chamber at the back of the court building, the place where Lucy had been sworn in with the aid of a shiny Bible.

She threw her hat at Ann's feet, the ostrich plumes shivering, and picked up her skirts. A fast hopscotch saw her over the stones of the crosswalk, and as she rushed down the hill, her ankle twisted in one of the road's dry ruts. Limping along the railing, she at last came to the corner. Mary Jane was already gone, leaving Preston and Gilmer's dire warnings about Mrs Heaster echoing in Lucy's head.

Here was the horror of the prelude, that moment when she must imagine Trout emerging to freedom through the front door of the courthouse, Constable Shawver slapping him affectionately on the back. He would return to the house in Livesay as if nothing had happened. And if Zona were to be remembered at all, it would be as a weak and muddled woman who had brought about her own demise.

Lucy struggled back up the hill, the sky white with heat. Turning into the courthouse, she saw the lobby mobbed with people, jostling for a chance to get into the gallery. *Make way!* one of the women shouted. *It's Lucy Frye.* A thrilled silence fell as the whole group looked at her, wide-eyed. A path cleared through their number, allowing her to walk, notorious, into the court-room, because she had a role, it seemed, in their vile theatre.

The benches in the gallery were filled to bursting, and she trembled with gratitude as she saw Bessie, dressed in her full weeds, arm held high in greeting.

Lucy rushed to her side. 'Did you hear?' she whispered.

'Yes, yes.' Bessie pulled her onto the bench. 'Last night I sent Armsted to town with beef tea for Mary Jane, and she begged him to bring her to Rucker's house, wanting to have her say. I reckon that old coot told the whole county. Wants a big audience while he tries to make a fool out of her.'

With that, Sheriff Nickell emerged through the door to the court, guiding the frail Mary Jane, until he succeeded in depositing her on the front bench. The terrific silence that met her arrival decayed into islands of muttering and laughter. She looked abject in the face of this ridicule, her usual pride extinguished; a ruin of her former self inside her copious black dress. But at her nape was a bow of green velvet, and Lucy supposed that Zona's heavenly hand might have guided her mother to the star-shaped pendant today, so that in some small way, Mary Jane might not be as alone as she felt.

In the row ahead of Lucy, Jacob and Alfred Heaster each had the rancorous air of a man unfairly detained, seeming to itch to be anywhere but here. The court went through the same clockwork motions that it performed every morning – the court reporter, the jurors, the attorneys, the swaggering defendant, the judge all slotting into place. Preston's mouth betrayed his irritation, while Gilmer beside him had a look of thunder.

'Mr Rucker,' McWhorter said, brisk, 'the defence will call its first witness.'

The attorney breathed loudly through his moustache. 'Your honour,' he said. 'Gentlemen.' He beamed a smile across the dozen faces in the jury box, allowing their curiosity to bristle. 'The defence calls . . . Mrs Jacob Heaster.'

'Silence,' McWhorter said.

This reproach was enough to dampen the thrill that rippled through the gallery, and in the riotous quiet, Mary Jane stood up. Spindly, she walked in creaking manner toward the stand, Rucker hovering alongside. He was persistent as a horsefly, offering one hand in support. She declined him, but he kept his arm out in readiness, as if to mock her stubborn refusal.

The cross-rails of the chair knocked the last of the wind from her lungs, hands resting loose in her lap. With the green lustre of Zona's star at Mary Jane's throat, Lucy could not decide whether she resembled an old woman or a delicate child.

'Would you like some water?' Rucker said as the witness licked her dry lips. He was drawing attention to her weakness, his hands posed as if ready to catch a falling house of cards.

'No,' she said.

There was shock in the gallery at her worsening condition; her dull eyes and vulnerable expression.

'Tell the jury, please,' Rucker said, 'what is your name?'

'Mrs Jacob Heaster,' she said, her voice much quieter than the bold, smoky tones that Lucy had once been used to hearing on the Heasters' porch.

'You'll have to speak up. Turn toward the jury and repeat your name,' Rucker said.

'My name is Mary Jane Heaster,' she rasped. 'And I live in Meadow Bluff, Greenbrier County.'

'And tell me, what was your relation to the deceased, Zona Shue?'

'She was my daughter. My only girl.'

'And you claim there was an extraordinary occurrence after her burial,' he said, the gallery seeming to hunker down with him, ready for the pounce. 'Mrs Heaster, do you believe that you saw your daughter's ghost?'

'I do.' Mary Jane's glance flitted to the counsel desk where Preston and Gilmer were seated. 'I said as much in my statement. My nephew Thomas gave a written account of my last vision.' The boy himself looked on from the bench, the speed of his bamboo fan increasing.

'You say that the child, Thomas, took an account of your final vision; does this mean that there were others? How many times do you claim to have seen Zona Shue's ghost, Mrs Heaster?'

Mary Jane seemed frantic, gripping the arms of the chair as if she could sense impending disaster. But there was no escape now.

'Mrs Heaster,' McWhorter said, exasperated, 'answer the question.'

Her lower lip bunched upward, chin trembling, and a type of satisfaction seemed to sweep the room. Mary Jane's exposure was delicious to this rabble, her impending humiliation mouth-watering. Trout leaned back, relaxed, boots sliding noisily across the floor, as blithe as Zona's mother was brittle.

'My girl,' she stuttered, 'she came to me four times. First night I saw her, well, she came back and told me that Trout got mad at her the night she died. Angry that she didn't have meat cooked for his supper.'

'To be clear, Mrs Heaster, you're telling the jury that you saw your dead daughter with your own eyes? The deceased Zona Shue?'

'I did.' She clutched at the fabric of her skirt, twisting handfuls of cloth. 'I saw her standing right there in the bedroom, not so long after I went up for the night.'

'And you are sure that this was not a dream, Mrs Heaster? Founded upon your distressed condition of mind?'

'No, sir. I've sworn to tell the truth.' Her words were choked, her tongue seeming to cleave to the roof of her mouth. Lucy froze as Mary Jane's face turned quite blank for a moment. But then she exhaled very deeply, before taking a coarse and cleansing breath. When she came to, it was with fresh vitality, blinking and shaking her head as if she had just emerged from water. 'I can tell you,' she said, 'that night I was wide awake as I ever was.'

The skin of her face was brightening, a little flush coming into her cheeks, her skin growing smoother. And as if she were trying to get more comfortable, she stretched her back up straight and her neck out long.

'Mrs Heaster,' Rucker said, amused, 'you claim to have seen your deceased daughter as if in flesh and blood?'

A toothy smile now, showing the chipped canine that Mary Jane was always careful to cover; a wide, impish, familiar grin. And perhaps feeling the same wildness that squalled in Lucy's own chest, Jacob and Alfred sat forward, almost lifting from their seats. Here was a red tinge to her lips as she chewed them, gathering her thoughts and honing them to a point.

'Yes,' she said in a bright tone. 'As if in flesh and blood, standing right there in the dark. In a chequered dress, brown and cream, the buttons sewn with that cornflower-blue thread. Trout remembers it, don't you?' she said, leaning to one side so that she might see past Rucker, eyes taking on new lustre. 'The only dresses and hairstyles allowed were the ones you liked. Tell them all how you wouldn't let Dr Knapp open the collar when he came to the house.'

Trout's lips parted in nervous astonishment. He held her gaze, quite bold at first, but soon flinched, uncertain where he might look to avoid the sting of her attention. She picked at her little fingernail – *tick tick tick* – just as Zona used to when she was hurt or angry. It gave Lucy a peculiar sliding feeling, the real giving way to the unreal as Mary Jane's jaw cocked after the same habit as her daughter's. Bessie's hand gripped Lucy's as they watched her eyes roving the gallery, seeming to see the room for the first time. Then just as the clouds might clear to reveal the sun, singular and radiant, here, suddenly and com-pletely, was Zona.

'Mrs Heaster, please drink a little water.' Wrong-footed, Rucker carried a dripping beaker from his counsel desk. 'There's no cause for this agitation,' he said, hinting at madness.

'No cause?' Eyes closed, she pinched the bridge of her nose and gave a pant of incredulity. Then came the uncanny sound of Zona's snorting laughter. 'I'll be the best judge of that. He had plenty for his supper that night, you know. Look at me, Trout,' she said. 'How many different jellies were there?' These were

Zona's urgent tones, every sentence seeming to burst out of a gate before smoothing to its end. 'You had apple. Pear. Cherry. Raspberry.' As she named each flavour, she bent back a different finger on her hand, the digits supple and curving; the same gesture that Zona had used so many times when accounting for pipes and rivets and ash pans on the Heaster Wagon. This was likely the reason why Jacob's face was setting hard as concrete, convinced by the evidence of his eyes and ears.

'Mrs Heaster, the supper menu aside . . . ' Rucker paused here to give the jury a knowing glance, 'what else did you discuss with your dead daughter?'

Her brilliant gaze lighted upon him, and she said, 'Beg your pardon, sir, but who are you?'

The intelligence of her expression was not only a match for her daughter's, but was even wiser and abler than Zona had been in life. *The dead are more perfect than the living*, Mary Jane had always said, seasoned by their knowledge of the beyond. Mistaking her question for confusion, Rucker hooked his thumbs into the pockets of his linen jacket, and addressed her as he might a child.

'I'm Dr William Rucker,' he said, very loud. 'For the defence. Remember?'

She stood up from the chair and offered her hand, her attitude making her look several inches taller than Mary Jane. 'Let me introduce myself,' she said. 'I am Elva Zona Heaster. Forgive me, all of you, if you cannot recognise me in this guise. But I have come here today to tell you the truth about Trout Shue. I repeat, I am the woman who was known as Elva Zona Heaster, and I was born in Meadow Bluff, Greenbrier County, in the year 1872.'

The fear and amazement of those many who had known her sent a blistering charge through the crowd. Mary Jane's earlier frailness was gone, replaced by Zona's poise and conviction. She advanced her waiting hand, giving Rucker no choice but to shake it.

He gripped her fingers, and whatever he felt at her touch, his complexion turned quite pale. 'I have no further questions for the witness,' he said, retreating toward his desk.

She laughed kindly, as if at his simplicity. And the ripple of a great swallow betrayed Trout's panic as he glared up at his counsellor. 'Dr William Rucker doesn't need to ask me any questions, does he, Trout?' she said. 'You and me. We know what happened. We can tell the whole story together, and everyone will see you for what you are.'

Rucker blanched, his pleading eyes on McWhorter. But with his every hair seeming to stand on end, the judge paid the counsellor no heed. There was something extraordinary in train – too uncanny for interruption – as she stepped down from the witness box and began to cross the floor. She walked with Zona's effortless gait, the same long strides. Trout whispered frantically to Gardner, elbows tight to his ribs as if shielding himself. And where there had been mocking and laughter in the gallery, there was now only the hunger to hear what this young and vivid and enlightened woman had to say.

'Why won't you look at me, Trout?' Drawing close to the opposing side of the counsel desk, she lifted Mary Jane's black skirts out to full width, making herself evident even in the corner of his eye.

Eager for the answer to this question, the gaze of every juror veered toward the defendant as he lifted his face to her.

An innocent man might have been angry with Mary Jane, or worried for her, or might have made light of things. But Trout wore a grim, resentful expression, lips very straight and white. Blotches of red bloomed on his cheeks, so florid that Lucy could almost feel them pulse. It took the full of his strength to look at the familiar spirit dwelling in those eyes; the soul whose glinting sweetness sent a blade falling through Lucy, as if preparing her, already, for inevitable departure.

'Put your hands on the table,' she said, resting the tips of her fingers on the wood.

'Your honour.' Incensed, Gardner rose to standing. 'The defence has no further questions for this witness.'

'But, Justice McWhorter,' she said, turning to the judge with an easy smile. 'The defence is trying to prove that my mother is insane. Give me the chance to say my piece, and you'll soon see if this is true.'

McWhorter did not bother to consult his shining gavel. Unstuck by her words, he stared as if trying to picture Zona the way she had once been. 'Very well,' he said. 'Continue.'

'Show me your hands, Trout. Like this.' She pressed her palms on the oak of the counsel desk, and waited for him to do the same.

Trout set his big, cramped hands on the wood.

'Hold them flat,' she said.

Bitter and insolent, he straightened his fingers. Whether he refused to speak, or was afraid to, Lucy could not tell, and all around her, the gallery crackled with awe.

'Blacksmith's hands,' she said, the sight of them turning her very sober. 'Strong from hammering metal, and breaking scrap, and working those bellows. Hannah knew these hands, too,' she said. 'Oh, don't look surprised. Of course I know about the snowstorm – what you did to her.'

Trout's chair squeaked backward, and his feet kicked out under the desk. But he held his tongue, pressed his hands even harder to the table.

'You thought you'd get your way,' she said, her voice hard with anger and pain. 'That you could take my life and I'd say nothing. You forced me from this world, Trout Shue. But I've found my way back to tell on you.'

Her spirit seemed to flare, and he welled up with cold tears of frustration and fury.

'These fingers,' she said, looking down at his scrubbed flesh. 'Do you know how long you kept them wrapped about my throat?'

She held his angry gaze, a jolt going through the gallery as her eyes lit with sudden fright. A shoal of purple shadows appeared stark on her neck, and her hands flew to her throat, desperate fingers grasping, as if struggling to release some terrible constriction. All the while, she was fixed on Trout with dread and confusion, gasping for breath. His feet scrabbled against the floor, chair skidding into the rail behind him, as all life seemed to vanish from her eyes, her head falling backward at the most unnatural angle.

She might have been dangling above the floor, her body was so limp. And the crowd watched on, in perfect suspense, until there was the first sound of air rushing into her lungs. Her neck drew back into alignment, and Trout sat shaking beneath her gaze.

'You remember,' she said, the scorch of betrayal in her hoarse voice. 'How many minutes was it, Trout? Five? Six? A long time to squeeze your hands around a woman's neck. You were in no hurry. Plenty of time to think.'

She closed her eyes, drawing her mouth into a line, as if trying to stem the immense force of her sadness. Only Bessie's hand – a steady anchor – stopped Lucy from running to her.

'He'll tell you,' she said, 'that I drove him to it. He'll tell you about my grandmother's fine tortoiseshell comb, and how he wanted me to run it through his hair while he sat in the rocking chair. Remember how I did that for you every night? From the day you asked me to marry you, no matter how tired or busy. Until I realised that it wasn't because you liked it. You just wanted me to obey you in all of these little ways – to be frightened of you.' Her fingers rested light on her temples. 'And I was so very afraid. Terrified to tell anyone. Even Lucy. You remember, don't you? How you threatened to kill me if I ever saw her again. I never got to tell her she was right about you from the start. Never told her I was sorry for all those mean letters you made me write.'

Her tormented gaze washed out over the gallery, and Lucy felt as if her blood were shining out in answer. But Trout shot to his feet, face disfigured, squaring his frame.

'Stop talking,' he said.

'Only reason I came here is to talk, and you need to listen. The men on this jury,' she said, drawing the tender gaze of every man in the box, 'they need to know how you arranged things. How I came to be lying, just so, over by the staircase.'

'I said stop.' A tide of alternations passed through Trout's body, returning him to his natural state. Big and stony and threatening.

'See?' she said, her sorrow infecting the whole of the

courtroom. 'You're not sorry you killed me. You don't care that I'll never see my girl again.'

Trout struck faster than a copperhead snake, squeezing his left hand about her neck so that her chin was thrown upward. And in that instant before Gardner could haul him back, Lucy saw the exquisite terror of her expression – the shock of suffering his hands on her again so that he might be exposed.

'Your honour.' Rucker rubbed Trout's back, though his client was rigid beneath his hand. 'The court is allowing undue stress on the defendant.'

With grave amazement, McWhorter lifted his gavel, feeling its weight and eyeing its polished silver. 'The witness,' he said, 'will return to the stand.'

Lucy watched as her friend's grief seemed to rise in a great surge, causing her to sway on her feet. Her nose and mouth were lifted high into the air, as if above rising water, the whisper of her black dress the only sound as she turned and walked toward the witness box, seeming all at once in desperate need of rest.

'Zona?' A shaky voice rose from the gallery, and Jacob stood up.

She stopped in her tracks, her expression growing distant as she faced the room, her head tilted with what might have been the surprise and pain of seeing her father. Alfred stumbled to standing by Jacob's side, and Lucy, too, felt herself rising to her feet, pulling Bessie up beside her. All four were motionless in the gallery, electrified, as she looked from one face to the next. When her gaze fell on Lucy, she pressed one finger to the green star at her throat, and a current of love and rage and understanding flowed between them.

A different memory seemed to rise behind her eyes, then. She looked down at Mary Jane's skinny, worn hands, seeming to recognise and adore them where they were clenched. A kind of twilight was claiming her, Lucy thought, as she extended her little finger, frowning at the old, rough piece of silver that Trout had passed off as a wedding band. She pitched to one side, twisting it off with what seemed to be the last of her strength, and let it slip from her hand so that the hoop rolled in a wide arc into the gallery. It rattled to a tinny stop, the flush and shine of youth waning as her skin greyed, until there were only the sharp bones and shadows of Mary Jane's vacant face. Then she crumpled, as if dropped from a height, head sounding on the floorboards.

from:

THE TRIAL OF TROUT SHUE

A TRUE STORY
CONTAINING HITHERTO
SUPPRESSED FACTS

by Lucia C. Frye

July 1, 1897 was the kind of day worshipped only by okra. The plants reached their broad leaves high and wide in praise of the merciless sun, while inside the Greenbrier County Courthouse, twelve men, exhausted by that very same heat, retired to a pan-elled room for deliberation.

They had spent the morning on the uncom-fortable chairs of the jury box, listening to the closing arguments in the case of the State v. Edward Erasmus Shue. Speeches were elaborate and lengthy on both sides, mean-ing that the men had taken page after page of notes, using the cheap journals and pencils provided by the court. Only the jury's foreman, Mr Terence McClung, had chosen to make his records in ink, at one time calling for recess to change the glass vial on his fountain pen.

It was their tenth day in the custody and care of the county sheriff, all dozen residing at the Tanager boarding house on the very eastern edge of town. Separated from their families and regular occupations, they were denied free movement around Lewisburg, where gossip and speculation was rife in every store, restaurant and drinking house. Only the evidence in the court reports – the records of speech made in mechanical shorthand by Miss Minnie Grose before being typed up in Roman alphabet – could now be considered by the jury. And they were instructed to dismiss all else from their minds.

The closing arguments that would have been ringing in their heads were as well matched as they were different. The Honourable John Preston, for the prosecution, chose to deliver his speech in intimate manner, his hand often seizing the rail that separated him from the jurors, ensuring that every point bit home. He drew a convincing picture of Trout's behaviour in those hours between Zona's death and her burial, miming the fake grief of the accused when he had 'shrewdly impeded Dr George Knapp's post-mortem examination'. He described how Trout had hidden his wife's injuries beneath 'an elaborate costume, dressing her without the consent of her family'. And he recalled the vivid testimonies of those witnesses who had seen Trout bolstering the loose head of the deceased in her casket. 'His only motive was to disguise her severed neck,' he said. 'It was not shock or grief that made him act this way. It was the fear of being caught.'

Dr William Rucker ably drew the jury into another scenario, his speech very quick and sharp, as if trying to shock the men out of Preston's near-hypnotism. 'Here,' he claimed, 'was a newly married man, who loved his wife in every manner that pleases God, the affection between them very great, as we have heard from Mr Walter Neely.' He insisted that the jury could not find a man guilty of first-degree murder – a capital offence – when the only evidence against him was weak and circumstantial. 'Dr Knapp let him down. Left the defendant to dress his wife for burial without any suggestion that her death had been caused by violence. With her proven naivety and easy morals, we can suppose that it was the victim herself who let the real killer into her home. Zona Shue was far from averse to . . . how should we say it? . . . low-flung rendezvous. The jealousy and appetites of another man lost her her life, her grieving husband subjected to rumour and slander.'

Mary Jane Heaster was not mentioned by either the prosecution or the defence, her testimony having been struck from the record the moment her slight figure was carried from the courtroom. But even as Minnie Grose carried out the judge's order, it was clear that Mrs Heaster's appearance had made an indelible mark on the mind of every juror.

Three months after the verdict was delivered, out on the plains of his cattle farm in Richlands, where the bluegrass has raised many of his shorthorns to exceptional size, the foreman, Terence McClung, reflected on the jury's deliberations. 'It was my signature on that verdict,' he said, 'but everyone in the jury room gave their opinion, very orderly and fair.' As for the testimony of Mary Jane Heaster, and whether or not it had any lasting influence on the jury, he said, 'I can't tell you what was on the mind of any other man. McWhorter told us all to ignore it, and that's what we did, the very best that we could. But seeing as we're free to talk about it now – the way Trout Shue put his hands on her when she was accusing him? Well, that was the first time I thought he was capable of it. Of killing a woman, I mean.'

The people of Greenbrier County are divided as to whether or not the spirit of Zona Heaster Shue possessed her mother in the courtroom that day. 'I think Trout Shue bullied Zona to keep her quiet when she was alive,' said Bessie Harford, a close friend of the Heaster family, 'and he killed her to shut her up for ever. Well, he might have silenced her body, but there was no controlling her soul.' Mrs Harford's remarks echo those of many others in the gallery who believed that Mary Jane had been taken over by the essence of the departed.

By contrast, Mr Gill Weber, who operates the largest glove store in Lewisburg, said that Mrs Heaster 'should be locked up with every other demented Ophelia who cannot manage her own distress. It's a bad example, a woman like that making things up to bypass every rule and regulation.'

None of those interviewed suggested a third possibility – that Mary Jane Heaster was neither a clairvoyant nor a fraud, but an ordinary woman whose instinct would not lie dormant. And against her own will, just as water always finds a path, her voice gathered strength until it burst through every dam that government and society had built to contain it. A person of her sex will not be heard when she argues or pushes or demands. She must, instead, transfigure, and break herself upon the wheel of power.

The married women of our communities are broadcast far and wide, like so many seeds, each anchored and isolated in her own furrow. If a husband chooses to entrap his wife, she must spend her life navigating his web, finding those strands of silk that will not land her in his jaws. And we are, perhaps, more likely to judge this woman for her behaviour – for her apparent silence, and absence from our lives – than we are to investigate her plight. Until that day when she is lost, her voice and testimony forever extinguished by his violence.

Deliberations lasted for one hour and ten minutes before the jurors returned to the court, Terence McClung gripping a folded piece of paper that Sheriff Nickell passed up to the bench. Justice McWhorter read the verdict to the court.

We the jury find the prisoner Edward Erasmus Shue, alias Trout Shue, guilty of murder of the first degree as charged in the within indictment, and we further find that he be punished by confinement in the penitentiary.

'The *Greenbrier Independent* got it right,' McClung says. 'It was the most horrible, cruel, revolting crime we've ever seen in this county.'

There is no such thing as true justice, because the life of the victim cannot be restored. No punishment, and no contrition, will ever return Zona to those who loved her, nor deliver them to the painless state in which they existed before. Because I will never see her again for as long as I live, I, Lucia Clementine Frye, best friend of the murdered woman, want to believe, if only for a moment, that in the courtroom, it was really she.

18 | MARY JANE HEASTER

Pier 54, Chelsea, Manhattan

June 23, 1913

Mary Jane looked up from the letter that she had smoothed across the desk in her top-floor hotel room to see that here at last was the ship, gliding monumentally along the green Hudson. The vast, brilliant phantom was sleek, its four enormous funnels crimson against the blue sky. And she was taken by the dizzying feeling that the land was sliding in place of the ship; that she was drifting in parallel to this black cliff of steel with a small white city stacked upon its summit.

Out on the flat, glinting water, the ocean liner was another realm filled with souls. None was visible from this vantage, though she knew that so many hundreds must already be out on deck, sucking in the American air, as elated by any stretch of muddy coastline as they were by the concrete skyscrapers that reared beyond. The rest of the passengers would be rattling around the interior, she supposed, preparing to be reborn when they docked on the island. Amidst all this imagined excitement and chaos, she tried to suspend one particular spirit in her distant care; as if, through concentration alone, she might hold the girl in a tender sling.

The RMS *Mauretania* stalled on the water, now, propellers reversing in roaring battle with foaming brine, getting ready to dock at Pier 54. The vast pink granite archway that led out to the pier was gleaming on the far side of the street. The window frames rattled with the ship's thrum, and Mary Jane's irritation collapsed into nothing, as if washed by a lapping wave.

The wait had been several hours longer than Eugenia had promised, the time very fraught. She folded Mrs Wylie's monogrammed letter along its deep creases and returned it to its cream-white envelope. Over the last year, all of Eugenia's letters had been short and blunt and dismissive, typed and signed by her secretary. Except for this final letter, which had arrived to Meadow Bluff written in the adoptive mother's own hand.

Mary Jane had expected it to bring nothing but more fury and disappointment. She pressed her fingers to the address; the way that Eugenia had scribed *Mrs Jacob Heaster* in narrow, elegant letters. The shapes were familiar to her in the same way that she knew the rise and thrust of every tree on the farm, the way they branched against hill and sky. She remembered the script from those dark nights before the child was born, when she sat wakeful in the parlour, reading and rereading that special letter in which Eugenia had first agreed to take the baby. The Richmond lady wrote in much the same neat cursive as any other wealthy, polished woman, she supposed. Still, to dull her fears, she had convinced herself that the script was full of special signs that Mrs Wylie was to make a fine mother.

There was no longer any need for such fear or desperation as she slotted the letter into her carpet bag. It fell, light and crisp, on top of the rest of her cherished cargo – that parcel of dog-eared letters, and that rolled-up portrait, which she had protected on both stifling trains to New York by holding the bag very steady on her lap.

The nose of the ship slid closer to shore, bringing the girl who according to Eugenia was *robust and healthy*, and sailing from Cherbourg with her tutor, who'd had *the pleasant duty of escorting her to Venice, Florence, Rome, Geneva & Paris*. She was learning to speak *French & Italian*, Mrs Wylie mentioned, among a list of her other accomplishments, like *ballet* and *piano*. Zona's daughter, Mary Jane thought, was exactly the type of darling creature who had never shucked an ear of corn or milked a goat. The type who could never survive alone, not if she was gifted the best farm in Greenbrier County along with one hundred head of strapping cattle. And she was pulling so close to shore, now, that there was nothing to be seen of the ship beyond the massive pier gate except for the dark rims of its funnels.

She picked up her small hat from the quilt and, fingers trembling, turned to the foxed mirror to pull it on. It was more of a cap, really; white silk with green velvet edging. Although she had paid little attention to her appearance since Zona died, she had chosen the moss-coloured velvet to flatter her eyes and to match the green pendant that she had worn for all these years about her neck. With the curls of her salt-and-pepper bangs pinched into a neat row, she practised a smile so that her cheeks didn't sink so much into those gaps where her molars had fallen away.

It doesn't matter if she's not like you, Jacob had said. *Do not judge, or you too will be judged.* She stooped to lift her bag, which felt impossibly light given the value of what was within, and coiled down and down the stairs.

Pushing out into the crowded lobby, she joined the swarm of men and women dressed in their Sunday best. A porter was cutting a path through the melee with a trolley of leather valises and hatboxes, and she followed in his wake, squeezing by an earnest couple where they unfurled a stretch of floral wallpaper on the polished brass of the reception desk. There was a name written on the reverse: *Jozef*, inked in big letters. Perhaps they were meeting a relative for the first time, too. The growing reality of all these strange yet familiar figures on the ship made her feel unstuck, her footsteps uncertain as she emerged onto the sidewalk.

She shaded her eyes, glancing through the liquid sunlight toward the big white letters of *Cunard* where they shone above the gate to the pier. It was the same kind of mellow afternoon as the one when she and Jacob had taken Zona up to Little Sewell for her christening. The air and light had been whisked to an even gloss as they set off. He had carried their girl while she drove, Zona's tufts of blonde hair pale and soft as corn silks against the dark sleeve of his coat. It was only as the holy water dribbled over her daughter's scalp that she had felt the urge to gather Zona's little body back to herself, shocked all over again by her smallness; this creature packed so tight with potential that it had frightened her. She had never known how to help her daughter contain it – this silent hum in her flesh. Her answer had been to convince Zona that she was worth less than she believed. And as she took long strides toward the pier, she could see, at last, that it had not been for her daughter's sake that she had drawn cloaks over everything that dazzled. It had been for her own, to drown out the strong feeling that she could not compare.

Walking ever closer to the shining *Miss Julia Elisabeth Wylie*, the years seemed to unravel in her wake. She could feel them streaming behind her, like so many tattered ribbons trailing into dust and smoke. It seemed to her that there was a clean note of Elisabeth on the air, sharp and fresh, slicing the brackish gust that funnelled through the opened gate.

How bitter everything seemed from this vantage; all those ways that she and Jacob had tried to live with their ungovernable grief. Trout had been no more than two weeks in Moundsville when she first noticed the quality of Jacob's agitation. He worked without rest, even taking on those jobs reserved for the smaller boys, like weeding the fields and scaring the birds. He had tired himself out for the distraction of it, craving a purer and more constant kind of pain. She had so few memories from those days after the trial, having been drunk on her own suffering. Yet she had a clear picture of Jacob in the wheatfield, remarkable for the fact that there was no yellow pencil in his cap, walking too close to the oncoming wheel of the McCormick reaper. She knew the meaning of it, that wavering intent on his face. And whatever it was that stopped her from running, or crying out – whether it was badness, or bottomless understanding – she still did not know.

The breaking of the flesh, the splintering of the bone had

been over in a second. Bruising and stitching had healed into a crooked tattoo of remembrance that brought him strange relief. Even now, when folks saw him limping, the toes of his left foot scraping along, they joked about wrestling angels. And while he might tell them about the terrible force of the reaper, he never mentioned that moment in the courtroom when he believed that his departed daughter was looking him in the eye. Seeing her wretched, he had been unable to survive his shame intact.

Motor cars trundled along the cobbles, heavy and low-set and dark, except for their headlamps, those huge, unseeing bug eyes that shone brighter than a fish's skin, even in the middle of the day. There was a jam where ten or more of the machines had parked right in front of the pier gate, their engines coughing and droning while a flock of stevedores weaved between them, shirts open and pants rolled above their boots. She followed them through the arch, and came upon the edge of the water, where the black hull of the ship rose sheer above her, causing her heart to quicken with awe as she elbowed through the crush of people gathered on the platform. Two dockers heaved the last of the big mooring ropes around a bollard, and a great cheer went up. A flotilla of handkerchiefs was set to waving in the breeze, signalling to those bright faces that smiled out of the portholes. Others, tiny and indiscernible, shouted down from the upper decks, voices drowned by the excitement below.

Amidst this happy confusion, fear and oil and smoke and brine seemed to swill in Mary Jane's stomach. *Lucia Clementine Frye has explained everything* – that was what Eugenia's letter had said. *About you. About Zona.* And while she could never thank

Lucy enough for her intervention, panic began to surge about what Elisabeth might hope or expect. She would prefer to meet Lucy in place of her grandmother, perhaps. No dried-out old countrywoman with twisted tobacco-stained fingers could compete with the vibrant and modern journalist, no matter how neat the cap that Mary Jane had pulled down over her ears. The Wylies were likely the kind of rich folk who collected eccentrics like Lucy Frye. She had told them about *The Woman Engine*, no doubt, and *The Main Stream*, and every other failed women's newspaper that she had founded. Her hare-brained career little mattered when she had a fellow writer for a husband, a younger man happy to ride around Chicago in the sidecar of her motorcycle, apparently admiring of the fact that his beat-reporting wife refused to cover anything but crime and politics.

But worst of all, what if Lucy had been pushy enough to send Eugenia her coverage of the trial – those precious papers that she never did get published, what with so many editors telling her that *the ghost part was good* but *nobody wants to hear about a man killing his wife*. If Elisabeth had read these accounts, what class of mortal did she think would be waiting for her on this jetty?

A small door opened where a long, soaring gangway had been secured to one of the upper decks, and a gong sounded within, its crash accompanying a stream of first-class passengers where they issued from the ship. They headed for the tower whose flights of stairs would bring them down to the platform, and very soon the pier was flooded with men in finely tailored suits, and women in silk mousseline and fur stoles, the brims of their hats nearly as wide as umbrellas.

With nowhere to escape to except into the slick green of the river, Mary Jane stood frozen in the corner. Until she saw her — Elisabeth — where she had stopped on the stairs to lean out over one of the rails. A white chiffon tunic fell to her thighs, her long, straight underskirt in pale satin. She wore a simple sash of rose-coloured velvet, her sleeves trimmed with tiny silk flowers. The shape of the head was astonishingly familiar, a white scarf tied about her dark hair in a fashionable band. And she searched the crowd with that same unapologetic enthusiasm that her mother always had; with those same wide-set eyes and open countenance.

Mary Jane lifted her carpet bag into the air — caught herself waving it, with both hands, like a lunatic. *Here*, she wanted to shout. *I have saved her words for you. And here is her picture, painted by her own hand. I promise you, Elisabeth — this is a mother who would have been brave enough, always, to tell her daughter the truth.*

Dearest Beth,

I am keeping too many secrets. And the trouble is most of them are not my own. You are the only secret that is fully mine — and as you can tell from my letters, I hope to tell the world about you one day if you will let me.

Remembering you is a fond feeling, like a jewel in the softness of my belly, a star crowning that place where you once grew. And I hold a picture of you in my mind so that I can gaze on your little face very often.

Not all secrets feel so easy or so nice, my darling Beth. I do not believe that you should hide anything that hurts — that feels sharp or raw in your brain, your ribs, your heart — because it will never go away. Not even if you keep it there until the very end of the world. Find a way to release it, a loving ear to understand.

I want you to know that <u>Love Is Warmth and Affection</u>. It shines like sunlight on all the shadiest places of the soul, and gives them air, so that they might start to green over and grow. Shame cannot raise its head as easily as before, clustering pale and strange as mushrooms in rotting places.

Love does not come in any other guise. It never wears a mask. We must always believe the face that we are shown — cast off our hesitation and our doubt.

There is so much more I would like to tell you. No woman, once she has lighted a lamp of knowledge, should hide it in a cellar, but should put it on a stand, so that all those who enter may live by its glow. Look, Elisabeth! This is my candle for you. Call to me wherever I am. And I promise you, my darling — I will always answer.

Yours ever truly,

Your mother,

Zona

Acknowledgements

Thank you to my agent, Nelle Andrew, for your talent, strength and integrity. It's been my great fortune to have you understand and steer this novel since its early days. You've helped me to grow as both writer and human. Many thanks, also, to the team at Rachel Mills Literary for your essential support; Charlotte Bowerman, Alexandra Cliff and Rachel Mills.

To my editor, Rose Tomaszewska, who has shone subtle light into every corner of this novel, I'm grateful for your intelligence, empathy, agility and elegance. If flaws remain, they can only be the author's own.

Astute, precise and collegial, my thanks to Joanna Kramer and Jane Selley for guiding this text to completion.

I remain delighted and amazed that The Red Bird Sings has found its home at the iconic Virago Press. My gratitude to the talented professionals at Virago, Little, Brown and Hachette without whom this book could never hope to set foot on stage. Let it be known that: Charlotte Stroomer designed the cover; marketing is by Celeste Ward-Best; publicity is by Stephanie Elise Melrose; production is by Marie Hrynczak; rights are handled by Helena Doree, Kate Hibbert, Andy Hine and

Jessica Purdue; sales are by Lucy Helliwell, Caitriona Row and Hannah Methuen. I am very lucky to work alongside each of you. I'm hugely grateful for the brilliant team at Hachette Ireland: Jim Binchy, Elaine Egan, Breda Purdue and Ruth Shern. My thanks, also, to those who have so kindly welcomed the novel to the Virago family: Beth Farrell, Lennie Goodings, Madeleine Hall, Zoe Hood, Anna Kelly, Charlie King, Sarah Savitt and Clare Smith.

My gratitude to Lucy Cavendish College and the judges of the Lucy Cavendish Fiction Prize. Your unerring support for women's writing continues to inspire. Thank you to Gillian Stern, in particular, whose grace and generosity embody the spirit of this wonderful prize.

To the Arts Council of Ireland, An Chomhairle Ealaíon, thank you for awarding a literature bursary to assist in the writing of this novel.

Very special thanks are due to the Greenbrier Historical Society for facilitating research in the archives of the North House Museum, Lewisburg, West Virginia. I am in debt to Jane Hughes for introducing me to the nineteenth-century biennial reports of West Virginia's agricultural board, and to Janice Cooley who furnished the work of Karen Fankhauser, PhD (*The Bunger Store: Eggs, Butter and Trade*). Many thanks to Toni Ogden and Nora Venezky for allowing access to the Barracks on North Jefferson Street, and for guiding me through the rich and extensive collection of nineteenth-century farm tools temporarily housed there. My thanks, also, to AmeriCorps member, Sarah Shepherd and to Jim Costa.

Sarah Elkins, I am grateful for your help in apprehending

the folklore of the 'Greenbrier Ghost' in a contemporary, local context. Greg and Libby Johnson, I deeply appreciate your kindness; the peach jam, the guitar and Freddie Mercury.

I would like to extend my thanks to the faculty of the MFA programme in creative writing at University College Dublin, in particular, Gavin Corbett, Professor Anne Enright, Sinéad Gleeson, Katy Hayes and Dr Paula McGrath; you kindled this book into flame. Many thanks, also, to my uncommonly talented cohort: Nidhi Zak/Aria Eipe, Aingeala Flannery, Sarah Gilmartin and David Morgan O'Connor.

Niall Williams, I am grateful for your invaluable guidance when I was first charting a course for this novel. And thank you, Christine Breen. The wisdom and generosity I've experienced in Kiltumper continue to map the way.

For ongoing faith and encouragement, I'm especially grateful to Sarah Jane Carroll, Jacqui Churcher, Colleen Connolly, Claire Kilroy, Samantha McCaughren and Simone Schuemmelfeder.

Kieran D. Fitzpatrick and Honor Marie Mills, though you will never hold this book, I believe that you would have thrilled at its existence.

And to Peter, my fellow traveller: if I only have one life to live, I'm grateful to spend it with you. All of my love, always.

Who Can I Call?

If you have been affected by domestic violence or coercive control, the following organisations offer free and confidential services. Domestic abuse can take many forms; if you are uncertain about the warning signs, information is available on the below websites.

Great Britain & Northern Ireland

National Domestic Abuse Helpline
Visit www.nationaldahelpline.org.uk for access to live chat, Monday to Friday, 3 p.m. to 10 p.m. Or freephone the 24-Hour National Domestic Abuse Helpline on 0808 2000 247 (7 days a week). Live chat available online, Monday to Friday, 3 p.m. to 10 p.m. A British Sign Language Interpreter service is available from Monday to Friday, 10 a.m. to 6 p.m., and is accessible through the homepage of the website. Confidential messages can also be sent through the website; you will able to choose your preferred method of reply.

Scottish Women's Aid

Visit www.womensaid.scot for information and live chat. Or freephone Scotland's Domestic Abuse and Forced Marriage Helpline on 0800 027 1234 (24 hours a day, 7 days a week). Services will be made available in your preferred language. Contact options are also available for those with hearing and/or speech difficulties, e.g., an email service is available through helpline@sdafmh.org.uk.British Sign language (BSL) interpreting via Scotland BSL, www.contactscotland-bsl.org.

Welsh Women's Aid/Cymorth i Ferched Cymru

Visit www.welshwomensaid.org. All services are available 24 hours a day, 7 days a week. Live chat can be accessed on the 'What We Do' page of the website. Or freephone the Live Fear Free Helpline on 0808 80 10 800. Services are available by text through your mobile phone on 078600 77 333; send a message to receive a reply. If you would like to communicate by text phone (landline with keyboard), contact the helpline via Type Talk on 18001 0808 80 10 800. Welsh and English are spoken, and extensive translation services are available.

Women's Aid Federation Northern Ireland

Visit www.womensaidni.org, or freephone the 24-Hour Domestic & Sexual Violence Helpline on 0808 802 1414 (7 days a week). Live chat through website homepage, Monday to Friday, 9 a.m. to 5 p.m. Translation services are available; state your preferred language, and hold to be connected with your interpreter. For support through text, message 'support' to 07797 805 839. Or email help@dsahelpline.org. This helpline is open to all women and men affected by domestic and sexual violence.

Respect Men's Advice Line

Visit www.mensadviceline.org.uk to access the information hub. Or freephone the Men's Advice Line on 0808 8010327, Monday to Friday, 10 a.m. to 8 p.m. For email support, send a message to info@mensadviceline.org.uk. Webchat support is available Wednesday, 10 a.m. to 11.30 a.m. and 2.30 p.m. to 4 p.m. If English is not your preferred language, translation services are available. If you have difficulties with hearing or speech, services can be made available by text.

Republic of Ireland

Women's Aid

Visit www.womensaid.ie for instant messaging, or freephone 1800 341 900 (24 hours day, 7 days a week). If English is not your preferred language, telephone interpretation services are available. State your language at the beginning of the call, and you will be put on hold. It may take a few minutes to be connected with your interpreter. If you have hearing or speech difficulties, a text service is available, 8 a.m. to 8 p.m., on 087 959 7980 (7 days a week); send a message to be texted by reply.

Men's Aid

Visit www.mensaidireland.ie, or telephone the Confidential National Support Line on 01 5543811, Monday to Friday, 9 a.m. to 5 p.m. For access to services by email, send a message to hello@mensaid.ie.

Emergencies (Great Britain, Northern Ireland, Republic of Ireland)

If you are in immediate danger, call emergency services by dialling 112 or 999. It is best to speak directly to the operator. If you cannot speak, or it is not safe to speak, the operator will stay on the line with you. Wait for them to engage the protocol for silent calls. Follow the operator's instructions, including those of any automated messaging service with which the operator may connect you.

If you have difficulties with hearing or speech, it is possible to access emergency services by text; however, **your mobile phone must be pre-registered** for this service. If you are concerned for your safety, register now; do not wait for an emergency. In Great Britain and Northern Ireland, text 'register' to 999 and follow the instructions sent to you by reply. In the Republic of Ireland, register your mobile at www.112.ie/emergency-sms-service.

Aoife Fitzpatrick is a native of Dublin, Ireland. Her debut novel, *The Red Bird Sings*, won the Lucy Cavendish Fiction Prize in 2020. The winner of the inaugural *Books Ireland* short-story competition, her work has also been recognised by the Séan O'Faoláin Prize, the Elizabeth Jolley Prize and by the Writing.ie Short Story of the Year award. Aoife received an MFA in Creative Writing at University College Dublin in 2019 and, ...   ʒ, she was the recipient of a literature bursary from the Arts Council of Ireland.

Praise for *The Red Bird Sings*

'A sparkling, unusual novel that demands you turn the pages. The spirits tell me that this Irish debut author is a talent to watch' *The Times*

'Written with a compelling, lyrical intensity, *The Red Bird Sings* is a historical drama whose characters are full of a suppressed fury and haunted by a need for justice. A deeply felt and accomplished debut' Anne Enright

'Genuinely brilliant ... offers a tangible slice of life from another time and place, one that feels both fantastical and utterly believable' *Irish Times*

'Stunning ... Fitzpatrick unspools an uneasy shimmering tale of coercive control, spiritualism and staunch friendship. It's a brilliant take on the Southern Gothic' *Daily Mail*

'An utterly engrossing read, I adored it. Aoife Fitzpatrick is a powerful new voice in historical fiction' Paula McGrath

'An atmospheric debut that keeps you turning pages right until the end. Loved it' Julie Owen Moylan, author of *That Green Eyed Girl*

'Truly superb ... Compelling and lyrical in equal measure' Victoria MacKenzie, author of *For Thy Great Pain Have Mercy on My Little Pain*

'I was spellbound by this incredibly accomplished piece of historical feminist fiction. Thrilling and beautifully written' Jennie Godfrey, author of *The List of Suspicious Things*

'A historical courtroom drama and ghost story that had me on tenterhooks until the very end. Fitzpatrick has a magpie's eye for detail and eccentricity, her prose shines . . . I loved *The Red Bird Sings*' Aingeala Flannery, author of *The Amusements*

'A beautifully crafted novel about loss, faith and justice set against the backdrop of nineteenth-century West Virginia. I had to keep reading to find out what happened whilst also not wanting it to end. A brilliant debut' Alison Stockham, author of *The Cuckoo Sister*

'Aoife Fitzpatrick gives voice to a murdered woman in this powerful, unflinching study of domestic brutality. The elegant, masterful prose hums with the righteous fury of women who cannot be contained and will not be silenced . . . at its core is the moving tale of a mother's ferocious love for her child. A triumph' Nikki Marmery, author of *On Wilder Seas*

'Seriously stupendous . . . a read-late-into-the-night tense, well-up-weeping touching, truly transformational read' Meg Clothier, author of *The Book of Eve*

'Excellent, immersive historical fiction inspired by a true story. Beautifully written, this is a brilliant novel that asks questions that we're still trying to answer today' Louise Hare, author of *Miss Aldridge Regrets*

'Exceptional . . . What a treat. It's that rare beast: beautiful and literary with an extremely compelling and readable plot' Nicola Garrard, author of *29 Locks*

'Beautifully crafted . . . wholly convincing in its historical detail and tone' Sarah Gilmartin, author of *Dinner Party*

'I loved *The Red Bird Sings* . . . a haunting story of love, revenge and grief' Stacey Thomas, author of *The Revels*

'An absolutely beautifully written story. Aoife Fitzpatrick's prose just lifts straight off the page and transports you to 1897 Virginia' Cailean Steed, author of *Home*